Other Bell Bridge Books
by Bill Allen

How to Slay a Dragon

How to Save a Kingdom

Dedication

To all who believe in Myrth

Special Delivery

"Wait, Greg, that's Manny up there."

Greg Hart hadn't been tardy once this year, but when Kristin Wenslow grabbed his wrist, he couldn't imagine leaving for class.

Would Mom notice if I never washed my arm again . . . ?

The smell of hyacinths drifted past his nose, and in spite of the fact he was crouched in a flowerbed, Greg truly believed the fragrance was coming from Kristin.

Ahead, Manny Malice and two other bullies loitered on the steps outside the school, tormenting any smaller children who tried to sneak past. It took all of Manny's attention, since every child was smaller, and Manny had little attention to give.

"I'm not afraid of him," Greg said, trying unsuccessfully to sound confident. In truth, he placed Manny somewhere between a troll and an ogre in the list of things he'd least like to meet on his way to school, but he didn't want Kristin to think he was a coward.

Kristin pulled her jacket tight. "Well, you should be. He's had it out for you since the first grade."

She stared intently at the steps. Greg stared just as intently at the curve of her cheek. "How'd you know that?"

"What do you mean how? You've been sitting across the room from me since Mrs. Dorman's first grade class, remember?"

"You knew that, too?"

Kristin turned to Greg, confused. "Of course. What do you mean?"

"I-I just didn't realize you knew who I was back then."

"Oh, now you're just being silly."

Something in her eyes caused Greg to look away. Over on the steps, Manny stole Tommy Ritter's backpack and began a rousing game of keep-away with his friends. Tommy ran between them, jumping and waving his arms, a frantic version of a mime trapped inside a box.

"We need to go," Greg said. "The first bell's already rung."

"Hang on. Manny's got to go in too, doesn't he?"

"Do you even know Manny? He's always late. I'll bet he's spent more afternoons in detention than all the other seventh-graders combined."

"I think you're exaggerating."

"Maybe. But I doubt waiting will help."

As if to spite Greg, Manny tossed Tommy's backpack in the dirt, and while Tommy ran in circles collecting homework scattered by the breeze, the three bullies ambled inside, laughing.

"See," said Kristin. "Let's go." She grabbed Greg's wrist again and pulled him toward the stairs. Exhilarated over the touch as much as the danger, Greg let himself be led along the sidewalk and up the steps, passing Tommy Ritter so quickly, the boy spun and nearly dropped his homework again.

"Sorry," Greg yelled over his shoulder.

He and Kristin burst through the doors and into the school. Not far ahead, Manny was working hard at stuffing a five-foot-tall boy into a three-foot-tall locker. Otherwise, the halls were empty.

Kristin yanked Greg toward a stairwell at the end of the corridor. "This way."

They reached the door just as the second bell rang, signaling the start of homeroom. Up the stairs they sprinted, their footsteps echoing loudly in the empty stairwell.

The first landing proved to be no problem, but before they reached the second, a door slammed from above. Greg stopped abruptly, nearly pulling Kristin over backward. There the two waited, listening. Light footsteps started down the stairs above. A woman's heels.

"Teacher," Kristin whispered.

"Shh," warned Greg. Getting caught out of class after the bell was bad, but nothing compared to the danger he'd just sensed. His skin began to prickle as the air became charged by a threat far greater than anything of this world.

"Down," he urged, turning Kristin around and nudging her back the way they'd come. "Go."

Kristin didn't argue. The pair fled down the stairwell, two steps at a time, no longer bothering to hide the noise.

"Who's there?" a woman called. "Is that you, Mr. Malestino? It'll be suspension for you if I catch you out of class again."

Kristin rounded the landing and started down the lower flight. Greg hung back, risked a glance over his shoulder. Behind, the air split open, revealing a tiny, unwelcome window in space. Halfway up the stairs, stars floated in a blackness deeper than any Greg had ever seen—unless of course you counted the other four times he'd been faced with this rift between his own planet and the magical world of Myrth.

"Come on, Greg," said Kristin. "Why are you stopping?"

"Wha—?" Greg couldn't tear his eyes from the sight, but at least he had the sense to grip the rail. It wouldn't do to be sucked through that gap.

Thankfully, Kristin couldn't see from the lower flight. Greg looked between her and the danger. Part of him wanted to flee with her, or for that matter do just about anything with her, but another deeper, far less sensible part longed to know why the rift was here for him again.

Whatever he did, he had to do it quickly. "Go on. I'll catch up."

Kristin hesitated. "What is it, Greg?"

"Go," he insisted, knowing he was in trouble if she took even one step closer. "I'll come in a second."

Reluctantly, Kristin turned and ran. Greg stared back at the hovering tear in space. Not far above, heels clomped down the stairs. What would he do if one of his teachers rounded the corner and disappeared through that gap?

Then, just as quickly as it opened, the rift zipped up with a flash. A small white envelope remained in its place, suspended in mid-air. It swished back and forth as it dropped to the stairs and landed with a barely audible clap.

The footsteps grew close. Greg snatched up the envelope just as Mrs. Beasley, his math teacher, rounded the corner from the upper landing.

"Mr. Hart. What are you doing out of class?"

Mrs. Beasley was a wretched old woman, Earth's version of Witch Hazel from Myrth, and the similarity grew when her voice squelched like a series of violin strings being stretched to their limits.

Greg forced a smile. He met her eye as he stuffed the envelope into his pocket.

"Morning, Mrs. Beasley. I'm on my way to homeroom."

"You're late. The bell rang just a moment ago. Didn't you hear?"

"That was the second bell?"

"Yes." She peered past his shoulder. "Was there someone else with you? I thought I heard another voice."

Greg didn't like lying. He thought carefully about his reply. "Well, *you're* here with me."

Mrs. Beasley frowned. "It's not like you to be late for class. I don't believe I've seen you in detention all semester."

"No, ma'am."

"Well, see to it I don't."

As long as Greg had known her, Mrs. Beasley had worn a tight bun high atop her head. From it she pulled a pen. Greg wouldn't have been surprised if she found a pad in there too, but she reached into her pocket for one of those. While she jotted down a note, her wide eyes darted about the stairwell, as if she might still spot the source of that second voice.

Greg silently wondered if her eyes might not be so wide if she wore her bun a tad looser.

"You're in Mrs. French's homeroom, aren't you?" Mrs. Beasley asked.

"Yes, ma'am."

"Fine. Give her this note, and she won't give you detention. But if I catch you out in these halls during class again, rest assured, next time I won't be so nice."

Greg had no reason to doubt her. He could hardly believe she was being nice this time. "Thank you," he said, taking the note and stuffing it into his pocket.

"Just get to class, Mr. Hart." She started down the steps again, not waiting for a reply.

Greg breathed a sigh of relief. "Yes, ma'am." He turned and ran up the steps two at a time.

"Walk!" Mrs. Beasley called from below. "Hurry, but walk."

Greg forced himself to a slow jog until he heard the stairwell door open and close with a bang. Then he raced up the remaining steps and out into the corridor. He reached Mrs. French's room a minute later and eased the door open.

Mrs. French was sitting at her desk, rather miraculously reading a newspaper through coke-bottle glasses. He doubted he would need the note Mrs. Beasley gave him. Mrs. French's hearing was even worse than her eyesight. Then again, he hadn't counted on Manny Malice coming to her aid.

"Ahem," Manny said in the worst interpretation of throat-clearing Greg had ever heard.

Mrs. French licked her finger and turned the page of her newspaper.

"AHEM," Manny tried again, at twice the volume.

Mrs. French blindly patted the desk for her coffee mug.

Manny grabbed his seat and hopped about the room, producing a ruckus that couldn't be missed.

Mrs. French allowed her paper to droop. "Did someone say some—? Oh, Greg. Are you just coming in?"

Greg shot Manny a disgusted look. "Uh, yes, ma'am."

"Oh, dear. I hope you have a note."

"Yes," Greg said. He hurried over to her desk. "Yes, I do." He reached into his pocket for the note Mrs. Beasley gave him and handed it to Mrs. French, who studied it curiously.

"What's this? An envelope? How formal."

Greg's head snapped up. "What? No—"

But she was already tearing open the letter. She pulled out a single piece of faded parchment and shook it, then lifted her nose to read the page through her thick lenses.

"Hmm, let's see what we have here . . . This writing is terrible, Greg, just terrible . . . *Dearest Greghart . . .*"

Greg's stomach churned. He silently measured the distance between himself and the door.

"Greghart?" Mrs. French said, staring at Greg past the note he'd given her. He thought about snatching it from her hand, but already she was back to reading, and he had an idea that as bad as her eyesight was, she might notice.

"*It is with depressed rugrats . . .* no wait, that's *deepest regrets . . . that I rescued the newts . . .* That can't be right . . . oh . . . *received the news . . . from Simon today. Please . . . allow me . . . to be the frost . . .* no . . . *first . . . to offer my sincerest convalescence . . .* no, that would have to be *condolences,* wouldn't it? . . . *on your rather unfortunate demise.* Hmm, that part's right. *Rest assured that you will mower . . .* er . . . *river? . . .* oh, *never! . . . Rest assured that you will never be frog rotten . . .* er . . . *forgotten.* Signed . . . *Brandy Alexander?*"

The class roared with laughter. Greg might have thought to be embarrassed if he hadn't been so stunned by Mrs. French's words. *Rather unfortunate demise?* Hopefully she'd read that part wrong.

"Is this some sort of joke, Mr. Hart? Because if it is, I, for one, do not see the humor."

"No—there's been a mistake."

"There certainly has. I do not like being made a fool. I'm afraid you leave me no choice. You will report to detention directly after school this afternoon."

"But—" Greg started.

"Take a seat, Mr. Hart. Homeroom is nearly over."

Greg groaned and shuffled to his chair to the smirks and chuckles of several of his classmates, not the least of which originated from Manny Malice. The huge boy's face was beaming so brightly, it looked as if he were using it to guide Greg in for a landing.

When the bell rang, announcing the end of homeroom, Greg was met at the door by Kristin Wenslow.

"What was up with that note?" she asked.

"Nothing. It was just a big mistake."

The two of them stepped from the room and ambled toward Greg's next class.

"I can't believe you got detention," said Kristin. "It's all Manny's fault. He's such a jerk."

"Yeah, well, it's early. I wouldn't be surprised if he's there with me by the end of the day."

"I suppose. But still . . . it spoils my plans."

"What plans?"

She eyed him coyly, holding back a smile. "I thought maybe you'd like to walk me home today."

Greg stumbled and banged his head into a locker but recovered quickly and pretended nothing had happened. "Really?"

"Sure. That is, unless you don't want to."

"No! I mean, yes, I want to."

Kristin smiled. "Well, I've got some homework I could work on for Mr. Heineke's class. Maybe I could wait around until they let you out of detention."

"Really?"

"Yes, really. Why do you keep saying that?"

"Oh, sorry." Greg could barely speak. "I don't think they'll keep me more than an hour. Want to meet out front around four thirty?"

Kristin's smile widened. "I'll be waiting."

And just like that she was gone. Two minutes later, Greg breathed again.

Hart Decision

Greg spent all day waiting for detention. At three thirty he grabbed up his knapsack and practically ran to study hall. Just as suspected, Manny Malice had crammed himself into one of the tiny desks near the back of the room.

Scattered about were several other students Greg didn't recognize, but each shared a certain commonality with Manny, and Greg had an idea he was better off not knowing them. He took a seat up front, as far from the others as possible, and immediately began to watch the clock.

Mr. Armbuster, Greg's gym teacher, had everyone sign an attendance sheet, but then, to Greg's dismay, left the room. Greg felt as if hundreds of eyes were upon him. He silently thanked the fates each time Mr. Armbuster popped his head in to ensure no one left or misbehaved.

Having never been to detention before, Greg wasn't sure what he was supposed to do. The others all either slouched with their heads lolling backward, drool running from the corners of their mouths, or slumped forward with their foreheads resting in their folded arms atop their desks. Greg would have liked to do the same, but he was way too anxious over his date with Kristin to sleep. Besides, he didn't feel safe closing his eyes with Manny Malice behind him.

The hour dragged by like a runnerless sled drawn up a rocky cliff by a lame husky. While he waited, Greg thought again about the strange note Brandon sent. *Greg's rather unfortunate demise?* Had Simon really prophesied Greg was going back to Myrth to die? If so, he knew one thing for certain. The next time he felt the unpleasant prickling of a rift about to open, the last thing he was going to do was stick around to see what came out of it.

The memory of that eerie prickling pressed so hard on his mind, Greg could almost believe he was experiencing it now. Suddenly the air beside him split open, and Greg realized the awful sensation wasn't a memory at all. He jumped up, screaming, and ran for the exit, knocking over two desks along the way.

As if he'd been standing with his hand on the knob, Mr. Armbuster threw open the door. "What's all the commotion about? Hart, what are you doing out of your seat?"

Greg snapped his head toward the front of the room, where the rift disappeared in that instant, leaving behind a second envelope that dropped soundlessly to the floor.

"What? Oh, nothing. I . . . uh . . . thought I saw a spider."

The other boys roared. Apparently they'd all been either sleeping or too distracted by Greg to notice the gaping hole that had floated at the front of the room a moment ago.

Mr. Armbuster scowled. "Take a seat, Hart, before I add another hour to your detention."

"Yes, sir. Right away."

"And put those desks back."

Greg righted the desks he'd knocked over and rushed back to his seat, where he stomped on the envelope and waited forever for Armbuster to leave. The instant the door closed, Greg snatched up the envelope. He struggled to keep his hands from trembling as he tore it open and peered cautiously inside.

The message was written on old parchment, just like the first, but this time the handwriting was perfectly legible.

Dearest Greghart,

It has come to my attention that my scribe has taken it upon himself to send a rather inappropriate message your way. Please allow me to offer my deepest apologies for his thoughtless action. I do not know exactly what he told you, but rest assured we do not expect you to deal with Witch Hazel for us. Our problems are our own, and we can handle them without your help, no matter how overwhelming the odds against us may seem. Simon's prophecy about the destruction of Pendegrass Castle is no doubt incorrect, and just in case it isn't, that's all the more reason why you should just go about your business as if you never heard from any of us. Again I apologize.

Hope not to see you soon,
King Peter Pendegrass III
(Please, call me Peter.)

Greg studied the note a long while, wondering what trouble Witch Hazel might be brewing. The witch was an ornery old hag whose idea of fair play might be to kill you slowly, so you wouldn't miss out on any of the experience. She could be dangerous even under the best of circumstances, but Greg had an even deeper reason to be concerned.

The Amulet of Tehrer.

Last time he saw Hazel, Greg had been forced to give her a small pentagon-shaped piece of metal, the crucial piece to an amulet that had been broken apart centuries earlier, after nearly causing the destruction of Myrth.

Even though at the moment the destruction of Myrth didn't sound like a bad thing, deep down Greg knew the Amulet of Tehrer must never be reassembled. With it, Hazel could control dragons, and while only one dragon remained on Myrth, an enormous creature named Ruuan who had helped Greg the last two times he visited there, Greg didn't want to think what might happen if Ruuan were forced to use his seemingly endless powers for evil rather than good.

Now, as the clock ticked slowly toward four thirty, Greg couldn't help but wonder if Hazel had already managed to locate the remaining amulet sections. Maybe King Peter really did need his help. But what about that first note and Brandon's talk about Greg's "rather unfortunate demise"?

Perhaps Mrs. French just read it wrong. Maybe it was supposed to say "rather unfortunate disguise" or "rather unfortunate devise." But no, then why would Brandon have been offering condolences? Maybe she got that part wrong too. Brandon's handwriting *was* pretty bad.

Mr. Armbuster came back into the room at twenty after four. After what seemed like another hour, he announced to the boys that their punishment was over for the day. Greg was first out of the room. For the moment, he gave up fretting over what might be happening on Myrth and fretted instead on his upcoming meeting with Kristin. As inconceivable as it seemed, he found her waiting outside as promised.

"You're here," Greg said.

"Well, of course," said Kristin, laughing. "Why wouldn't I be?"

"It's just . . . I thought this morning . . . well, maybe I'd been dreaming or something."

Kristin's cheeks flushed in a way Greg found particularly pleasing. But then he realized she might just be cold. He debated putting an arm around her for warmth but couldn't shake the vision of her shooting mace into his eyes and using some Judo move to send him somersaulting into the shrubbery.

They cut across the grass toward the start of a path that led within three blocks of Kristin's house. Last month, Manny Malice had cornered Greg on this very same lawn. Fortunately, Greg had just returned from Myrth and was recovering from a spell that allowed him to rip a four-inch-thick limb from one of the trees and threaten Manny with it. Of course, Manny knew nothing of Myrth or the spell. He just assumed Greg possessed superhuman powers, so naturally he'd given Greg a wide berth ever since. Still, Greg scanned the woods. Seven-year-long habits were hard to break.

"So what was up with that note?" Kristin asked as she and Greg stepped into the woods.

Greg stooped to pick up a fallen branch to use as a walking stick, another habit he didn't acquire until his first trip to Myrth, last fall. "You know about the note?"

"Of course. Everyone knows."

It took Greg a moment to remember the incident in homeroom that morning. "Oh, you mean the first one."

"There was another?"

"Huh? Oh, no, of course not."

"Sure there was. What did it say? And who's writing them?"

Greg sighed, wondering if there'd ever been a boy who could get himself into trouble quicker. "It was nothing, really."

"Come on, Greg. How about the first note? What was that? Who's Brandy Alexander?"

"Brandon," Greg corrected. "I mean, he's nobody. I just made him up."

Kristin frowned. "I can't believe you're lying to me."

Greg didn't know what to say. This walk wasn't going anything like he'd planned. "No, Kristin, wait. I'm sorry, but—well, I can't tell you who he is."

"Why not?"

"I just can't, that's all. You wouldn't believe me if I did."

"Try me." Her eyes gazed up at him, pleading, and Greg tripped over a root for not watching where he was going.

"Careful," Kristin scolded.

Greg nodded and limped along, nursing a newly sore toe. "I tried to tell you once before. As I recall, you asked me to go see the school nurse."

"You're not talking about that silly story you made up about traveling to some other world, are you?"

"It's not a story. It really happened."

Kristin reached for his forehead, but Greg ducked her hand. "I'm not sick. I knew you wouldn't believe me."

She folded her arms across her chest and stared forward, avoiding Greg's eye. It seemed an awkward way to walk, but it did effectively convey her mood.

"Okay, you're right," she said. "But look at it from my point of view. You're claiming to have been abducted by space aliens."

"Not aliens. People. Good people, just like you and me. And according to their note, they're in serious trouble."

"I heard the note," Kristin said. "It sounded like you were the one in trouble."

"Not that note. The second one."

"So you did get another?"

"Yes, while I was in detention."

She frowned at him. "I'll bet Mr. Armbuster found that interesting."

"Armbuster didn't see it. He was out of the room. And neither did anyone else. They were all asleep."

Kristin quit walking and propped her hands on her hips. "Do you know how ridiculous you sound?"

"I'm not making this up. I can prove it."

Greg slipped his backpack off his shoulder and loosened the straps. For a moment he debated pulling out his pet shadowcat, Rake, but he was trying to sway Kristin, not find out if she really did carry mace. Instead, he withdrew the second note from under his journal and handed it over.

Kristin eyed him doubtfully but took the parchment and read it. "Oh, so this one's from a king now."

"Yes, King Peter. You'd like him." He wasn't sure, but he thought he saw her roll her eyes.

"Maybe we should start small," she said. "Do you know any kings on this world you could introduce me to?"

Greg scowled. "Okay, you're right. I'm making it all up." Furious, he turned and stomped down the path without waiting to see if she would follow.

"Hey, wait up."

Greg watched her come. As mad as he was, he couldn't help but admire the way her hair jostled from side to side when she ran. He wished there was some way to convince her he was telling the truth. Then the secret of Myrth could be something only the two of them shared.

"So, who's this Witch Hazel the king mentioned?" Kristin asked.

"What do you care? You don't believe me anyway."

"I'm trying to understand, all right? Are there witches on this other world of yours?"

"It's not my world. It's called Myrth, and yes, it has witches and magicians and monsters and all kinds of scary things."

"I see," said Kristin. "Then it sounds like they're used to trouble."

Greg knew she was just patronizing him, but still her statement caused him to recall King Peter's note. "Not trouble like this. I think Witch Hazel may be threatening to destroy their whole world."

"Why would she do that? Isn't it her world too?"

"Yeah, but I think she might be crazy. She kind of lost it when everyone started calling her a witch."

"Oh, then she's not a witch?"

"No, she is. She just doesn't like being called one."

Again Kristin frowned. She was staring at Greg's face but not into his eyes, probably checking his color. "Hardly worth destroying your world over, I would think."

"Look, I know you don't believe me."

Kristin wasn't paying attention. "What *is* that?"

"What's what?"

"That creepy buzzy feeling in the air."

"Buzzy?"

Despite the two earlier occurrences, Greg was caught completely off guard when the air suddenly split between them, revealing an endless sea of floating stars. As if from far off he heard Kristin scream, but he couldn't see her face behind the gaping hole that hung in mid-air between them.

The opening remained for only a few seconds before it flashed and disappeared, leaving behind a third envelope that dropped harmlessly to the path. Greg could now see Kristin clearly. Her face had lost all color, and her mouth had gone slack.

"Believe me now?"

"W-what was that?" Kristin managed to say. "Greg, did you see that?"

"Of course I saw. It's what I've been trying to tell you. That was the rift I went through to get to Myrth."

"B-but that's impossible."

"You'd think so, wouldn't you?"

Greg stooped to pick up the envelope. He tore it open and pulled out another letter, identical to the others. This one was written in a flowing script, though it was harder to read than King Peter's, as it looked to have been written in a hurry.

"What does it say?" Kristin asked.

Greg suspected she'd rather have spent a month of detentions with Manny Malice than hear the answer. He certainly understood her reluctance. He still had a lot of trouble accepting the concept of Myrth himself.

Dearest Greg,

Lucky just told me Dad sent you a note. I know he asked you not to come, but Lucky says he worded it in such a way that might make you ignore the warning. Listen to me. YOU MUST NOT COME HERE. Simon says you'll get killed when you do, and whether you save the kingdom first or not doesn't matter. I won't see you harmed.

Love, Priscilla

Greg looked up from the note.

Kristin's earlier expression of terror had been replaced by something else. "Love, Priscilla?" she said.

Greg tried his best not to smile. "That's what it says."

"Who's Priscilla?"

"She's a princess. Didn't you hear? She said Dad just sent me a note, and that last one came from King Peter, remember?"

"I meant, who is she, and why is she signing notes, 'Love, Priscilla'?"

Greg blushed. "I don't know. It's just something people say in notes. You know, like 'Sincerely' or 'Yours truly.'"

"I don't think I like it."

"Really," he said, feeling quite the opposite. "Oh. Well . . . sorry."

"So, what are you going to do?"

"What do you mean?" He started walking again, slowly, so Kristin could follow on trembling legs.

"It sounds like these people really need your help," she said.

"You did hear the part about me dying if I went there, right?"

"Yes, I heard." She fell silent for a few steps. "So, who's Simon?"

"Simon Sez. He's a prophet."

Kristin glared at him. "Are you messing with me?"

"What? Oh, no. His name really is Simon Sez, and he's a prophet, I swear."

"Really?"

"Yes, and he's never wrong. If he says I'd get killed if I went there . . . well, then I might as well take a headstone with me."

Kristin looked even more upset now than she had when the portal opened. "If he really is a prophet . . . well, he didn't say you *would* get killed, did he? He said you *will* get killed."

Greg gulped. "Not if I don't go there."

"But you will. Simon says."

Now it was Greg who fell silent. How was it Kristin seemed so comfortable with the whole notion of prophecies when Greg had already lived through two of them and still refused to believe? Anyway, she had a valid point, even if it was one he desperately wished to ignore.

They eventually reached the end of the woods and followed the sidewalk to Kristin's house. The whole way Kristin grilled Greg about the world of Myrth, but mostly she wanted to know about Princess Priscilla and what Greg thought of her.

As much as he liked her, Greg was glad to drop Kristin off at her porch. As soon as the door closed, he rushed back to the woods, eager to follow the trails home before his mother got too worried.

Along the way he tried not to dwell on the inevitable. He didn't know when or where it would happen, but surely it was just a matter of time before the rift would come for him, pluck him from this world, and drag him off to his doom.

A twig snapped, and Greg spun toward the sound, fully expecting to spot a gaping hole in the universe.

Nothing. Probably just a monkeydog.

Oh no! Already he was thinking like he was back on Myrth. Small creatures, never seen but always heard making impossibly loud noises in the brush, monkeydogs existed only in that other world.

Or did they? Greg had once been told that long ago Earth had real magicians. Who's to say they didn't have monkeydogs, too? After all, when it came to monkeydogs, the fact no one had ever seen one could be offered up as irrefutable proof that the whole planet was littered with them.

A second rustling caused Greg to jump. He searched the path

behind. What if Manny Malice had followed him out here? He gripped his walking stick tighter and hurried forward, listening to the many noises of the woods. Again he thought about Priscilla's note. She must really be in trouble this time. Too bad there was nothing he could do to help.

Or was there? Simon had already predicted Greg's return to Myrth. He was going there no matter what. But if he waited for the magicians to come for him, who's to say they wouldn't take too long about it and botch up the whole prophecy?

Because then it won't come true—which is impossible, right?

No. His friend Nathan once told him the reason prophecies always come true is because the people who act them out work so hard to see them fulfilled. Maybe Greg did need to take action now. He debated the matter a long while. And then, thankfully, a longer while.

What about his "rather unfortunate demise?" It seemed an important detail, one that kept him spinning around and flailing his walking stick each time he heard a rustling in the brush behind.

He continued to debate the issue nearly the whole way home, but in the end, as horrible as it was to accept, he arrived at the only conclusion possible. Simon had already predicted he was going to die. There was no way around it. But why die for nothing? At least he could save Priscilla and her family first, not to mention all the other citizens of Myrth. Many would have said it was a noble viewpoint. Greg recognized it for what it was. Utter resignation.

His fingers closed around the ring he wore on his right hand. Given to him by the dragon Ruuan, it was no ordinary piece of jewelry. With it, all he had to do was say one magic word, and he'd be transported to Ruuan's lair in an instant, and from there the dragon could carry him back to the castle in minutes.

He slowed to a crawl, debating what to do. Again, a noise behind. Greg spun toward the sound.

Maybe Manny *was* following him. Maybe when Simon predicted Greg's demise, he also knew Greg's time had come no matter which world Greg stayed in.

Greg knew then what he must do. He removed the ring from his finger and held it up to what little light bled through the trees.

"Well, this is it," he said to the empty woods. The monkeydogs quietly rustled in reply. "I wish I could say I'll see you again soon."

For a moment the woods fell silent. Then Greg said the one word that would forever seal his fate. "Transportus."

Behind him the brush rustled. Greg's world shifted and began to fade from view. But then a voice screamed out, and something hit him hard about the waist, reminding him of the time Princess Priscilla had latched onto him and hitched a ride all the way across the kingdom to Ruuan's lair, risking her life to protect him.

The image was still floating in his mind an instant later, when Greg found himself standing at the center of a huge cavern surrounded by glowing rock. Around his waist he felt the arms of a young girl. He realized then the thought of Princess Priscilla had been more than just a memory.

Only this time it wasn't Priscilla who had risked her life to protect him. It was Kristin Wenslow.

Mass Reunion

Kristin's screams echoed throughout the enormous cavern.

"Don't let go!" Greg warned. He wrapped his arms around her just in case, and in spite of the horror of his situation, couldn't help but notice how soft she felt.

"Where are we?" Kristin cried.

"Ruuan's lair." Greg dragged her toward a storage chamber nestled in one corner, where he knew the air would be magically cooled. It was there that Ruuan stored his food, while it was still breathing.

"Who's Ruuan?" said Kristin. "And why does he have a lair?"

"Because he's a dragon."

"What?" Her grip tightened until Greg could hardly draw a breath.

"Don't worry," he gasped. "He doesn't seem to be here right now. This happened to me last time, too."

"Last time?" Kristin shrieked. Greg shoved her through the narrow gap that separated the chilled storage chamber from Ruuan's lair. Light cast from the molten rock outside illuminated her face with heavy shadows. It might have lent a ferocious quality, had Kristin not been so enraged already. "You've been here before, and you came back?"

Greg could tell from her tone that Kristin couldn't see how this was possible. Odd, since she was the one who pointed out he should come. "Ruuan's okay," he tried to reassure her. "He likes me, I guess, on account of I didn't slay him the first time I came here."

"I didn't slay him either. Do you think he'll remember?"

"You'll be fine, as long as you stick with me. Oh, by the way, you can let go now."

Kristin remained clamped to him like a vice. In theory Greg liked having her arms around him, but in reality it made breathing nearly impossible. After several reassurances, she reluctantly let go, though Greg suspected she would tackle him again at the first hint of a dragon.

"Why did you grab onto me like that?" he asked.

"I heard you talking crazy and thought you were about to do something stupid. As it turns out, I was right."

"You were the one who said I was going to get killed here whether I ignored the note or not."

"Yes, but at least my way there was a chance the prophecy could be wrong. Your way has you charging right into an early grave. Why don't you just go back outside and call for the dragon to eat you?"

"Ruuan wouldn't eat me," Greg said. "At least, I don't think so. Besides, I came to save the kingdom."

Kristin regarded him doubtfully. "How do you plan to do that?"

"I don't know. I'm not even sure what the problem is. But I bet it has something to do with the section of amulet I gave Witch Hazel last month."

Kristin's mouth dropped open. "How often do you come here?"

"I've only been twice, to fulfill two different prophecies. Now I guess there's been a third."

Kristin begged to know about Greg's other two trips, but Greg shook his head. "They'll be plenty of time to talk on the trail. If what I suspect has happened, we better not wait for Ruuan. He may never come back, and it's a long way to the castle. Let's just hope the spirelings aren't home."

"The what?" Kristin asked.

"Believe me, you don't want to know. Take my hand, and whatever you do, don't let go."

"Don't worry."

As Greg guided her back into Ruuan's lair he remembered that Ruaan's ring would protect Kristin whether she held his hand or not, but he conveniently forgot to tell her. He led her to a magical door that hid the secret Passageway of Shifted Dimensions, the only route a mortal could take to the ground, as the lair was nestled halfway up an infinitely tall spire. Greg was nearly as concerned as Kristin when the door opened to welcome them, but they stepped through anyway. Again a cool breeze hit them, as the passageway possessed a special magic of its own.

"This way," Greg said, though that should have been obvious, since there was but one way they could go.

They descended a steep staircase that gradually melded into a sloping tunnel through the rock. Before long Greg heard a high-pitched whine from over his shoulder.

"What's that?" Kristin asked, her eyes wide with fear.

At first Greg thought it might be the sound of Ruuan soaring up the spire on his way back from the hunt, but then he realized the true origin of the sound.

"Rake."

He slipped his backpack off his shoulder and loosened the straps to allow the little shadowcat to escape.

Kristin took one look at the creature with its blue-black fur and unnaturally long tail and screamed. "What is that, Greg? Watch out."

"Shh. It's okay. It's just Rake."

A sudden shuffling sounded in the passage ahead. The pair froze in place and listened, afraid to breathe.

Whatever was coming was coming fast. Again Greg was reminded of the soaring dragon. He nearly told Kristin to run, but just then two short, stocky creatures rounded a bend in the rock. They looked a bit like rocks themselves, only Greg knew they were not. He also knew he couldn't possibly outrun them.

Kristin screamed, a sound that was becoming all too familiar, but Greg could hardly blame her. He felt like screaming himself.

The spirelings bared their teeth, or so it seemed. Six inches long and sharp as razors, spireling teeth jutted out at all angles from their jaws, even when the creatures' mouths were closed. As if the expressions weren't threatening enough, the two warriors carried heavy double-bladed axes, which they thrust forward now.

"Gnash?" Greg said hopefully. "Gnaw?"

These were the names of the only two spirelings Greg knew. Gnash and Gnaw were relatively friendly for monsters, but Greg wouldn't have had the slightest idea how to tell them apart from others, as all spirelings looked the same to him.

"No, I am Grunt," said one.

"And I am Growl," said the other. "But Gnash and Gnaw are with us now, as are all of our kind. We are most honored to meet the Mighty Greghart, though of course, in one respect we already have."

"Mighty Greghart?" said Kristin.

"It's a long story," Greg said. "I'll tell you later."

"If we survive this, you mean."

"We shouldn't need to worry now," he told her. "What one spireling sees they all see, and apparently I've already been recognized and accepted. Oh, by the way, they think I'm some kind of hero."

"Why would they think that?"

"Greghart is a legend among our people," said Grunt. "He has fought monsters we have never even heard of on this world, and he has always emerged the victor, no matter how overwhelming the odds."

"Is there more you're not telling me?" Kristin asked Greg.

"Later, remember?"

Grunt suddenly screamed and jerked backward. Growl yelled and raised his axe. As if she thought it was the fashionable thing to do, Kristin joined in with a scream of her own, but Greg knew what had disturbed the spirelings so.

"Get back in the pack, Rake."

The shadowcat hissed and arched its fur, clearly reveling in the sight of the spirelings shrinking back, their axes raised to protect their faces. After what Rake surely must have felt was a sufficient interval, he chattered playfully and crawled nonchalantly into Greg's pack.

After a longer interval, Growl lowered his axe. "Queen Gnarla wishes a word with you. You will come with us."

"You mean I really do get to meet a queen?" said Kristin.

"She's not what you think," said Greg, and from the look on Kristin's face when they met up with Queen Gnarla later, he was correct in his assumption.

"You're a queen?" Kristin said before Greg could warn her not to speak.

"Silence," ordered Queen Gnarla, who was not particularly friendly, even for a monster. She wore a cloth robe and a jagged crystalline crown, while the guards who surrounded her wore tattered pants and chain mail, but otherwise she looked identical to the others.

The guards leaned close and showed off their axes.

"You shall not speak unless spoken to," Queen Gnarla announced in a haughty tone.

"Well, I'll admit you sound like a queen," said Kristin.

"SILENCE."

Greg shot Kristin a glare she couldn't possibly misinterpret. Even so, she nearly apologized. Instead, she caught herself and simply nodded.

"Have you not heard about the dragon?" Queen Gnarla asked Greg.

"Ruuan? What about him?"

"He has been taken against his will," the queen said, "by the human Witch Hazel. Apparently she holds some sort of amulet that grants her power over dragons."

Greg gasped. "The Amulet of Tehrer."

Even though spirelings could communicate clearly without a sound, they started up a whisper that shook the walls as it echoed its way down the tunnel.

"Does no one listen to Us?" Queen Gnarla held her hands over her ears and glared at Greg. "As We recall, you were responsible for the loss of the key piece of the Amulet of Tehrer. Why would you give something that powerful to the witch?"

Greg gulped. "Because Nathan told me to?"

"Nathan? He is that magician who was with you when last We met, no? He warned Us that there may come a time when he needed Our section of Ruuan's amulet, yet We have not seen him since. If not now, when?"

"Nathan hasn't come?" Greg said. "Maybe I should take the amulet with me."

Queen Gnarla's expression suggested otherwise, far better than words. "I will give it to the magician, when he asks."

After a long moment of awkward silence, the queen indicated Kristin with a wave of her hand. "Tell Us, who is this?"

"Kristin Wenslow," Kristin answered.

"Silence. We were not speaking to you."

"Sorry," said Kristin. She realized she'd talked again too late and quickly placed a hand over her mouth. Queen Gnarla rolled her eyes before looking to Greg for an answer.

"Her name is Kristin Wenslow," Greg repeated. "She's a friend of mine from my own world."

"Ah." Queen Gnarla looked her up and down without seeming to notice Kristin's discomfort. "She is a warrior too, then?"

"Women aren't warriors where I come from," answered Greg.

"I could be a warrior if I wanted," said Kristin. "Oh, I know," she told the queen. "Silence."

Queen Gnarla frowned. "Well, that is a shame. She has a lot of spunk for a human."

Kristin smiled and regarded Greg smugly. He took only a second to notice how cute she was. Then he told the queen of the letters he'd received and how he'd traveled between worlds to do what he could to save the kingdom. Queen Gnarla glared at her guards.

"Why are We always the last to know of these prophecies?"

The guards cleared their throats and quickly looked away.

"I don't suppose you would be willing to help us?" Greg asked the queen.

"Normally no," said Queen Gnarla, "but then normally We would have eaten you the moment We found you trespassing in Our tunnel. Since you are the Mighty Greghart, We are making an exception. Today you may have anything you need . . . aside from Our amulet. How might We help?"

Greg felt embarrassed to have to say what he was thinking, but these were desperate times. "We need to get to Pendegrass Castle. Even if we found our way, it would take weeks on foot. Obviously your warriors can get there much quicker."

"Your point?" Queen Gnarla asked impatiently.

Greg looked to Kristin and back to a spot somewhere near Queen Gnarla's feet.

"Do you think they might be able to . . . well, you know . . . carry us?"

Whirlwind Tour

And so it was that Greg and Kristin found themselves riding atop a litter carried by four spireling warriors, watching the blurred forms of snow-covered trees whiz past on both sides, close enough to touch.

Two of the litter-bearers were Grunt and Growl, who Greg and Kristin had met inside the spire. The others claimed to be Greg's friends Gnash and Gnaw, though in truth, Greg had no way of knowing for sure. Not only did they look just like every other spireling Greg had ever seen, but when Greg traveled with Gnash and Gnaw on his last visit, all the other spirelings shared the experience. There was nothing these two alone would know that could prove they were the actual pair who accompanied him during the last prophecy.

"This is incredible," shouted Kristin. "How can they move so quickly?"

"It is something, isn't it?" said Greg, "Next to traveling by dragon, I don't see how we could make better time."

"Dragons can move faster than this? You're kidding?"

"Much faster. Ruuan could have carried us to the castle in a matter of minutes."

"I'm not sure if I'd like to see that or not," Kristin admitted.

"You'd like Ruuan," he told her. "He's really cool for a dragon."

Kristin began to relax after that. She looked to be enjoying her adventure, and Greg accepted his, too, partly because he was glad to be there with Kristin, but mostly because he'd temporarily forgotten all about Simon's prophecy and his "rather unfortunate demise."

Earlier, just before the group left the spire, Queen Gnarla gave the children vests identical to the kind her spireling warriors wore.

"Is there going to be another battle?" Greg had asked worriedly.

"These will keep you warm," Queen Gnarla told him, which was hard for Greg to believe, since it was freezing outside, and the chain mail was little more than a collection of holes. But amazingly, when he slipped the gift on under his windbreaker, he felt quite cozy, and he had since discovered that with it he could barely feel the torrent of wind that threatened to lift him off the litter at any moment.

Since all four spirelings were dressed alike, in tattered pants and light chain mail, shortly into the journey Greg suggested they each wear some accessory he could use to tell them apart. At first they thought he was joking, as there was clearly no way one spireling could be confused with another, but later, when Kristin admitted having trouble telling them apart too, they knew Greg had been serious.

Quickly they did as he asked, and Greg was only mildly insulted when Growl suggested that it might be helpful if Greg and Kristin each wore some identifying accessory, as well. Greg found an oddly shaped twig he tucked into his belt. Kristin picked a cluster of bright red berries to adorn her hair, which Greg felt Growl might have noticed was easily five times as long as Greg's.

Gnash had managed to find a bright purple flower peeking up through the snow just outside the spire. He'd plucked it out of the ground and poked the stem though a hole in his chain mail, which was the only way Greg could be sure it was Gnash who cried out now.

"Attack!"

The group stopped in an instant. If not for the spirelings' dexterous manipulation of the litter, Greg and Kristin surely would have been hurled into the woods.

"What's going on?" asked Greg. "Why are we stopping?"

As one, the spirelings dropped their respective corners of the litter and lifted their axes. Greg felt the ground rise up to slap his backside. A horrifying shriek broke the stillness, and a wyvern shot down from the sky, its claws splayed to capture anything slow enough to remain in its path. Unfortunately, Greg and Kristin were the only two around that met the description.

"Watch out!" said Greg. He dove into Kristin, who surely would have been cut in half by a talon if one of the spirelings hadn't diverted the thrust aside with a blow of his axe.

Kristin cried out too, partly from fear of the wyvern, partly from the way the spireling had just swung an axe at her, but mostly from surprise over being tackled. "I thought you said Ruuan was friendly."

"That's not Ruuan," Greg cried. "That's not even a dragon."

Kristin stared wide-eyed into the sky. "It sure looked like a dragon to me."

Greg decided nothing could be gained from pointing out that dragons were about thirty times as large.

"He's coming back around," warned one of the spirelings. The fern poking through his chain mail helped identify him as Grunt.

"Watch yourself," Greg warned Kristin. He wished he had the magic sword Lucky carried with them the other times he'd traveled these woods. But no, here he was with only a walking stick for protection. Then the guards moved in to surround him and Kristin, and Greg felt safer, for he knew the warriors would die to protect them. The spirelings were very respectful of prophecies.

The wyvern came in low on its second attack, barely clearing the trees with its enormous wings. So close, Greg could see blood dripping from its injured talon. For just an instant he felt sorry for the creature. Sure it wanted to tear Greg's limbs off, but no doubt for a fair reason. To a wyvern they must have looked quite tasty.

Again the wyvern was turned aside. More cautious of the spirelings' blades now, it managed to pass unharmed. Greg was left with a mental image of the beast long after it disappeared through the trees. There was something familiar about its brilliant teal scales and iridescent streaks, and the gold ovals encircling its eyes.

"I know that wyvern," he said suddenly.

"What?" said Kristin.

"It's the one that saved us at the base of the Smoky Mountains last month—the same one I saved on the ridge near the Infinite Spire a couple of weeks before that."

"You do get around, don't you?"

"Here it comes again," Gnash announced.

Greg jumped to his feet. "That's him," he cried out as the beast soared toward the campsite.

With a blur of one hand, Grunt pulled him aside. Growl shifted his identifying evergreen branch so he could raise his axe above his head.

"No!" Greg shouted, and dove into Growl. He would have expected a less jarring impact had he dove into a rock wall, but Growl's toss was affected just the same. It missed the wyvern by no more than an inch. Greg and Growl were both lucky not to lose their heads.

"Why did you do that?" Grunt demanded.

"Yes, why?" said Growl. "You could have got us both killed."

"Here it comes again," said Gnaw. The identifying strand of ivy he'd wrapped about his neck flapped in the wind as he pointed to a tiny patch of sky.

Greg couldn't see a thing in the direction Gnaw pointed, but the remaining spirelings unanimously agreed that the wyvern was indeed approaching. And then Greg saw it too, headed straight for them. He was just regretting his earlier decision to interfere, when suddenly the wyvern's eyes grew, as if it were the one that was terrified. Greg watched in amazement as the creature veered about and retreated in the direction it had come.

"It's leaving," said Kristin.

Greg breathed a sigh of relief. "I wonder why." He was still watching the wyvern fade in the distance when from behind he heard another screech, ten times as terrifying as what the wyvern had offered.

Greg dove to the ground. He couldn't help himself. Kristin landed beside him. To his surprise, the four spirelings landed beside her. All six of them craned their necks to search the sky.

To Greg's horror, a huge black shape moved across the sun. The silhouette quickly grew as it moved closer, until suddenly it was passing directly overhead, and Greg could see clearly what it was. The dragon Ruuan let out another ear-splitting cry and soared after the retreating wyvern, releasing a searing jet of flames that would have annihilated all of them if it had been directed at the ground. Within seconds Ruuan had reached the spot where Greg had last seen the wyvern. The dragon released another jet of flames, but Greg could make out little else from this distance.

Kristin's face had lost all color. "I'm guessing *that* was a dragon."

Greg nodded. "Lucky he didn't see us. I may have been wrong before about him not eating me."

Grunt stepped forward. "Oh, he saw us. The dragon could not possibly have missed our movements. Fortunately the witch did not."

"You saw Hazel up there too?" Greg asked.

Growl stepped up to Grunt's side. "Steering the beast, yes. She must be practicing controlling his movements in battle. Grunt is right. We were lucky to pass unnoticed. If Witch Hazel had spotted us, she would have ordered her attack on us, and I'm not sure the dragon could have resisted. It seems the witch is quickly gaining mastery over the use of Tehrer's amulet."

"We need to get to the castle and warn them," Greg said.

The spirelings agreed. They quickly regained their litter, and soon Greg and Kristin were once again soaring through the trees toward the heart of the Smoky Mountains.

Kristin stared wide-eyed as the scenery whizzed past. "That dragon was terrifying. How could you have possibly made friends with a creature like that? I can't believe you've been coming here, doing all these incredible things, and you've never told me any of it."

"But I tried—"

"You need to tell me now. It's the least you can do."

Greg started to speak, but decided against trying to yell over the rushing wind. He removed his backpack, flipped open the flap and pulled out his old journal. He could no longer carry it in his pocket, as he had long since filled the last of the pages, and now the book was crammed full of loose slips of paper and bulged twice as wide as in the beginning of the year.

"Everything I've done on Myrth is in there," he said.

Kristin stared at the book with the same reverence the spirelings had shown when they returned it to him on his last visit. The moment she cracked the cover, several loose slips of paper soared off in the rush of wind.

She snapped it shut again. "I better save this for later."

Soon before dusk they reached Death's Pass, a narrow tunnel of stairs cut through solid rock, connecting the highest peak of the Smoky Mountains with a point about halfway to the base. Under normal conditions the pass provided a quick descent, but at the speed the spirelings negotiated it, Greg had to wonder if they'd dropped their load and were still standing somewhere near the top, watching the litter free fall to the bottom. Fortunately, when the base drew near and the level ground rushed up to meet the litter, the spirelings were there too. They screeched to an uneventful halt.

"We will camp here," Gnash announced. "It is not safe to travel after dark."

"Did they think we were traveling safe before?" Kristin whispered to Greg.

"Safely," all four spirelings corrected at once.

"Oh, I forgot," said Greg. "Whispering doesn't work around spirelings. They've got really good hearing."

Kristin looked at Gnash. "Greg says you can see in the dark without any trouble. Why is traveling at night so dangerous?"

"We are not the only creatures who can see well in the dark. Some of the others you might find . . . well, let us just say you do not want to find them."

Kristin scanned the surrounding shadows. "What if they find us?"

"Do not worry. We will be prepared for them if they do."

Neither Greg nor Kristin felt completely reassured by that answer, especially since Greg remembered his friend Nathan once telling him that dragons hunted at night. Even though he knew there was little the spirelings could do if Hazel and Ruuan returned, he was glad to have Gnash guard over them while Grunt and Growl set out for firewood.

The pair emerged from the trees seconds later, both with full armloads of wood, just in time to prepare a dinner Gnaw had captured. Whatever it was continued to protest rather loudly while he dragged it toward the fire.

"I think I'm going to be sick," said Kristin.

"You get used to it," said Greg, though in truth he was only hypothesizing, since he'd never gotten used to it himself.

The four spirelings offered a wide berth while Greg fed Rake, as they were deathly afraid of shadowcats. After dinner Greg showed Kristin some of the chikan moves the magician Nathaniel Caine had taught him on his first visit.

"That's terrific," cried Kristin, clapping and whistling over Greg's antics.

"Yes, very good," said Gnaw, "but I think it is time you and the human girl got some sleep."

"My name is Kristin."

Greg couldn't help but notice how much she sounded like Princess Priscilla.

"Yes, well, Kristin then," said Gnaw. "You humans need your rest. We want to be on the trail again at first light."

"What about you?" said Kristin. "Don't you need your rest too?"

"We spirelings do not sleep," he told her. "But thank you for your concern."

"Is that really possible?" Kristin whispered to Greg.

"I don't sleep much on Myrth either," he admitted.

At least they wouldn't be spending more than one night on the trail. On his own, Greg would have taken over a week to get this far, but the spirelings had done it in less than a day. At this rate, Greg estimated they would reach Pendegrass Castle before nightfall tomorrow, provided Ruuan didn't eat them along the way.

But as happy as he was with their progress, Greg was apprehensive as well. Arriving at the castle sooner just put him closer to his expected confrontation with Hazel and, as Brandon had put it, his "rather unfortunate demise."

When he was sure the spirelings weren't watching, Greg unstrapped his knapsack and allowed Rake to wander freely. The shadowcat stretched its legs for a few seconds and then returned, intending to curl up in its usual spot atop Greg's chest, but Greg was still standing, staring into his pack.

"What's wrong, Greg?" Kristin asked. "What are you looking at?"

"My math and history books. When I was here before, Lucky's backpack had everything we needed. We don't even have bedrolls."

"You will not need a bedroll tonight," said Gnaw—no wait, purple flower—Gnash. "You will find the chain mail Queen Gnarla gave you quite comfortable."

"It's just a vest," said Greg.

"Try it," Gnash told him. "Then argue."

Greg wouldn't have argued with the spireling no matter what happened next, but when he lay down in the snow, wearing nothing but his light windbreaker over his new chain mail, he found he was just as comfortable as if he'd crawled into a snuggly warm featherbed. Rake found it quite comfy as well. He was happy to curl up on Greg's chest, where Greg's warm breath rhythmically ruffled his fur.

Within seconds both children were sound asleep, as it was impossible to remain awake long once Rake began his monotonous purring. Fortunately, neither was conscious when Rake's purr drifted across the campsite to knock out all four of their spireling guards.

Greg woke shortly after dawn, but still before Kristin. Surprising neither had awakened earlier, seeing as the spirelings had apparently loaded the two of them on the litter while they slept and were already racing between the trees when Greg first opened his eyes.

Kristin snapped alert. "Oh, my. When they said first light, they weren't kidding."

Panicked, Greg checked his backpack. To his relief, Rake's bright eyes peeked out at him.

The spirelings reached the base of the Smoky Mountains and passed into and out of the Weird Weald in record time, stopping only once for lunch. They were happy not to see the witch again, and by dinnertime emerged from the forest onto Pendegrass Highway, a trampled-down section of weeds that bordered the farming fields east of the castle.

Within seconds they completed the last two miles to arrive at their destination. There they were met at the castle's huge wooden gate by a mysterious man in a black robe, his face completely hidden beneath the hood he wore pulled up over his head.

"I thought you might come," said the dark figure.

Greg shivered in spite of the warmth of his magical chain mail. "Mordred?"

The magician lowered his hood, confirming Greg's suspicion. Greg had to stop himself from shrinking back. Mordred held little respect for him, tolerating him only because the Mighty Greghart, as Greg was better known, was named in prophecies Mordred deemed important. He studied Greg with indifference before glancing Kristin's way.

"And who is this?"

"Kristin Wenslow," Kristin answered.

Mordred's brow furrowed. "I don't remember any Kristin Wenslow in Simon's prophecy."

"Well, just because he didn't mention me doesn't mean I won't be around."

Greg cringed. He probably should have pointed out to Kristin that she shouldn't aggravate someone who could conjure a bolt of lightning with a wave of his hand. To his surprise, Mordred turned back to Greg and smiled, an expression Greg had never seen him use before.

"I like her," Mordred said. "She reminds me of Hazel."

"Hazel?" said Kristin. "The witch? Well, I never."

Mordred actually laughed, but then his face turned grim. "You two had better come inside. King Peter will want to see you."

"What about them?" Greg asked, indicating the spirelings.

"I'm not sure the king would approve of the entire spireling race listening in on his private conversations."

"They'll probably just hear everything anyway," said Greg.

"Believe me, they won't."

Greg nodded. He had an idea if Mordred really didn't want to be heard, the entire kingdom might suddenly turn up deaf. The spirelings stayed behind while Greg and Kristin followed the magician inside. According to Mordred, King Peter was in his study, but before they'd walked even halfway there, they were intercepted by Princess Priscilla and Lucky Day.

"Greg," Lucky called.

One of Greg's best friends on Myrth and without a doubt the luckiest person Greg had ever met, Lucky wore his usual bright orange tunic and wide smile. Priscilla was dressed in her usual attire, too: torn pants and a button-down shirt. She rushed forward to give Greg a big hug.

But then she pushed away and shot him a stern look. "I told you not to come here."

"Ahem," said Kristin.

Priscilla noticed Kristin for the first time. "Greg, who is this?"

"This? Oh, this is . . . um . . ."

"*Kristin*," said Kristin, looking more than a little irritated. "Don't tell me *you're* the princess?"

Priscilla brushed back a loose strand of flowing red hair. "Princess Priscilla, yes. And how do you know Greg?"

Kristin looked Priscilla squarely in the eye. Neither girl blinked. "We're dating."

"We are?" said Greg.

"He walked me home from school just yesterday," Kristin said, ignoring him.

Priscilla's voice sounded a bit higher than usual when she asked, "Greg, is this true?"

"Well, yeah, I guess so."

"I see."

Kristin smiled smugly and slipped her arm around Greg's. Greg gasped and shook himself free. Knowing he was prophesied to die here made him uncomfortable enough. This was too much.

"Father will want to see you," said Priscilla, stepping forward and taking Greg's arm in her own. Kristin took a more secure hold of his other.

Helpless, Greg glanced pleadingly at Lucky, who shrugged and gave him a look to indicate he sympathized. Even so, Greg was pretty sure he saw the boy crack a smile when the two girls tightened their grips and dragged Greg away.

Shaping Destiny

King Peter's study was nothing like Greg imagined. He'd expected an enormous room with splendid decor and thousands of ancient-looking tomes. Perhaps a few maps of the kingdom or intricate, richly woven tapestries. But this was just a small room, with a single comfortable-looking chair resting before a small wooden table. The air smelled faintly of smoke, as the room was lit by a dozen or more torches flickering in sconces lining the walls. On the table sat a single candlestick, which King Peter used to cast additional light on the pages of the book he was reading.

"Greghart," he said, when he first spotted Greg. "What are you doing here?"

"Oh, Father," said Priscilla, "there's no use playing innocent. I heard about the note you sent."

"But I distinctly told him *not* to come," the king insisted.

"As if you thought he'd stay away. Really, Daddy, this is embarrassing."

"Actually, I came because of *your* letter," Greg told Priscilla.

The princess blushed. "Mine? But I told you not to come under any circumstances."

"Yeah, but I couldn't stop thinking about you being in trouble. I wanted to help."

Behind the redness, Priscilla's face broke into a smile. The expression faded when Kristin stepped forward and took Greg's arm. "My Greggy is so brave, isn't he?"

King Peter's eyes widened. *Oh my,* he mouthed. "And who is this?"

"Kristin Wenslow, Your Highness," Kristin said, grasping an invisible dress and pulling it to the side as she curtsied. "Greg's girlfriend."

"My what?" said Greg.

King Peter pushed back his initial unease and smiled. "Please, call me Peter."

"But you're a king," said Kristin.

"So? I still have a name, you know. I'll make a deal. You call me Peter instead of Your Highness, and I'll call you Kristin instead of That Girl Who Came With Greg."

"Deal," Kristin said, smiling.

Priscilla crossed her arms and glared at the two of them. Kristin smiled even wider. She moved closer to the king and put a hand on his arm.

"What are you reading?" she asked in a lilting voice.

King Peter glanced at his daughter, then at Greg. Suddenly he looked as uncomfortable as Greg felt. He cleared his throat and spoke in a strained tone. "It's, er, something Brandon wrote. A prophecy, about Greg, and all of us."

"You call that writing?" Kristin said after one glance at the book lying open upon the desk.

"Yes, well, that's what Brandon calls it anyway."

"Brandon Alexander?" she asked.

King Peter regarded her with surprise. "You know him?"

"Just what my Greg has told me."

"Do you mind, Your Majesty?" Greg asked quickly, gesturing toward the book.

"Peter, Greghart. No, by all means."

Greg studied the book for only a moment. If he had to guess what happened here, he'd have bet a swarm of beetles had landed in an inkwell and then struggled to escape across the page. "This writing is awful. How are you going to figure out what it says?"

"Oh, I already know—Brandon told me two days ago—I was just taking a second look, hoping maybe there was something we overlooked."

"And is there?" asked Kristin.

"Beats me. These lines look like little more than random smudges to me."

"Does it really say Greg's going to die?" asked Lucky.

King Peter stiffened. "According to Brandon, I'm afraid so."

No one said a word for several uncomfortable seconds. Finally Lucky broke the silence. "Sorry, Greg. If there were any way to change all of this . . . If it makes you feel better, you're going to save us all before you go."

Greg tried to smile. "Yeah, that helps."

"What does Brandon say Greg's supposed to do?" Kristin asked.

"Yes, Father," Priscilla said, stepping between the two of them.

"What did he say?"

"Witch Hazel has managed to reconstruct the Amulet of Tehrer," Mordred told them both. "And she's been wasting no time. Already she's using it to control Ruuan."

"We know," said Kristin.

Greg quickly explained about their encounter with the witch along the trail.

"Oh my," King Peter said. "It's good Hazel has not yet figured out how to use the amulet to its full capacity. Once she does . . . well, I'm afraid Ruuan will do anything she asks."

"This is terrible," said Greg. "Where's Nathan? He'll know what to do."

Mordred grunted, but said nothing.

King Peter frowned. "We don't know. He left here soon after you did, right after he helped fulfill the last prophecy."

"Probably out researching the Dark Arts," said Mordred with disgust. "It does not surprise me he's not here during our time of need."

"That's not fair," said Greg. "Nathan would do anything for this kingdom. If he *is* trying to learn about Dark Magic, I'm sure he has his reasons."

"Yes, because he can't decide whether his loyalties rest here or with his old friend Hazel."

Greg was so mad he wanted to hit Mordred, but he wanted even more to live out his final days as a boy rather than as a newt. Still, he found it impossible to hold his tongue. "I seem to remember you were the one making deals with Hazel when I was here before."

"Yeah," Kristin jumped in, "and her name sure brought a smile to your face earlier."

"I do like her," Mordred said, indicating Kristin with a nod. "She's got spunk. Just like Hazel did when she was your age."

"There's that smile again," accused Kristin.

"Who has the questionable motives now, Mordred?" said Greg.

The magician's smile dissolved away. He stared at Greg with such intensity, Greg nearly slipped beneath King Peter's table.

"Er . . . *Mister* Mordred."

"I made a deal with Hazel," Mordred explained, "because years ago Nathan told me she would trade four pieces of Ruuan's amulet for the key piece of the Amulet of Tehrer. Only, Hazel didn't have all the pieces to trade, so I did what needed to be done. I saw to it she got them. Consequently the prophecy was fulfilled, and all turned out well for the kingdom."

"Except now Hazel's got the whole Amulet of Tehrer," said Priscilla, "and she's going to use it to destroy us."

"Not according to Simon," said Mordred. "The boy, here, is going to help us."

"What can *I* do?" Greg asked.

"Well, for starters, I had hoped you might have the Amulet of Ruuan."

"Me? Why would I have it?"

"You were the only logical choice to watch over it. Hazel would be looking for it here on Myrth, and even if she suspected it was safe on another world, she would have no way to find it. She doesn't have Lucky Day's talent to help her home in on its location."

Lucky smiled behind a complexion nearly as red as his hair.

"And you didn't understand how to use it," Mordred added in a tone that suggested Greg barely knew how to use a fork. "Nor would you be able to expand your knowledge without returning to Myrth. No, more than likely Nathan kept the amulet for himself, and he is the most dangerous person to have it. Without it, he is one of the most powerful magicians on Myrth. With it, well . . . "

He left the sentence unfinished, but Greg knew what he was implying. "You don't have to worry about Nathan."

"If only that were true. An artifact like that can have a tremendous pull on a man of power, especially one who has repeatedly shown an interest in the Dark Arts."

"Nathan is not evil," Priscilla insisted, crossing her arms over her chest in the same manner Kristin had been using ever since the princess stepped between her and Greg. "I won't hear of it."

"Nathan doesn't have the amulet yet," Greg said. "At least not all of it. Queen Gnarla still has her section."

"Maybe that's why he's not here," said Lucky. "Maybe he's at the spire now."

"But what if he's not?" Greg said. "We need to find him, make sure he knows to assemble the amulet and bring it here to show us how to use it. Then we'll be able to fight Witch Hazel on her own terms."

"Good luck," said Mordred. "Nathan's not on his way to the spire, I can assure you. He's not even within the kingdom. Or in the Styx. Or the Outer Reaches. Perhaps you'll find him in the Void, but even my magic can't locate him there."

"You can tell from here if Nathan's in the kingdom?" Greg asked.

"I can do many things."

Something about his tone reminded Greg of Nathan. It was a side of Mordred he'd never witnessed before—one that he might have liked on any other man, but in this case only made Greg question why all this time he'd trusted Nathan.

"I've tried to help the magicians find Nathan too," said Lucky, "but—" He shrugged.

Greg's hopes plummeted, for he knew if Lucky Day couldn't find him, Nathan was not about to be found.

"I can't believe he just left when we needed him," said Priscilla.

"Doesn't surprise me," said Mordred.

"To be fair, he didn't know we needed him," said Greg. "He didn't even know about Simon's third prophecy, and no one knew Hazel would reassemble the Amulet of Tehrer so quickly."

Kristin moved away from the table and took up Greg's arm again, to which Priscilla frowned. "Of course Nathan didn't know about the prophecy. You said this Simon guy just came up with it."

"He did," said Greg, "but that didn't stop Nathan before. It was really weird. He knew all kinds of things about those first two prophecies before they ever happened."

"How?"

Greg thought a moment. "He said I told him about them."

"That's right," said Priscilla. "I forgot. Just before you left us last time. What do you suppose he meant?" She eased up to Greg and took his other arm. Kristin's grip tightened. Greg hoped the two weren't preparing for a tug-of-war. Everyone was staring at Mordred, so Greg stared at him too.

"Don't look at me," said the magician. "Nathan may have confided in me some when we were children, but when it came to these prophecies, he remained quite secretive. Probably worried about me knowing too much about my own future."

"That does sound like Nathan," said Priscilla.

"Didn't he also say he learned about the prophecies when he was still living on Gyrth?" asked Lucky.

King Peter's eyebrows lifted. "You kids know about Gyrth, too?"

"Just that Nathan says that's where he's from," Greg said, "and that he didn't come here until he was about my age."

"But how could you have told him anything on Gyrth?" said Priscilla. "You weren't even alive when he was a boy. And even if you had been, you wouldn't have known about the prophecies until they happened."

"Maybe you're supposed to go there now," said Lucky.

Greg gave him a skeptical look. "What are you talking about?"

"Think about it. We need Nathan and the Amulet of Ruuan here now, right? I'm sure if Nathan knew that, he'd be here, so obviously he doesn't know."

"Okay, so?"

"So, Nathan claimed he knew all that other stuff because you told him. Maybe you were supposed to have told him this, too."

Greg frowned. "Let's hope not, because obviously I didn't."

"But it's not too late. King Peter's magicians can send you to any time and any place, remember? Just have them send you back to Nathan's past, and tell him to be here with the amulet when we need him."

"That's crazy."

"No, it makes perfect sense," said Priscilla.

Greg could feel Kristin tugging his arm, trying to pull him away, and he nearly let her. She leaned past him to better see Priscilla. "You think sending people back in time makes perfect sense?"

Priscilla spoke to Greg as though the two of them were alone. "Don't you think it's funny Nathan knew all those details about the first two prophecies and nothing about the third?"

"Sounds like us," Lucky said.

"Exactly," said Priscilla. "If Greg goes back to talk to Nathan now, he can tell him all about the first two prophecies, like Nathan said he did, but just like Nathan, he knows nothing of the third."

"I know it exists," argued Greg. "That's more than Nathan knew."

"Yes, but you don't need to tell him, do you, dear?" The princess looked up into Greg's eyes and batted her lashes.

Greg felt his face flush. "Dear?"

Priscilla's brow furrowed. She squeezed his arm a little too hard to be a sign of affection. "Well, do you?"

Greg struggled hard to shake loose of her grip. "No, I suppose not."

"Excellent," said Lucky. "When do we go?"

"We?" said Priscilla. "Who said *you* were going?"

"Who else could be lucky enough to find Nathan? He could be anywhere on Gyrth."

"Yes," Priscilla said, "but you don't need to go there. You just need to tell the magicians when to open the portal, like you always do."

"But what if Greg needs help?"

"I think I can handle it," Greg said. "All I need to do is tell Nathan a few stories."

He and Lucky started arguing, but nothing compared to Priscilla and Kristin, who practically got into a brawl over who could better defend Greg's abilities.

"Hush," said King Peter. "Quiet, everyone."

The children's bickering faded away, though Kristin and Priscilla each continued several seconds longer, each trying to get in the last word.

"I agree with Greg," said the king. "It would seem his future looks quite bleak, and I think it's only right he be the one in charge of his own destiny." Under his breath, he added, "however short that may be."

"Huh?" said Greg.

"Mordred, I want you to gather the other magicians. Lucky, you go with him and assist with the opening of the portal. Girls . . . well, I think you better stay here with me."

"But—" said both girls at once.

"Sorry, the matter is not open for discussion. Now, we all know what we're supposed to do. Let's get to it. And good luck to all of you."

Lucky smiled. "Don't worry. We won't need it."

"Speak for yourself," Greg muttered. Then he realized Lucky was right. No amount of luck could change the fact that Simon had already spoken. Regardless of Greg's success or failure on Gyrth, once he returned, he held not even a glimmer of hope for survival.

Greg could see very little within the gloomy Room of Shadows, a small anteroom off the Great Hall, where he had begun and ended two previous trips to Myrth. He should have been exhausted. All day he'd been traveling, and even if he *had* ridden atop a litter the whole way, he felt he had every right.

But as he waited for the magicians to cast their spell, Greg felt oddly restless. Well, perhaps not *oddly* restless. He was often afraid on Myrth, particularly in the presence of the magicians. The fact he was about to leave did little to help.

"You worried, Greg?" asked Lucky.

"A little."

"Well, don't be. King Peter will make sure the girls don't tear each other apart."

"What?" Greg realized Lucky was smiling. "Oh, right . . . So, you think I'll recognize him?"

"Why wouldn't you? How many kings do you know?" Again Lucky was smiling.

"I'm serious, Lucky. It's hard to imagine Nathan as a kid."

"Relax, Greg. We're going to set you down right next to him."

"Let's hope so."

A hooded figure stepped out of the shadows. "Ready, boy?"

Greg recognized the voice, even if Mordred's face was completely lost in the shadows. "I guess."

"Then let's get on with it."

Lucky handed Greg a walking stick, which Greg clenched to his chest with one hand while he passed back his knapsack with the other. Lucky grimaced. The magic packs of Myrth could carry countless objects far bigger than the packs themselves, and Lucky once told Greg no matter how much he carried inside his, he never once noticed the weight, not even the time he stuffed Princess Priscilla into the bag.

But if Lucky had been surprised by the weight, it was nothing compared to the shock he must have felt when the knapsack in his hand let out a shriek.

"Sorry, Rake," said Greg, "you need to stay here."

The whining only grew stronger.

"Sounds pretty serious," said Lucky. "Maybe you should take him with you."

"I guess I could."

Greg took back his knapsack. He removed his text books and handed them to Lucky, then placed Rake in the pack, slipped the straps over his shoulders, and took up his walking stick again. The two boys moved to the center of the room, and Greg fought the urge to run while the magicians moved in to surround them. "Wait."

"Yes, what is it?" said Mordred.

"How will I get back?"

"The spell we've prepared will keep you there a short time only. Complete your business early, because when you're brought back, it will be without warning."

"But what if I haven't found Nathan yet?"

Mordred glanced at Lucky and back again. "I don't think that will be a problem. Now, we're wasting time."

"Yes, sir."

The magicians joined hands, and Greg instantly felt a charge in the air. Within seconds the space before him split and revealed a hidden dimension beyond. Thousands, maybe millions of stars floated by while Lucky stared intently into the gap. An eternity passed, until Greg was so tense he nearly screamed.

Then Lucky did scream. "Now!"

Instantly the world shifted beneath Greg's feet. The gloomy chamber full of dark hooded figures disappeared. In its place, Greg faced a world far less cheery.

Nate

The building ahead was buried in graffiti, or perhaps should have been. Boards had been nailed over the lower windows, but shards of glass from those above littered the ground by Greg's feet, along with bricks and bits of crumbled mortar fallen from the dilapidated wall. Behind, the buildings resembled little more than enormous piles of rubble. At first Greg thought he was in a war zone, but something told him a war zone would have been safer.

A shuffling to his left caused him to spin and raise his walking stick. The familiar feel of wood in his hands restored his confidence, even if the rat that scurried away looked big enough to take it from him.

Then he spotted someone standing atop the rubble. Nathan might look different as a boy, but Greg had an idea this was someone else. For one thing, he was the wrong color. In fact, Greg felt blue was the wrong color for any boy.

"Hello?" Greg called.

The blue-skinned boy stared without speaking. In one hand he carried a fist-sized rock. He tossed it to his other hand and back again. Greg shifted his grip on his walking stick.

Behind came the clink of metal on rock. Greg spun to find a second boy leaning against the closest building. This one was olive-skinned, but not like anyone Greg had ever seen before. The boy's complexion was actually a bright olive green. He carried a two-foot-long pipe in one hand, and Greg had an idea he and the other boy had not come here to play baseball.

From around the corner stepped a third, larger boy, his skin a bright red. At least Greg could pretend this one was badly sunburned. The boy carried a short length of chain, which he swung in a lazy circle.

"Uh, hi guys," Greg said. "How's it going?"

From behind buildings and scattered piles of rubble emerged several more boys, each more threatening than the last. They sported skins of every color of the rainbow, and even the few who had complexions of a more familiar hue looked no less odd due to the extreme contrast. A few laughed, but not in a friendly way. They ambled toward Greg, separating as they approached.

Greg blew out a breath. He raised his walking stick, adopting the *sensen* stance Nathan had ingrained in him, and waited to see what they would do.

Suddenly one boy lunged forward, swinging a length of pipe. He obviously thought to surprise Greg, and he did, but only because Greg had imagined him doing something far worse.

The thrust came as if in slow motion, and Greg easily diverted it away with his stick. The boy stumbled and nearly fell, but Greg made no advance against him. Instead he planted his walking stick on the ground before his feet.

"I don't want to fight."

"I'll bet you don't," the boy said, and launched a second attack.

Greg slapped away that thrust just as easily as the first, but a second boy took advantage of the distraction to come at Greg with a chain. Greg's eyes widened. He'd never tried deflecting a swinging chain before. But then, he *had* once managed to deflect an enraged troll, not to mention a couple of angry spirelings. The thought might have calmed him, if the memories themselves hadn't been so terrifying. Even so, he caught the chain on the point of his stick and yanked it away before it completely unfurled.

The boy with the pipe launched another attack. Greg barely managed to dodge the blow. He flailed his stick around for protection, accidentally striking the boy across the shoulder.

"Ow!"

"Sorry," Greg said.

The boy looked even more terrified than Greg felt. He hesitated, his pipe dangling loosely at his side. But then he grinned, and Greg caught movement out of the corner of his eye.

Greg ducked and spun and extended his stick, feeling the solid impact of wood on bone. A third boy had joined the fight and paid dearly for it. He screamed and fell to the ground, holding his side.

"Really sorry," Greg added.

"Get out of the way," growled a large purple-skinned boy. He shoved one of the others aside and lumbered forward, tossing up a large rock and catching it again. "Let's see how far he can reach with that thing."

Greg was just about to try reasoning with him when the boy lurched forward and unleashed the stone. Greg gasped, but months of practicing his chikan skills on the trail took over. His head jerked back, and he batted down the toss with his stick.

The purple boy's jaw dropped. "What the—?"

"Get him!" someone shouted, and Greg nearly panicked when attackers rushed him from all sides.

He didn't focus on any particular one, but instead began to dance through the chikan moves Nathan had taught him, adjusting the routine ever so slightly to slap away each strike that came his way, never hesitating long enough to see the results of his efforts. The attacks seemed to rain in on him forever, but not one of the boys managed to reach him with their makeshift weapons. Finally, when Greg felt he was about to collapse, a voice rang out above the crowd.

"Stop!"

Greg continued pushing his walking stick through his practiced movements for several seconds before he realized the attacks had ceased. He spun the stick a final time and planted one end in the ground at his feet.

His attackers pulled back to allow another boy to pass. This one stood smaller than any Greg had faced, but he walked with an air of confidence that worried Greg even more. His skin was dark but human looking, and he seemed vaguely familiar.

"Nathan?"

The boy stopped several feet away and eyed Greg, clearly confused but in no way intimidated. "Nate. Only my father calls me Nathan."

Greg exhaled shakily. Who'd have thought Nathan would have been just as confident as a boy as he was as an adult? Was it possible Nathan knew magic before he ever left for Myrth? Greg shuddered at the thought. Then he had an idea.

"How *is* your father? I heard he was sick."

The length of turned wood Nathan carried might have once been a baseball bat, or it could have just as easily been a table leg, or a banister spindle. Whatever it was, Greg had an idea it would cause major damage to anything that got in its way. Nathan held it up much the way he'd raised his staff on hundreds of occasions as an adult. Greg gulped, remembering the man's impossibly fluid skill.

"What do you know of my father?"

Greg didn't know anything about Nathan's father, except that the man had passed away just before Nathan came to Myrth. Still, he knew he better say something.

"Just that he depends on you and probably wouldn't want you

fighting."

Nathan smiled. "Well, he can rest easy, because I won't be fighting long." And with that he lunged forward so quickly, Greg barely had time to duck.

Nathan's bat cut the air just above Greg's head. Before Greg could even congratulate himself on his quick reflexes, a second blow came out of nowhere.

He parried the swing and stabbed out with his stick, catching Nathan by surprise. Still, Nathan was a natural athlete even then. He dodged aside with nearly the same fluidity he would achieve in later years and launched a third attack, which Greg deflected just as skillfully.

"Come on, Nate," yelled one of the others. "Quit fooling around. Finish him off."

Nathan focused on Greg, searching for a weakness. Ironically, Greg followed the very advice his opponent would one day teach him. He took the moment to clear his mind, and his body naturally moved to sensen position.

Nathan, if anyone, should have realized the significance of the stance. But instead of taking the moment to prepare himself, he struck. Greg read the blow and knocked it aside. At the same time his foot stabbed out and caught Nathan's ankle. His mentor stumbled and fell, but then rolled back to his feet and struck out with his bat before he was even halfway up. Once again Greg met the blow and pushed it aside.

Nathan's confidence was shaken. His next attack was sloppy, more desperate. Greg easily stepped out of the way and reached in with his own stick, leveraging the wood from Nathan's grip. The bat flew to one side, and a few of the other boys nearly knocked each other over scrambling to get out of the way. From all around him, Greg heard gasps. He waited to see what Nathan would do. It wasn't what he expected.

Nathan's face broke into a wide grin. "What's your name, kid?"

"Greg."

"Where'd you learn to fight like that?"

"I had a good teacher."

Nathan looked nearly as surprised as he did when the weapon flew from his hands. "What teacher? Nobody knows how to fight like that but me and my dad." He studied Greg's face for a moment. "How come we've never seen you around before?"

Because I just came here from another planet, Greg thought. "I'm not from around here," he said instead, "and everybody there knows how to fight."

Nathan stepped forward and reached out a hand, causing Greg to flinch. His grin widened. "Relax," he said, laughing. He put an arm around Greg's shoulder and pulled him around to face some of his friends. They each stepped up in turn to shake Greg's hand, and while they seemed much less threatening now than they had a moment ago, Greg still felt far from comfortable having them all within arm's reach.

"Now will you tell me how you know my father?" Nathan asked.

Greg wondered how long everyone would stay friendly if he told them the truth. "Uh, I don't really. I just know *of* him."

Nathan stooped to pick up his bat. "Well, I'm sure he'd like to meet you. There aren't many kids around here who know chikan, and none who can beat me."

"None except Greg, you mean," said one of the boys, but he shut up rather quickly when Nathan's bat soared past his head.

"It's almost dinnertime," said Nathan. "You should come eat with us. My dad and me, I mean. I was serious before. I'm sure he'd like to meet you."

"Sure," said Greg. He needed to get Nathan alone so they could talk.

Nathan said good-bye to his friends and led Greg away. Behind them a couple of boys began sparring with their crude weapons, mimicking the moves they'd seen Greg use, but Greg could tell they knew nothing of chikan.

Nathan led him past two buildings, then turned and walked down a desolate alley. Greg became increasingly nervous, but he still had his stick. He felt confident he could defend himself if need be.

Ahead, a large pile of bricks had spilled out onto the sidewalk. Nathan turned there and stepped through a hole in the wall, motioning for Greg to follow. The building they entered was little more than a shell. They passed through it and into another alley. A few hundred yards further, Nathan stopped and pulled back a weathered piece of plywood used to seal up a hole in yet another building. He stepped through the opening, and Greg followed.

The plywood fell back into place, cutting off all light. Greg's grip tightened on his stick.

"This way," said Nathan, and Greg felt a touch on his elbow.

The area was deafeningly quiet. The two of them moved through the darkness to a stairway, up two flights, and into a hallway lit by a single window set in the far wall. Nathan knocked on one of the doors midway along the hall. Two quick taps, a slap, and another quick tap. In a few moments Greg heard the sound of a latch being drawn back.

A second latch was pulled back, then a third. After five more, the door opened. Greg's breath caught in his throat.

The last thing he'd been expecting was for Nathaniel Caine's face to poke out and greet him.

Story Time

It wasn't quite Nathan's face. The features were similar, but the eyes were more sunken, or maybe they just seemed that way because the skin was so sallow. At the moment the mouth was frowning.

"There you are. I've been worried sick. Out fighting again, I suppose."

"Uh, no, Dad," said Nate. "Just messing around. I found someone who knows chikan."

"Hah. I knew you were fighting."

Nate exchanged glances with Greg. "But he's really good. His name's Greg. Say hi, Greg."

"Uh, hi," Greg said awkwardly.

Nate's father looked at him for the first time. "You sick, son? You look pale."

"Dad."

"Well, if he's sick you'd want to know, right?"

"He's not sick." Nate motioned Greg inside and closed the door.

Mr. Caine hobbled across the room to a chair that looked like some sort of elaborate mousetrap. He started to say something but began coughing instead and couldn't catch his breath for a long while. Finally he looked back to Greg through watery eyes.

"Well, he sure looks sick. I haven't seen skin that fair since . . . well, I'm not sure I've ever seen skin that fair. Maybe in Grandpa's old photo album. People seemed a lot lighter-skinned in those days . . . then again, that may have just been the film." He coughed once or twice more, then spoke in a strained voice. "Say, are you sure you're not sick, son?"

"Dad, he's not sick. I just told you he beat me at chikan."

"No, you said he knew chikan. You didn't say nothing about him beating you." He winked at Greg. "So you beat him, did you?"

"I guess," Greg muttered.

"You should have seen him," said Nate. "He fought Benny and Bobby Bristo, Danny, Sam, and Big Pete, all at the same time."

Nathan's father regarded Greg with renewed respect. "Five at once?

Impressive. So, where'd you learn the art, son? Your parents, I'd wager. They obviously have Earthen roots, no?"

"Earthen roots?"

"Dad has this crazy idea that only the Spectrals originated here," said Nate.

"You have ghosts here?"

"Not specters. Spectrals . . . you know, every color of the spectrum. Say, where are you from, anyway?"

"You wouldn't believe me if I told you," Greg said.

Mr. Caine's head snapped toward Greg, and in spite of the deathly look about his face, his eyes flashed with excitement. "What do you mean?"

Greg pretended not to hear. "You were saying something about spectral people?" he said to Nate.

"Yeah. Dad thinks the Spectrals evolved here, but the Earthtones, as he calls people like us, originated on another world he calls Earth. Pretty crazy, huh?"

Greg wasn't sure how to respond. Nathan once told him that magicians from both this planet and his own were brought to Myrth to fight the Dragon Wars, and that some from Earth may have returned here instead of their own world. Calling them Earthtones didn't make it any crazier.

"I said, 'Pretty crazy, huh?'"

Greg realized he'd been daydreaming. "Who's to say?"

Nate scowled. "Don't humor him," he whispered.

Mr. Caine took to coughing so hard, Greg wasn't sure he'd ever regain his breath. "I knew it. You're from Myrth, aren't you?"

Now it was Greg who started coughing.

"What are you talking about, Dad?" said Nate.

Mr. Caine pried himself from his chair and motioned the boys toward an old wooden table. "Come, sit. There's much we must discuss."

"What's going on, Dad?" said Nate, but Mr. Caine wouldn't speak again until the two boys were seated and he'd poured himself a large cup of water from a chipped pitcher. His hands trembled so badly, water spilled over half the table, but he managed to drink a few drops and then offered some to Greg out of the same cup.

"Er, no, thanks."

Mr. Caine took a second drink for himself, then set the cup back on the table with a clatter. "So, you *are* from Myrth then?"

Greg wasn't sure what to say. He wondered how long these two would wait if he said nothing at all.

"Where's Myrth?" Nate asked again.

His father frowned. "You'd know if you ever listened when I'm talking."

"Dad."

"Myrth is a world of magic."

Nate laughed. "I think I'd have remembered that."

"I've never told you much about it because you always roll your eyes at me whenever I bring up your origins."

"But that was about Earth. I thought this time you said Myrth."

Mr. Caine shot Greg a see-what-I-have-to-put-up-with? look. He stifled another cough and poured himself a second cup of water.

"Well, maybe next time I talk, you'll listen." He turned back to Greg. "You never answered me. You are from Myrth, right?"

Greg debated ignoring the question again but guessed the man might notice. "I did come here from Myrth, yes."

Mr. Caine looked as if he might faint. Of course, he'd looked like that from the start.

Nate regarded Greg doubtfully. "You're from another world."

"Of course he's from another world," said Mr. Caine. "Just look at him."

"He looks normal to me."

"Ridiculous. Normal people can't do magic."

Nate turned back to Greg. "You can do magic?"

"He came here from another world, didn't he?" said Mr. Caine.

"No, you've got it all wrong," said Greg. "I'm not a magician."

"You're not?" said both Nate and his father. Greg couldn't decide who sounded more disappointed.

"If it makes you happy, I did get sent here by one. Actually, a whole group of them. And they're going to bring me back soon."

"You're kidding?" said Nate.

"I knew it," said Mr. Caine, banging his fist on the table. His cup bounced up and clinked into the pitcher, but didn't topple over.

"Why would a bunch of magicians send you *here*?" Nate asked.

"Yes, tell us," said Mr. Caine. "Did you do something bad? Were you exiled?"

Greg started to answer, but then caught himself. Sure, this was why he had come here, but how much should he tell them? On Myrth, the adult Nathan was always saying how dangerous it was to know too much about the future. Greg needed time to think.

"Sorry, I can't say."

"Why not?" asked Nate.

"Magicians," his father said. "Terribly secretive lot."

"I'm not a magician," Greg objected.

"Wouldn't know it to listen to you. I've been waiting all my life for proof that Myrth exists. Now here you are, and I can't pry a word from you."

"Can you at least tell us something about it?" asked Nate.

"Um . . ." said Greg. He at least had to tell Nate about the first two prophecies, or they might never come true—er, have come true—either way, he had to tell him.

"We'll give you dinner," Mr. Caine bargained, and Greg's expression must have changed, because the man banged the table again. "I knew it. Don't tell me I don't know how a young boy thinks."

Nate stood and walked to a counter in what might have passed for a kitchen. He removed a loaf of bread from a dented canister, returned to the table, and tore off one piece for Greg and another for his father.

"Er, thanks," said Greg. In his mind he ran through every moment he'd ever spent with Nathan. How much did the man already know about the future when he met Greg, and how much did he learn along the way? Well, he at least knew about the existence of the first two prophecies. Greg started out by telling them how he once set out to slay a dragon.

Nate and his father listened with awe as Greg discussed meeting a strange man in white among the shifting pools of lava within the Molten Moor, but he made sure to mention being alone when he set out to confront Witch Hazel, remembering how Nathan had refused to step foot across Black Blood Creek.

Soon he was describing how he and Lucky hauled a large sled up the winding tunnel through the Infinite Spire, and of his confrontation with the dragon, Ruuan. But he skipped the part about running into the Army of the Crown along the way. Nathan seemed just as surprised by that chance encounter as Greg was. Likewise he didn't mention the bollywomp attack, or the stampeding falchions in Fey Field.

"This is incredible," said Nate. "You're making it up."

"No," said Greg, "I'm not."

"Of course he's not," said Mr. Caine. "You don't lie to magicians."

"Dad, we're not magicians," said Nate.

"No, but the people in Greg's world are. You don't just go breaking habits overnight." He returned to coughing then, and Nate and Greg exchanged worried glances as he fought to catch his breath.

"You okay, Dad?"

"I'm fine," Mr. Caine insisted. "Tell us more," he said to Greg, his voice little more than a gasp.

"Uh, okay." Greg thought hard about how much advance knowledge Nathan had of the second prophecy. His memories were getting all mixed up. It seemed as if Nathan knew very little about Greg's last trip to Myrth beyond the fact that Greg exchanged the key piece of the Amulet of Tehrer for the missing pieces of Ruuan's amulet. But Greg wasn't sure, and he couldn't help but worry as he relayed even this much.

He made sure to hint that it wouldn't take the witch long to restore the amulet, so Nathan would know to be there when they needed him, but he was careful not to mention a third prophecy at all. Unfortunately there was not much more he could reveal.

Nate looked disappointed. "But you hardly told us anything about the battle."

"There's not much to tell. We were surrounded by trolls, and a lot of good men died. I might have too, if not for my skill in chikan."

"Lucky you're so good," said Nate.

"Not luck. I worked hard to learn."

Mr. Caine shot his son a look. "See?"

"You could be just as good if you wanted," Greg told Nate.

"Who says I'm not?"

Greg laughed. "I thought we settled that earlier."

"Who are you kidding, boy?" said Nate's father. "You'll never be as good as you could. All you're interested in is the mechanics. You never listen when I tell you about the important things."

"Aw, Dad."

"No, he's right," Greg said.

"What would you know about it?"

"Chikan is more than just a way of fighting. It's a whole way of thinking. True power can only come from inner peace."

"You sound like Dad."

"Oh, then you have heard me," Mr. Caine said. He started wheezing again, and once again Greg was afraid he wouldn't stop.

"Maybe you should go to bed, Dad," said Nate. "You don't look so good."

Mr. Caine nodded but was unable to speak. He allowed the boys to guide him to a cot in one corner of the room. Nate draped a blanket over him while Greg adjusted the single pillow beneath his head. Then, as Greg started to draw away, Mr. Caine reached out and grabbed his hand.

"Thanks for coming here," he whispered. "About the chikan . . . I'll try to tell him again. Maybe now that he's met you, he'll listen."

Greg wasn't sure what to say. "Yes, you should do that. He needs to know about sensen and the meditation. I can't tell you why, but it's important."

Mr. Caine offered a faint smile and nodded as if he understood, even though there was no way he could. "I'll teach him," he said. "I promise." He closed his eyes then and lay still, drawing breath in ragged gasps. Nate and Greg both stared at him worriedly. Finally Nate motioned for Greg to follow him to the door.

"He's not going to make it this time, is he?" Nate asked, as if it would be perfectly normal for Greg to know the future.

"I-I don't know," Greg admitted, but then he remembered what Mr. Caine had just said. Nothing was likely to happen to him before he finished teaching his son the philosophy behind chikan. "I think he's going to be okay for a little while."

Nate looked doubtful.

"You should listen to whatever he has to tell you," Greg added. He didn't know if it was the right thing to do, but he decided to add one other thing, his voice little more than a whisper. "You might not have a lot of time left together."

Nate turned away, as if to hide his tears, but then was quick to recover. "Thanks for all those stories you made up. I think Dad really enjoyed them."

"I didn't make them up."

"Yeah, right."

"No, I swear."

"Do I look like an idiot?"

Greg's backpack let out a yowl. He slipped it off hurriedly when he felt Rake struggling to get loose. Before he could do anything to stop it, the shadowcat wriggled free and jumped to his shoulder.

"Whoa," said Nate. "What is that?"

"Uh . . . it's a shadowcat. You'll learn all about them if you come to Myrth."

Nate's jaw fell slack. "Then you *were* telling the truth. You are from another world?"

Greg nodded.

"I wish I could see this Myrth place for myself. Maybe I'll come see you when . . . you know."

Greg shooed Rake back into the pack and slipped it over his shoulder. "Yes, you should come . . . but you won't be able to see me, at least not right away."

"Why? Are you invisible in your world?"

"No . . . I can't tell you . . . but we will meet again, I promise."

Nate smiled sadly. "I hope so. How does somebody get to Myrth anyway?"

Greg stared back at him dumbly. All along he'd been thinking he just needed to relay a few stories to the young Nathan. He'd never stopped to question how the boy was going to get to Myrth when the time came. It's not like he could just say a magic word and expect to pop between dimensions. Or could he?

"My ring."

Greg slipped the special ring from his finger and held it out. Suddenly everything made sense. Of course Nate had to take it. Someone had to give it to Ruuan so the dragon could offer it to Greg years from now, when Greg faced him in his lair.

Nate reached out cautiously for the ring while Greg explained how to use it and cautioned him about what he might find on the other end of his trip. Ruuan could seem a bit intimidating if you didn't know him—and even if you did. Afterward Nate seemed twice as reluctant to take the ring, but he accepted it anyway and slipped it over his finger.

"But then how will you get home?" Nate asked.

"Don't worry," said Greg. "I've made other arrangements."

Nate stared at him, looking more than a little overwhelmed. "Tell the truth. I mean, I know I've never seen one of those cat things before, but . . . you weren't just putting us on, were you . . . for Dad's sake? This Myrth world really exists?"

Greg didn't need to answer. Before he could speak, he felt his world shift. Nate's questioning face was still gawking at him, refusing to believe, when it blinked out of existence.

In its place hovered the shadowed features of the dark magician, Mordred.

Missing Pieces

"What happened?" Greg asked. "Nate?"

Lucky stepped up next to Mordred's shoulder. "Greg, you're back."

"I am?"

"Obviously," said Mordred.

Lucky squeezed past the magician. "What happened? Did you find Nathan?"

"What? Oh, yeah . . . is he here?"

Lucky glanced around the room. Dozens of hooded figures stood motionless in the dark, but Nathan was not among them. He shrugged. "Maybe he's outside."

"Nathaniel is not in the area," Mordred said. "If he were, I would sense his presence."

"But I don't understand," said Greg. "I did everything but tell him what Hazel would do. He wouldn't have abandoned us now."

"This does not surprise me," said Mordred. "You can't trust a man who would dabble in the Dark Arts."

"Would you get off the Dark Arts thing?" said Greg. "Nathan's the most trustworthy man you'll ever meet." He shared a worried look with Lucky. "I wonder what happened to him?"

Mordred's mouth worked itself into something vaguely smile-shaped. "I rest my case."

"Let's go find King Peter," said Lucky. "Maybe he's heard something . . . and even if he hasn't, he's been watching over the girls for three days now. I'm sure he'll be grateful for the reprieve."

"Days?" said Greg. "You mean hours."

"No," said Mordred. "Time passes differently here than it does on Gyrth."

"But when you sent me between here and Earth, I got back the same instant I left."

Mordred frowned. "Gyrth isn't Earth."

"Wow." Greg couldn't believe he'd wasted so much time already. "Poor King Peter. Have the girls killed each other yet?"

54

"Don't know," said Lucky. "I haven't seen either of them since you left."

The two boys rushed off to seek out King Peter, whom they found alone in his study, reading a book. The girls were conspicuously absent.

"Maybe they did kill each other," whispered Lucky.

"If you're referring to the girls, they're fine," said the king. "Much better than expected. So, how did your trip to Gyrth go, Greghart? Did you find Nathan?"

"Yes, Your Majesty—"

"Peter, Greg. Just Peter."

"Right. Anyway, I did find him, and I warned him about Witch Hazel. I'd hoped you would have heard from him by now."

"Oh dear, not a word."

"Great, what do we do now?" said Lucky.

The door opened, and a harried-looking Brandon Alexander rushed in carrying a large tome. Behind him walked Mordred, his face nearly concealed by his hood.

"Sorry it took so long, Sire," Brandon said, "but someone placed it back on the shelf in the wrong spot."

"Peter, Brandon. Just Peter."

"What's that?" asked Lucky, motioning toward the book Brandon carried.

"It contains the first of the Greghart prophecies," the king said. He took the book from Brandon. "I've gleaned all I can from the current prophecy and the last, but haven't learned anything that will help us. I had hoped the first might hold some clue we've overlooked."

"I doubt you will find anything there, Sire," said Mordred. "If you ask me, Nathaniel Caine is the only man who can tell us what we seek. He's known about events to come his entire life, and has spent all of that time preparing for them."

"Nathan's not here?" said Brandon. "That's odd."

"How so?" King Peter asked. "He's been gone for over five days."

"Nonsense." The scribe's face reddened. "I-I mean—"

King Peter waved away the words. "Are you saying Nathan's back?"

"I don't know if he's back or not, but I do know I saw him yesterday morning. He told me if Greghart arrived before he got back to let him know not to worry, that he would return before sunset with a solution to our problem."

"This is great," said Lucky.

Greg frowned. The situation seemed anything but great, but it was not the first time Lucky was happy to be in a spot that would have brought Greg to tears.

"Don't you see?" Lucky said. "Your trip to Gyrth must have worked. Before you left, Nathan had been gone for days. Now you changed history, and Nathan was here just yesterday morning."

Greg would have been ecstatic, except for one thing. "But he's still not here now."

Mordred grunted. "I told you. Nathan can't be trusted."

"He can too!" Greg's voice echoed throughout the King's chambers for several awkward moments.

Finally King Peter cleared his throat. "I believe Greg is right. I'd trust Nathanial Caine with my life. If he's not back, I'm sure he has a very good reason."

"He must be in terrible trouble," said Lucky.

Mordred frowned. "You don't know that."

"No, but he could be. Couldn't he, Sire?"

"Peter, Lucky. Please."

"Perhaps it's nothing," said Brandon. "Maybe his note can tell us more."

"His note?" King Peter said.

"Well, the note he asked me to put to parchment."

The king stared at the scribe expectantly.

Brandon stared back. His eyes grew wide. "Didn't I give you the note?" He patted down his tunic until he heard a crinkling sound, then hastily dug out a wrinkled swath of parchment. "Sorry, here you go." He passed it to the king, who studied it for a few seconds.

"I can't read this."

"What do you mean?" said the scribe. He peered over King Peter's shoulder, moving his lips silently as he scanned the page.

"Just tell us what it says." Mordred's tone suggested he was more annoyed than any magician ought to be.

"Well, it's all right here, plain as day. *Dear Greg, I have gone to the Netherworld to see a man named Dolzowt De* . . . What's this word?" he asked Greg, holding the parchment out and pointing at a spot where it looked as if someone had swatted a fly.

"You're asking me?"

"Deth," said Mordred. "He's gone to see Dolzowt Deth."

Brandon's eyes brightened. "Yes, exactly. I don't know why I didn't see it. Anyway . . . *I have gone to the Netherworld to see a man named Dolzowt*

Deth about a matter of highest imprint—er *import. I should be back by nightfall, but if you are feeling anxious about events to come, you can start making separations*—no, *preparations*—*without me. Get the king's magicians to assist you, but warn them to avoid using too much magic. They will want to conserve their strength for our upcoming battle, as we will need every resource we can find to overcome the throat that lies before us.*"

Greg's stomach was beginning to churn in a peculiar way he'd come to associate with the world of Myrth. "The throat that lies before us?" he repeated.

"I think he means *threat*," King Peter said with a wink.

"Oh, right," said Brandon. "*We will need every resource we can find to overcome the* threat *that lies before us.*"

"This is terribly helpful," said Mordred. "Does Nathan have any other profound words of wisdom for us?"

"Uh, let's see." Brandon used a finger to guide himself through the lines on the parchment. "Oh, yes, here we are. *I would start by eliciting help from the spirelings. Their race far outnumbers our own, and as they are masters at battle, they may have a few useful suggestions. Queen Gnarla should be receptive to our needs. If not, remind her that she and her people share in our flight.* Er, I mean *our plight. Remember, if you can find one of her kind, you will hold her ear.*"

"Hold her ear? That can't be right." Brandon started reciting other options to himself until Mordred interrupted.

"He means she will hear you, imbecile. The spirelings share a single mind when it comes to matters of the senses."

"Now, now, let's not be rude," said King Peter. "What else did he have to say, Brandon?"

The scribe took a moment to find his place again. "*You may want to contact Marvin Greatheart, as well, and his father, Norman, since both have experience battling dragons.*" The churning in Greg's stomach took on a more gnawing quality. "*Even Melvin may have a part to play in this. I cannot be sure. Finally, I would suggest you work closely with my old friend Mordred.*"

"Me?" said Mordred. "It does not say that." He snatched the parchment from Brandon's hands and scanned the page for himself. "Were you having some sort of fit when you wrote this?"

"Is there anything else?" asked King Peter.

Mordred stared at the note with a bewildered expression, eventually shrugged, and handed it back to Brandon. The scribe glared at the magician over his nose before turning his attention back to the page.

"*Mordred knows Hazel better than even I. If anyone there can second-guess what she will do, it will be he. If all goes well, when I return I will bring with me a solution to our troubles. If you just do your best until then, I am sure Simon's prophecy will play out as predicted. Wait, no, don't write that. The prophecy says Greg is going to die, remember?"*

Brandon looked up, rather embarrassed. "I guess he wanted me to leave that part out."

"Yes," King Peter quickly interjected, "well, I'm sure Simon must have . . . that is to say, the prophecy is clearly . . . well, I hardly think it's possible . . . "

"I'm going to die, aren't I?" said Greg.

"No, of course not," said everyone in unison. All except Mordred, who did his best to offer a sympathetic, "I can't see how not."

"Mordred, please," scolded the king. "Well, I guess we shouldn't be standing around wasting time. This note makes it quite clear what our plan should be."

"But what about Nathan?" said Greg. "Lucky's right. He must be in terrible trouble."

Mordred scowled. "Which is exactly what he should expect."

"Enough," said King Peter. "You heard Nathan's advice. We'll all need to work together if we're going to live through this latest threat."

And even if we're not, Greg thought.

"Of course, Sire," said Mordred. "I would never let Nathan's senseless disregard for his craft stand in my way of protecting this kingdom."

"Glad you're being so big about it," said the king.

"I will see to his recommendations myself."

"Very good. And you'll take Greghart with you, of course."

Mordred glared at Greg as if he were seriously contemplating conjuring up a bolt of lightning to clear the spot where Greg stood. "Of course, Your Majesty."

"Peter, Mordred. Why can't anyone just call me Peter?"

Breakthroughs in Communication

"Wait," said Greg. "What about the girls?"

He and Mordred were striding down the hall away from King Peter's chambers when Greg slowed. Mordred stopped and turned, his robe wafting out around him, making him appear twice as large as he really was. Greg couldn't say he liked the effect.

"Why are you stopping?" the magician hissed.

"I forgot about Kristin and Priscilla," Greg told him. "King Peter said the two of them are together somewhere."

"How fascinating."

"No, you don't understand. They're both very headstrong. I'm afraid they might . . . you know . . . kill each other or something."

A giggle echoed down the corridor. A short way off the two girls came strolling in Greg's direction, engaged in an animated conversation broken only by their wide smiles and exuberant laughter.

"Yes, I see what you mean," said Mordred.

"Greg!" both girls cried out. They ran at him so quickly, Greg nearly bolted away. Once they reached him, they squeezed him fiercely until his face turned blue.

"I should think you'd be more worried about *them* killing *you*," observed Mordred.

"When did you get back?" Priscilla asked.

"Yes, when? We've been so worried," added Kristin.

"We?" said Greg.

"Prissy and I."

"Prissy?" Greg said, cringing. "She hates being called that."

"No, I don't mind," said Priscilla. "Krissy likes it. That way we rhyme."

"Krissy?"

"Right," said Kristin. "She's Prissy. I'm Krissy. Cute, don't you think?"

Greg wasn't sure, but he thought he liked it better when the girls were fighting.

"If you're about through here," interrupted Mordred, "do you think we can get back to saving the kingdom?"

"Oh, right," said Greg.

Kristin smiled at the menacing magician and back at Greg. "You came up with a plan? That's great."

"Then you must have found Nathan," Priscilla said. "Where is he?"

"We still don't know." Greg started to tell her about the note, until Mordred stopped him with an impatient groan.

"We really don't have time for this," Mordred said. "Hazel is surely becoming more adept at the use of that amulet with every passing hour. If we don't put a stop to this right away, we may find her too powerful to fight."

"You're going to fight Hazel already?" Kristin asked Greg.

"Not yet. We still have some things we need to do first."

Priscilla breathed a sigh of relief. "Good. We'll come with you."

"Yes," Kristin said, placing a hand on Priscilla's shoulder, "we want to help."

"Wonderful," said Mordred. He turned and stalked off down the hallway. Greg and the girls ran to keep up.

"Hang on," called Lucky, who was just leaving King Peter's quarters.

Greg couldn't risk slowing down. Lucky didn't catch up until many hallways later, when Mordred was approaching the castle entrance that Greg and Kristin had used days earlier. A guard rushed up and swung open the door so Mordred could pass without breaking stride. The others followed. Outside Mordred scanned the area, a frown across his face.

"What are you looking for?" asked Priscilla.

"The spirelings who delivered Greghart and your friend to us," Mordred answered.

"The spirelings brought you?" Priscilla said to Greg, excitedly. "Gnash and Gnaw, I hope."

Greg started to answer, but Mordred waved him into silence. The magician signaled to the guard. "What happened to the spirelings who arrived here three days ago?"

"Ah, that lot. They hung around here patient enough for a couple days, but then one said something about their queen needing them, and off they went. You should've seen it. I never saw a body move so fast—let alone four of them."

"Great," said Mordred. He stormed back through the gate toward the Great Hall, leaving the others to scurry after. The dark magician passed through the expansive room and into the antechamber, where King Peter's staff of magicians waited in the shadows lining the walls.

"Do these guys ever leave here?" Greg whispered to Priscilla.

"I don't really know. They've been here every time I have."

"What are we doing?" Kristin asked.

Mordred scowled at the interruption. "I am hoping to be able to contact the spirelings from here."

"Why don't you just send one of those apparition things like you and Nathan used last time I was here?" asked Greg.

"That's precisely what I intend to do. I'm just not sure they'll be able to see it."

"Why not?" said Priscilla. "We all saw it fine when you did it with Nathan."

"Yes, well, Nathan is a magician. You were able to see me because he tuned into my signal for you. Had he not been there to act as a receiver, I'm sure you would have walked right past."

"Then how do you expect the spirelings to see?" asked Kristin.

"Fortunately spirelings are not all as dull-witted as your average man. Or in this case, child. The Canarazas even count a few hundred mages among their race. If we can locate one of them, chances are good they will hear us."

"How exciting," squealed Kristin.

"I know," Priscilla said. She squeezed Kristin's hand while the two of them waited to see what the magicians would do next. Lucky glanced questioningly at Greg, who shrugged.

Mordred settled on the floor, shut his eyes and concentrated on forming an apparition.

"What's he doing?" Kristin asked.

"Could we have a bit of silence?" Mordred asked. His eyelids drooped, and his breathing slowed, as if he'd fallen into a deep trance.

Eventually Mordred raised his head and stared at the center of the room before him, where the air suddenly shimmered and revealed a picture of two spireling warriors, ambling along a forest path at what to Greg would have been a dead run. They looked just like any other spirelings, short and stocky, with razor sharp teeth jutting out at all angles from their jaws, and each carried a heavy, double-bladed axe that was longer than the spirelings were tall.

"Gnash," cried Priscilla.

"Shh," said Greg and Lucky as one. Kristin shot them both a look that suggested they might try being a bit more polite to the princess.

Mordred called out to the spirelings, but the two did not hear. Greg found this particularly surprising, as his previous experience with spirelings suggested the pair might have heard even without the apparition.

Mordred called out a second time, and when again he got no reaction, his brow furrowed, and thunder began to rumble throughout the tiny chamber. A bolt of energy shot from the room and split the ground between the two spirelings' feet. They jumped a full three feet off the ground and spun wildly, trying to look all directions at once.

Again Mordred called out, and to Greg's surprise, one turned to face the room. The spireling's mouth dropped open, highlighting an intimidating array of teeth that caused Kristin to gasp.

"What sort of magic is this?" asked the spireling, but then he took a second look and nodded. "Ah, another apparition. You are the human magician Mordred. We have seen you before."

"Gnash?" said Greg, amazed that Priscilla could have recognized him. But when the spireling did not respond, he tried a second guess. "Gnaw?"

"Quiet," said Mordred. "He can't hear you. Besides, you don't know him. He only recognizes me because his whole race shared your friends' experience."

"Are you talking to the Mighty Greghart?" the spireling asked Mordred. "Is he there with you now? If so, I am honored. Oh, sorry. I did not introduce myself. My name is Gniblet. I am but a boy, but I am told I have more potential as a mage than any others of my hive."

Mordred nodded. "I have a message for your queen."

"She is with us now and always," Gniblet told him. "State your message, please."

Mordred explained about Witch Hazel's progress and the threat she posed to everyone on Myrth, whether they counted themselves among those who pledged allegiance to the king or not. He also told of the Amulet of Ruuan and how it must be reassembled if they were to stand any chance of defeating the witch. Gniblet listened intently, though something about the spireling's expression left Greg wondering if he was really there at all. When Mordred finished, the spireling waited several seconds before replying.

"We are already well aware of much of what you say. As you know, Ruuan shares his spire with us. We regret to admit, it looks as though the witch even used our passageway to gain access to the dragon, though we were unable to sense her presence."

"Hazel is a very skilled magician," Mordred said.

"You mean witch," corrected Gniblet.

"An orchid by any other name."

"Queen Gnarla would also like you to know that the human you call Nathan has already come to us to retrieve our section of amulet. He left with it more than a week ago."

"Then your trip to Gyrth really did work," Lucky told Greg.

"He also warned us you would need our help soon," said Gniblet. "What is it you desire?"

"We'd like you to rally your hive and meet us at the castle," said Mordred. "If you have any tricks up your sleeves, you should bring them along. We'll need every advantage at our disposal when we confront the witch."

"We do not have sleeves," Gniblet told him, holding out his arms to give an unobstructed view of his chain-mail vest. "Queen Gnarla is already aware of your trouble. She and the rest of our hive left for your castle the day before yesterday. She wants me to inform you that she will be there late tomorrow. She apologizes for the delay, but wants you to know that it is unavoidable, as she needed to make a side trip along the way."

Greg could barely restrain his excitement. Even one as powerful as Hazel would be hard pressed to fight the entire spireling hive. But then he remembered Simon's prophecy and realized the good news meant little toward his own fate.

"Excellent," said Mordred. "We will be anxiously awaiting your arrival." He ended the apparition a bit abruptly in Greg's mind, but then the magician had never been particularly gifted in social graces. "Very well. Next I suppose we'll need to go retrieve the dragonslayers. Do you have everything you need?" he asked Greg.

"What do you mean?"

"We can cut off a lot of time by traveling though the Enchanted Forest, but it's still a long trip. We'll be gone about a day."

"Whoa, you're not talking about actually hiking to Marvin's house? Why not just use another apparition?"

Mordred laughed, but not in a happy way. "You expect those dolts to spot an apparition? They'd be lucky to spot a dragon on their doorstep."

"Doesn't sound lucky to me," said Kristin.

"It is, if the dragon's about to spot you," Greg muttered.

"Get your things," said Mordred. "We'll leave straight away. That will put us in the dark within the Enchanted Forest for only a short time."

"You're not seriously thinking of traveling through the Enchanted Forest at night?" Greg said, remembering his horrific experiences there. The peculiar forest seemed to have a will of its own, opening wide to lure travelers deep inside but then closing the trail behind them as they walked, forcing them to its center. There a path might clear if another person stepped up to the edge to be lured inside, but more likely the trail would lead toward something horrifying, like one of the many hungry monsters that waited inside.

"Enchanted Forest?" said Kristin. "That sounds pretty."

"Oh, it can be," said Priscilla, and the two girls started chattering among themselves while Greg argued with Mordred about the wisdom of willingly marching to their deaths.

"We won't be marching to our deaths," Mordred said. "At least, *I* won't be. Most creatures of the forest, dim-witted as they might be, are smart enough to sense when a magician is in their midst. I expect they'll leave us alone."

"But monsters were always attacking us when we were with Nathan," Greg argued.

"You weren't in the Enchanted Forest then. Those woods are different than most. The creatures there respect magic, as they are immersed in it every day. They know no other way."

"What about the trails?" asked Lucky. "They won't clear unless someone happens to step up to the edge of the woods on the other side."

"Yes, well, again you boys are showing your ignorance. Magical plants are far more sensitive to a magician's presence than all but the most clever animals. I'm confident the vines will be quick to pull out of our way, as well."

Greg hoped the magician was right. He tried not to contemplate what might happen if Mordred wasn't. "Even without monsters, how can you say we won't be in the dark long? It takes all day to cross that forest."

"Ah, not if you know the shortcuts."

"But there's no way to go but to follow the trail it shows us."

Mordred met Greg's eye. "I suppose you're right. The forest is the only one that needs to know the shortcuts. We just need to follow whatever paths it opens for us. As I said, we shouldn't be more than a few hours each way."

"Nice," said Lucky. "I wish we'd had you along when Greg and I set out to fulfill the first prophecy. Could've saved us a lot of trouble. When do we leave?"

"We?" said Mordred. "King Peter insisted I take this one," he said, motioning toward Greg. "He said nothing about you."

"But I'm Greg's lucky charm. I've been keeping him alive throughout all his adventures."

"So you're to blame."

"You don't like me much, do you?" said Greg.

"I don't like you at all," Mordred answered without hesitation, "but the truth is I'm glad you've kept yourself alive thus far. If you had gone and gotten yourself killed, it could have had terrible repercussions on the last two prophecies."

"Stop, I'm getting all teary-eyed."

"As long as you keep yourself alive a little while longer, I'll be happy," Mordred continued. "But not too much longer, of course. We don't want to disrupt this latest prophecy."

Greg felt his stomach lurch.

"Then you'll be needing me," Lucky told Mordred.

"I want to go too," said Kristin.

Mordred rolled his eyes. He turned toward the girl and opened his mouth as if to speak.

"Of course you're going," said Priscilla. "I'll want someone to talk to."

"Neither of you is going," said Mordred.

"Of course we are," said Priscilla. "You work for my dad, remember?"

Dragonslayer Roundup

Mordred wasn't happy about the delay, but the children insisted on gathering bedrolls into packs for the trail, just in case something went wrong and they were forced to spend the night outdoors. Priscilla even prepared one especially for the magician, and while normally Mordred would have scoffed at the idea of needing to take something as mundane as a pack, he accepted it once Lucky reminded him that Nathan had advised against using magic.

Greg took the opportunity to grab a few brief minutes of sleep, since his trip to Gyrth had left him the only one without a good night's rest, or in this case, three nights' rest. Lucky woke him up to give him a proper hero's tunic for the trail, and by late afternoon the group was headed across the castle grounds toward the edge of the Enchanted Forest.

"Look at those trees," Kristin cried as they approached the woods. "They're beautiful."

"We'll see if you still think so in a minute," said Greg, and while Kristin didn't understand at first, she caught on pretty quickly once she stepped closer, and the trees slithered out of her way.

"They moved."

Even though Priscilla had witnessed the sight hundreds of times, she squeezed Kristin's hand and squealed.

Mordred growled and headed into the woods.

Greg was relieved to find Mordred was right about the monsters avoiding them. And about the trees. While normally the path would have closed in behind them as they came, today it remained clear, both ahead and behind, long after Mordred announced they had crossed the halfway mark.

Still, Greg thought it best to keep his eyes open. The first time he traveled these woods, he and Lucky ran into an ogre just minutes from the southwest edge of the forest. Exactly where they were headed now.

After a while Greg let Rake out of his pack, and the shadowcat scampered about, investigating each moving tree root with great interest. Within a couple of hours, darkness settled in, and Greg found that keeping his eyes open for danger had little effect. He wondered if Mordred planned to continue walking blindly through the dark, or worse yet, if he planned to camp within the forest.

"We don't have time to stop," announced Mordred.

Greg couldn't say the announcement disappointed him.

The magician held up his staff and stared at it. Greg and the others stared too. For a moment, the darkness of the forest seemed to press in on them. Greg was straining so hard to see that he nearly jumped into Lucky when the tip of Mordred's staff burst into flame, illuminating the trail around them.

Priscilla looked horrified. "Nathan said you're not supposed to use magic."

"This is one time where urgency overrides precaution," said Mordred. "If the monsters in this forest saw us wandering about without light, they might question whether I was able to use my power. Believe me, it's better for us all if they maintain their fear. Come. We still have far to travel."

Greg hadn't eaten since sharing a few nibbles of stale bread with young Nate and his father in Gyrth. "Do you think we could stop for dinner?" he asked.

"Certainly," said Mordred, "but you probably won't make much of a meal."

"Oh," said Greg, "maybe we should just keep moving."

Mordred chuckled. "Maybe so."

"I'm hungry too," announced Kristin.

"Me too," said Lucky, though he was always hungry and probably didn't need to tell anyone.

Princess Priscilla slipped her knapsack off and dug around inside while she walked. She pulled out some finger sandwiches she'd taken from the kitchen and offered them to the others, but clearly the tiny morsels were designed more for display than for satisfying hunger.

"I have some chewing gum," Kristin said. "Sorry I don't have more, but I've been watching my figure lately."

"Watching it do what?" asked Lucky.

Kristin frowned at the remark, but Greg knew Lucky wasn't joking. He probably had just never heard the expression.

"How much farther?" Kristin asked Mordred.

"A couple hundred miles. Don't worry," he said, after seeing her reaction. "The magic of the woods will make it feel much shorter. We should be out soon."

Greg grunted. He doubted they'd be out of the woods at all, as long as they were on Myrth.

As the minutes ticked away, and the southwestern edge drew near, Greg became more and more concerned about the ogre he and Lucky had run into the first time they attempted to pass this way. But as Mordred predicted, they saw no monsters of any kind the entire way. Eventually Greg noticed stars above and realized they had emerged from the forest.

"We made it," said Priscilla.

"Of course," Lucky said, obviously believing himself responsible.

"It didn't seem that bad to me," said Kristin. "So the trees moved around a little. I don't see what the big deal was."

"Be thankful for that," Greg told her.

"It was nothing," Lucky told them both.

"You're slowing down," Mordred called over his shoulder.

Greg spotted the glow of Mordred's staff outlining his black form and rushed to keep up. He didn't mind the harried pace. He was plenty anxious to leave the Enchanted Forest behind, and just as anxious to see the Greathearts—well, all except Norman, anyway. The retired dragonslayer had a dreadful habit of sharing one gruesome story after the next, and each one alone was enough to leave Greg afraid to so much as walk outside.

Come to think of it, Norman's eldest son's continual boasting over his successes as the greatest dragonslayer who ever lived could get quite annoying too. And the best thing Greg could say about Norman's youngest son, Melvin, was that recently the boy had stopped trying to kill him.

So really Greg was just anxious to see Edna Greatheart, Norman's wife. Her role as a mother to Marvin and Melvin seemed to spill over to Greg, and on this strange world, where danger lurked behind every bush, Greg was grateful for the reassurance she provided.

It took another hour to reach the Greathearts' tiny shack, as the trees in this area were just stupid, non-magical trees that wouldn't know a magician from a troll in the ground and couldn't have moved to reveal shortcuts even if they'd wanted to. Greg was glad to see Edna answer the door, even if the look on her face suggested she was strongly considering slamming it shut again.

"Oh, dear," she said. "Norman, they're here."

"You've been expecting us?" said Mordred.

"More like dreading, but here you are, just the same."

Greg and Priscilla exchanged curious looks.

"Aren't you going to invite us in?" Priscilla asked.

Mrs. Greatheart looked as if she never realized she had a choice in the matter. It bothered Greg she took so long to decide. "Yes, of course," she finally said. "Where are my manners? Do come in, Highness. Norman, where are you? I said they're here."

Now retired, Norman Greatheart had once been the greatest dragonslayer Myrth had ever known, though he'd paid dearly for the reputation. He now wore a patch over one eye and walked with a shifting limp. And the sounds his bones made. Why, the only time Greg had heard worse crackling was once at the movies, when the entire family behind him couldn't seem to break into their bags of chocolate mints. Norman was the human equivalent of a scrapheap, although Greg would have bet on the scrapheap as the more likely of the two to be responsible for the sounds that rapidly approached from behind Edna.

Melvin Greatheart's face popped out from behind his mother's shoulder, grinning from ear to ear. Greg could swear the boy had grown three inches in the few weeks Greg had been away. He unconsciously stood a bit taller.

"They're here!" Melvin shouted. "They're here!"

"I just said that," Edna told him.

"You also said you were going to let us in," Kristin reminded her.

"Yes, of course. Sorry."

Mrs. Greatheart backed into the room to allow the others to pass, though the room was so small, they required a quick strategy session before everyone could fit. "Norman," she called, "where are you?"

"Coming." Now came the meandering shuffle more in line with what Greg expected. But it wasn't Norman who stepped from the back this time either. It was Marvin, Melvin's older brother. As always, he was dressed only in a loincloth, his frame so large, it was hard to believe he could fit into the room.

"Princess Priscilla," he said, "Greghart, it's good to see you again."

Of course it is, Greg thought. *It gives you someone to boast to.*

Kristin's eyes nearly popped out of her head. She ran her fingers through her hair. "Uh, Greg," she said in a nervous titter, "who is this?"

Greg observed her glossed-over look and scowled. He realized the shuffling noises had stopped. Norman Greatheart's face peered out first from behind Marvin's elbow, then grimaced and rose level with Marvin's shoulder. The cacophony of popping noises that accompanied the movement drew even Kristin's attention. She witnessed Norman's missing eye and the network of scars covering every inch of his face, and screamed.

"Oh, sorry," Norman said with a wink. "Didn't mean to startle you. Greghart, my boy. You did come. Good, I'll get my cloak."

Mrs. Greatheart scowled. "Who are you kidding? They didn't come all this way for an old coot like you. They're after our boys."

"Actually we're after all three of them," said Mordred.

"Oh, dear."

"Told you so," said Norman, puffing out his chest with a crackle.

Kristin sidled over to Marvin and peered up at his massive chest from beneath his armpit. "Hi, I'm Kristin."

Marvin glanced downward, observed Kristin's expression, and quickly looked away again. "We heard about Hazel getting hold of Ruuan. Figured it was just a matter of time before you came looking for me. But what do you want with Dad and Melvin?"

Melvin frowned. "Why wouldn't they want me? I'm a legend."

Your brother must be very proud, Greg thought, not for Melvin's status as a living legend, but for his legend-worthy bragging skills.

"Of course you are," said Edna, "and so is your father."

"Sure, but he's like a thousand years old."

"He's not. He only looks that way."

"Thank you, dear," said Norman. "Like I said before, I'll get my cloak."

"But . . ." Greg found he could barely maintain the energy to stand. "I haven't slept in days. I thought we were going to stay the night."

"Oh, I think that's a splendid idea," Edna said, pulling her youngest son's head to her bosom. Melvin struggled to escape, but he was no match for his mother. Good thing she wasn't a dragon, Greg thought, or Melvin would have shown her what a real hero could do.

Kristin cleared her throat. "That's Kristin, like in piston, but with a 'Kr' instead of a 'P.' Get it?"

Marvin clearly had no idea what Kristin was talking about. The look on her face caused him to take a quick step back.

"Sit down, everyone," insisted Mrs. Greatheart. "You should eat."

By Greg's count, they were at least two chairs short. Mordred wasn't interested in sitting anyway. He paced back and forth throughout the meal, though as small as the room was, he looked to be just twirling about. Norman gave up his seat as well. Greg suspected he wanted to join the others but couldn't get his knees to cooperate. In the end,

Marvin had to carry him to the living room sofa, where he could lie flat with his feet hanging above the edge of the kitchen table.

When Marvin returned, the only empty chair was next to Kristin. He chose instead to stand, hovering over the table while Edna served up piping hot bowls of stew.

"Out of the way," Edna scolded. She pushed past Marvin to place a steaming bowl in front of Greg. Marvin squeezed his massive form in behind her, only to end up in her way again when she tried to retreat. "My word, always under foot. Would you go sit down?"

"But Mum—"

"Don't argue with your mother. Now sit."

Marvin pulled in his stomach, nearly launching Edna into the kitchen with his expanding chest. "Sorry, Mum."

"Who's your friend?" Melvin asked Greg, his eyes fixed upon Kristin's cheek. Kristin continued to stare at Marvin, trying her best to ignore the younger Greatheart, much the same way the older Greatheart tried to ignore her.

"Her name is Kristin," Priscilla told him, "and stop staring. You're making her uncomfortable."

"I'm not staring," said Melvin.

"Yes, you are," Kristin said without looking his way. Edna placed a steaming bowl in front of her. "Thanks. This smells good. What is it?"

"Fresh wyvern stew," said Edna.

"Wyvern?"

"They're kind of like small dragons," Melvin said helpfully.

Kristin grimaced and pushed the bowl aside. "Ugh, no thanks."

Greg made a show of eating a large spoonful. "Try it. It's delicious."

"I don't think so."

Melvin leaned forward to draw Kristin's attention. She promptly turned the other way. "I can get you an ogre patty from out back," he told the back of her head.

"Yuck."

"Are you sure you don't want to try some stew, dear?" Edna asked. "You don't want to go to bed hungry."

"Yeah," said Lucky, "we haven't eaten all day."

Kristin regarded her bowl as if it might suddenly sprout limbs. She picked up her spoon and dipped it cautiously, withdrew a morsel barely large enough to see, and guided it toward her lips. The others looked on expectantly.

"Hey, this is good."

"There now, glad you like it," Edna said with a smile. She turned then and started toward the kitchen, frowning at Marvin, who was trying his best to blend in with the wall.

"Aren't you going to eat, Mrs. Greatheart?" asked Greg.

"Oh, don't worry about me," Edna said. "You all eat up. I'll get some later if there's any left."

"Oh, for goodness sake, sit down, Edna," said Norman from the couch. "You're driving everyone crazy."

"Can I get you seconds, dear?" Edna asked Lucky as he scraped the bottom of his bowl with his spoon.

"Some of us would like firsts," said Norman.

"Hush. I'll get yours in a minute."

Marvin cleared his throat. "I'm kind of hungry too."

"Would you *please* sit down?" Edna said, exasperated.

Marvin considered the empty chair next to Kristin, who smiled widely and patted the seat. Slowly he slid his back down the wall until it at least appeared as if he were sitting. His knees bumped the table and sent it screeching across the hard wood floor, sloshing everyone's stew nearly out of their bowls.

Mrs. Greatheart shook her head. She ladled out more stew for Greg, who, after glancing at Marvin's and Norman's empty bowls, hid his eyes. A moment later, when Edna dished up a second small bowl for Rake, Greg debated crawling under the table.

Kristin waved to capture Marvin's attention and pointed to her stew. "Want to share mine?"

Greg forced himself to look at Norman. "You said you already knew of the next prophecy? How did you find out?"

Marvin leaned to one side to see around Kristin. "I told him. The Sezxqrthms are getting on in years, and I like to go check on them now and then to see they're all right."

"Such a good boy," Edna said, smiling proudly at her son.

"Simon told you?" said Lucky. "How'd you ever understand him?"

Greg had met the prophet only once, but that one meeting was enough to make him wonder, too. Well over a century old, the man could barely hear and just naturally assumed everyone else shared the same problem. The only one who could understand his shouting was his wife Gabby, whose hearing was even worse than her husband's. On his first visit to Myrth, Greg had cringed as the two screamed at each other, Gabby with her grating squawks, Simon with his garbled grunts. They shared their own little world, and no outsiders could communicate with them there.

Greg was happy to give them their space.

"Everyone's always saying they have trouble understanding Simon," said Marvin. "I just don't get it. He makes perfect sense to me."

"What did he tell you?" Priscilla asked.

Marvin relayed all he could remember. Kristin listened intently, resting her elbows on the table with her head propped in her hands, and while Marvin provided nothing Brandon hadn't already relayed to the king, Greg listened intently too. This was the first he was hearing most of it.

According to Marvin, Hazel was preparing to unleash a horrible power held in check since the Dragon Wars of centuries ago. She planned to use the Amulet of Tehrer to turn Ruuan against his will and force him to attack Pendegrass Castle, and while the spirelings would come to the aid of the Army of the Crown, as they had done against the trolls when Greg was last here, there was only so much they could do against an airborne dragon. The real fight would be up to Greg, and though he was prophesied to win in the end, he would pay for his victory, rather unfortunately, with his life.

"Are you sure about that last part?" Greg asked, though he held little hope.

"Afraid so," said Marvin somberly.

The room was quiet for a long moment. Kristin stopped staring at Marvin and looked to Greg instead, a mixture of shame and concern in her eyes. Even Melvin, who Greg would have expected to stifle a snicker, held his eyes cast to the table in respectful silence. Greg guessed the boy was a lot less jealous now that he'd become a great hero himself in the recent Battle of the Spirelings.

"I'm sorry, son," said Norman. "It's a very noble thing you do for us."

"It certainly is," said Edna, wringing her hands nervously. "I just wish there was something we could do for you."

"Yeah, I'm sorry too, Greghart," said Melvin. "That's tough luck."

"I just don't understand it," said Lucky. "If luck has anything to do with it, you should be fine. I don't plan to leave your side for an instant."

Greg frowned. He remembered Nathan once telling him how Lucky's confidence might one day get him in over his head. As afraid as he was for his own life, he couldn't help but wonder what fate awaited his friend.

The two girls sat on either side of Greg. Each took up one of his hands in their own, and where a few days ago Greg might have thought they were about to tear him in half, competing for his affection, today they meant only to console him. Tears welled up in both girls' eyes.

"Yes, well, no point getting all choked up," said Mordred. "The boy's death has already been prophesied. Nothing can be done about it now. Has everyone finished their stew? We really need to be getting back."

"But I haven't had any yet," said Marvin.

"Hush," Edna scolded. "Our guest was speaking."

Shaping Destiny – Take Two

To Greg's relief, Mrs. Greatheart insisted they stay the night, and then again for a huge breakfast of basilisk chops, before they resumed their journey. After the meal, her husband popped out of the bedroom, ready to hit the trail.

"Norman! Put some clothes on."

Norman scowled and lifted his sagging belly to reveal that he had, in fact, donned his old dragon-hunting loincloth. He went back and changed anyway, supposedly because Edna pointed out that spring was still a ways off and it was sure to be cold, but Greg had an idea it was more because Norman wasn't happy with the expressions on the two young girls' faces.

A few minutes later he came out wearing a refreshingly concealing tunic. Still it was barely hiding tights that were disturbingly true to their name.

Once again the monsters of the Enchanted Forest knew better than to mess with a magician of Mordred's caliber, so the group was able to complete the lengthy journey back in little more than three hours. They might have even finished sooner, except the first quarter hour was wasted watching Norman creak and pop his way across the living room at a snail's pace.

"Maybe we should stuff him into Lucky's pack," Melvin had suggested, but when Norman wouldn't fit, even when he sucked in his gut, Marvin had a better solution.

"I'll just carry him till I get tired."

Now, with noon come and gone, the powerful dragonslayer was finally setting his father down, although probably only because here they were, at the end of their journey.

"Let's see if Nathan came back," Greg suggested.

Mordred strode deliberately for the castle. "He didn't."

The others ran after him.

"How do you know?" Priscilla asked.

"I would feel him if he did."

"Why, where's Nathan?" Marvin wanted to know.

"Didn't I tell you?" Greg asked. He realized after three hours on the trail he'd never once mentioned anything about the prophecy or Nathan being missing.

Not that it was his fault. The beginning of the trip no one could get a word in past Marvin's boasting. Even Kristin lost interest in the dragonslayer after a time, which inspired Melvin to hop along after her, asking question after question, while she tried hard to ignore him.

Then, once Melvin grew hoarse, the conversation was completely consumed by foolish chatter between the two girls over clothes and hairstyles and the ten cutest boys at school, which probably would have worked out better if they went to the same school, or at least schools on the same world. Now that they'd arrived, Greg ignored the fact Kristin hadn't included him on her top-ten list and filled Marvin in on Brandon's note about Nathan going off to see Dolzowt Deth.

All color drained from Marvin's face.

"What's wrong?" Greg asked.

"He went to see Dolzowt?"

"Who's Dolzowt?" asked Melvin.

"Dolzowt Deth is a legendary sorcerer who lives deep within the Netherworld," Mordred answered. "He's a master of the Dark Arts, and if Nathan has gone to him and not returned, I cannot say I'm surprised, or that he did not deserve his fate."

"Nathan doesn't deserve anything," argued Priscilla.

Mordred nodded.

"I mean, he doesn't deserve to have anything bad happen to him."

"He went to discover secrets about the Dark Arts," said Mordred. "He deserves whatever he gets."

Everyone started arguing then, including Kristin, who didn't even know Nathan but must have felt obligated to defend him since her BFF Priscilla seemed so adamant about it.

"We shouldn't be standing around arguing like this," Greg finally said. "We need to go find this Dolzowt person and get Nathan back."

Mordred cackled. "And just how do you expect to get to the Netherworld?"

"I don't know," said Greg. "Can't you send me?"

"Sorry. Your friend Nathan said I'm not supposed to use my magic, remember?"

"He's your friend too," Lucky reminded him. "And how else can we get there?"

"*We?*" said Mordred. "I don't remember the prophecy saying anything about *you* going to the Netherworld."

"Yeah, well, it doesn't say anything about Greg going, either."

"Which is precisely why neither of you should go."

"But we must," Kristin said. "We owe it to Nathan."

Greg gazed at her dumbly, wondering how she could possibly owe anything to a man she'd never met.

"Kristin's right," Melvin insisted.

"Leave me alone," she told him.

"No, she *is* right," said Greg. He stared defiantly at Mordred. "And even if you care nothing about Nathan, he has the Amulet of Ruuan with him. We don't stand a chance against Hazel without it. If you won't send us, then we'll just have to hike there ourselves." He looked to Lucky to see if this was even possible, as he had no idea what or where the Netherworld was.

"I'm afraid that would be impossible," Mordred said, confirming Greg's suspicions. "You don't have time. The Netherworld is months away, clear on the other side of the Styx."

Priscilla frowned. "But we have to go." Her face brightened. "I know, Greg. You could use your ring to get us to Ruuan's lair, and then we could walk to that portal Nathan showed us and be in the Styx within a day or so."

Greg remembered the portal she was talking about. It existed somewhere in the middle of a barren desert, completely undetectable to the human eye. Well, to everyone's eye except Nathan's.

"You think you could find that portal Nathan showed us?" Melvin said. "I know I couldn't."

"That's where I come in," said Lucky. "With my talent, I should be able to lead us out into the Barren Reaches and straight into that portal on my first try."

"That sounds like a reasonable plan," said Mordred, his tone assuring just the opposite. "Then you'll just need to walk for a month or so to the south side of the Styx . . . Oh, but the spirelings were going to be here tonight to help us launch an attack against Hazel. I would think you'd want to be here for that."

Not really, Greg thought to himself, but aloud he said, "It doesn't matter anyway. I can't get us to Ruuan's lair. I gave away my ring."

"You what?" Priscilla said.

"I had to. It was the only way I knew for Nathan to come to this world as a boy."

"Very resourceful," said Mordred, and for a change Greg believed the magician actually approved of something he'd done. "This prophecy business is more complex than I ever imagined. I must say, I'm not really sure how best to proceed. I didn't tell you before, because I didn't want to worry you, but I have reason to believe it is too late to save your friend Nathan."

"Stop calling him *our* friend," Priscilla insisted. "What do you mean, too late?" She gripped Kristin's hand tightly in her own and didn't even object when Melvin tried to slip his in too.

"I've never been to the Netherworld myself, of course," Mordred started, "because only the Dark Arts are practiced there . . ."

"Nathan said when you were kids you did all sorts of stuff with the Dark Arts," Priscilla interrupted.

The look on Mordred's face suggested Priscilla was lucky to be King Peter's daughter. "They say," he continued quite slowly, "time does not pass there."

"Say what?" asked Lucky.

"Well, that's not completely accurate. It passes there. It's just, from our point of view, no time passes here. No matter what sort of delay Nathan experienced inside the Netherworld, he should have been back the moment he left." He paused to let the others come to their own conclusions about what he'd said. "I can't say he didn't deserve his fate, but still I am sorry this has happened."

"Are you really?" Priscilla asked, a tear in her eye.

"Most certainly. If something has indeed happened to Nathan, then he won't be here to fulfill his role in the battle."

Greg frowned at the man's callousness. "The prophecy says Nathan has a role in the battle?"

"Did I not mention that?" said Mordred. "To be exact, it says both he and you will take to the skies to fight atop the backs of magnificent flying beasts."

"You mean dragons?" said Melvin. "Nice."

"But wait, that's impossible," said Marvin. "Hazel has control of Ruuan now, and he's the only dragon left. There might have been a couple dozen around when I was born, but between me and Dad we've taken out every last one of them."

Norman Greatheart coughed suddenly. He avoided the others' eyes, busily stretching out the fabric of his tights, which, after being carried a thousand miles through the Enchanted Forest, looked to be riding up in an uncomfortable way.

"Did you have something to say, Mr. Greatheart?" Priscilla asked.

"Um, maybe not *every* one."

"How's that, Dad?" said Marvin.

"Er…it's possible one or two dragons may have slipped through the cracks."

"What?"

"Well, one for sure."

Marvin's face reddened as he pulled his father off to one side. "What are you talking about, Dad?"

"I should've told you sooner, son. That mean-spirited offspring of Tehrer . . . you know the one . . . when I, er, slayed him, he ended up . . . well, less dead than we might have hoped."

"Are you saying he got away?"

"Not exactly. More like he let me get away. Truth is, he agreed to let me live if I would just go back and tell everybody I'd slayed him. That way folks would quit coming looking for him, and he could finally get some peace."

"I can't believe you would trick everybody like that," Kristin scolded, and now it was Greg who avoided the others' eyes, as he'd made a similar deal with Ruuan and knew better than anyone how to mislead a kingdom full of people.

Norman fidgeted uncomfortably. "It seemed a pretty good deal at the time, considering it was that or be incinerated. See, Tehrer was actually born in the Netherworld. He lived just a couple hundred miles from the Styx border most his life. Before I met him he'd been harvesting stray cattle for years, scooping up anything foolish enough to step across the border. But—and this seemed a bit odd for a dragon of Tehrer's disposition—he still respected the monster-free zone that had been agreed upon centuries earlier with the people of the Styx. Least until his one slip up, shortly before I was called upon to help."

"Tehrer crossed the line?" said Marvin.

"Yep. In more ways than one. One day on a whim he soared into the Styx, scorched a couple of villages, and flew off with a half dozen maidens. Oh, you can imagine the people were furious. All this screamin' and hollerin'. But do you think one of them would step up to do a thing about it themselves? No. As always, they called upon me to clean up their mess for them.

"But I didn't mind," he said, and for a moment Greg thought he sounded a lot like his son Marvin. "No, I did what I always do. I came to their rescue and headed out after that bloody dragon with no thought for my own safety. Only this time was different. I'd never been to the Netherworld before. Lot of strange things down there, by the way. Never been back since. Kinda sorry I went the once.

"Anyway, when I finally tracked Tehrer down and cornered him in his lair, he seemed quite apologetic. Said he'd just been feeling a bit giddy that day and how I could rest assured it would never happen again. I tended to believe him, what with him having me pinned to the floor of his cave under one of his talons, so we quickly scratched out an agreement instead of my entrails, and well, you know the rest."

"Oh my," said Priscilla. "We have to get Nathan out of there."

"I already told you, it's too late for Nathan," Mordred said, "and if Tehrer's still flying about snatching up anything that steps foot into the Styx, I'm certainly not going to let you go wandering about down there foolishly trying to save anyone."

For a second Greg thought he sensed a note of compassion. Then he realized Mordred was just concerned about the prophecy.

"Wait," said Kristin, "maybe it's like when Greg went to that Gyrth place. Maybe the reason Nathan didn't come back on time is because Greg hasn't gone to get him."

"That's preposterous," said Mordred. "It doesn't make sense."

"No," Priscilla insisted. "She may be right. Don't you see? If something did happen to him down there, then your precious prophecy can't work out. Nathan must still be alive. Now we have to go more than ever."

"She's right," said Greg. "Nathan always knew I'd do whatever it took to make Simon's prophecies work out. Maybe the only reason he's not back is because I haven't put forth my best effort."

"I agree," said Kristin.

"That's because he was agreeing with you," Mordred noted.

"Me too," said Lucky. "Agree with both of them, I mean."

"I agree with Kristin," Melvin admitted.

Marvin was keeping quiet. Perhaps he was contemplating the matter, but Greg had an idea he was still struggling over the truth about his father never slaying Tehrer.

"Then it's settled," said Priscilla. "Mordred, you need to use your magic to send us all to the Netherworld."

"Nonsense," said Mordred. "This settles nothing."

Priscilla crossed her arms over her chest and shot the magician a challenging glare. "Do we really need to go discuss this with Daddy?"

Even after receiving a direct order from King Peter to send the children wherever Greg wanted to go, Mordred was still reluctant to cooperate. Time was of the essence, yet he insisted on filling the children in on what they could expect to find in the mysterious depths of the Netherworld.

"They like children there," he told them, which might have eased Greg's mind if Mordred hadn't added, "They use them for spare parts."

Greg gulped. "You're joking, right?"

"Have you ever known me to flaunt my sense of humor?"

Priscilla squeezed Kristin's hand. "What do you mean, spare parts?"

"Dark Magic is not for the weak of heart, or stomach," Mordred told her. "Nearly all spells require ingredients from living things. Even ordinary, everyday magic usually involves some aspect of life: a certain plant, a hair of bat, eye of newt, or some such thing. But for the darker spells . . . well, eye of child might be a better place to start . . . though a worthwhile spell might take a kidney, or a few feet of intestines, or worse."

Not until Greg bumped into something squishy did he realize he'd been unconsciously backing away. To his surprise he found he'd run into Lucky, who had backed into the same corner, along with Melvin and the two girls.

"Our best bet is to get you some magicians' robes," said Mordred. "The more powerful you look, the bigger you will seem. Not that an adult would be safe in the Netherworld either, but parts from an adult are not as valuable as those from a child. I suggest you tighten that hood up around your face, Highness."

"What about the rest of us?" asked Greg.

"You do what you like. It's what you seem best at, anyway."

"Hey, I—"

"Just remember," said Mordred, taking in all of the children in a single glance, "keep those robes cinched and your hoods snug, and maybe, just maybe, you'll live to see your next birthday." He glanced specifically at Greg. "Well, most of you, anyway. Hopefully, they'll believe you are sorcerers and leave you alone—or at least be more hesitant to attack you."

"They who?" asked Priscilla.

"They everyone," Mordred answered. "There are few you will meet south of the Styx who will not try to cause you harm. And those who appear to want to help . . . well, they can be just as terrifying as any other."

"Maybe we want to reconsider this rescue," suggested Kristin, who was possibly just now coming to realize she didn't know Nathan.

"But if this place is as bad as you say, then it's even more essential we rescue Nathan," said Priscilla. "Who knows what kind of trouble he might be in?"

"Who indeed?" said Mordred. "Oh, did I mention I can send you there, but I can't bring you back? You'll have to figure that out on your own."

"Great," Greg muttered. And he thought this was going to be a simple matter of rescuing Nathan from an evil sorcerer—Nathan, the powerful magician incapable of rescuing himself.

The six of them entered the Room of Shadows, where twenty of King Peter's magicians had gathered to weave their magic—or perhaps they'd been there all along. Who could say?

Greg and the others waited in expectant silence, with Lucky in the center of the room, waiting to give the signal that would send them all through the rift and into the Netherworld. Greg's hands were so sweaty he could barely hold his walking stick.

"What's taking so long?" asked Kristin.

"Take your time," said Melvin, who found himself pressed up against Kristin in the cramped surroundings.

"Would you back off?"

"Shh," said the others.

Priscilla draped an arm over Kristin's shoulder. "We don't want to break their concentration."

"I'm going to break this kid's arm in a second."

"Quiet," insisted Lucky. He waved frantically at the surrounding magicians. "Not yet."

Greg thought Lucky's worry was a bit unfounded, considering the portal hadn't even opened yet, but then he wondered what would happen if the magicians actually did try to send them through now, before the portal existed. He quickly turned his mind away from the thought, but his mind was not easily swayed.

A familiar buzzing formed in his ear and shot about inside his head like a trapped fly. Rake shifted uneasily and let out a low growl from within Greg's knapsack, which Greg wore under his magician's robe but above the chain mail Queen Gnarla had given him. Earlier Greg had argued about wearing the pack, claiming it made him look like some ridiculous hunchback, but the others had all assured him it helped him look more sinister. Lucky and Priscilla didn't bother to wear theirs, since

Mordred shocked them all by stating that the type of magic used in the packs wouldn't work within the Netherworld, and without magic they were too small to carry anything worthwhile.

Soon Greg's skin began to prickle. Suddenly the air before him split open to reveal a bright light behind. Lucky stared into the gap, but Greg could see nothing but spots before his own eyes.

"What's happening?" asked Kristin.

"Shh," said the others.

Greg blinked away the spots. Lucky's face was a mask of concentration. Where before the portal had always revealed the blackness of space, today it was dominated by a slurry of colors, like objects close to the window of a speeding train. Greg watched for only a moment. The sight reminded him too much of his nearly-fatal slide down the Smoky Mountains last time he visited Myrth.

"Now!" shouted Lucky, and Greg was pulled from his feet in what might have been described as a tug in the same way getting flattened by a truck might be described as feeling under pressure. An instant later the ground rushed up to meet Greg's feet. It then met his hands and knees, and finally his face. It was unpleasantly hot.

Greg jumped to his feet. Screams sounded all around him. Thick smoke hung suffocating in the air. Through it he could make out the licking flames of a raging fire. Scattered sparks swept up by a blistering wind rained down from the sky.

This really is the Netherworld!

Then, through the smoke, he spotted the source of the fire. The sky was black as night, but the silhouette that soared his way was blacker still. A terrifying screech rent the air, like the sound of a car being pushed along steel tracks by a braking freight train. Ahead, the three-hundred-foot-long dragon spotted movement and prepared to launch another searing jet of flames.

The Netherworld

"Watch out!"

Garbed in the black robe Mordred gave her, Priscilla was nearly invisible within the gloom, but Greg didn't need to see her to recognize her voice, and he didn't need to hear her words to know to watch out. He dove face first into the dirt. Hot as the soil was, he far preferred the feel of it to the scorching jet of fire that soared above his head.

Again the dragon screeched. Banking hard to the left, it began the lazy mile-long circle that would bring it back to this spot.

"Let's get out of here," said Melvin.

Greg snugged up his hood to protect his face from the sparks. Toward the sound of Melvin's voice, a dark mass was sprinting away. Two more figures followed, so Greg ran that way too. His eyes burned as he struggled to keep the others in sight. The smoke bit his throat and lungs, and he coughed without relief.

"This way," someone shouted.

Greg was so terrified as he veered in that direction, he didn't even realize the voice was not familiar. He emerged from the smoke into a hazy clearing, blinked the tears from his eyes and spotted three hooded figures before him. A fourth rushed up from behind.

"You okay, Greg?" It was Lucky's voice.

"Yeah, you?"

"Of course. Where are the girls?"

"There," Greg said, pointing, "and Melvin too." Then he noticed the taller silhouette of a man with the others, and his heart jumped.

"Who's that?" asked Lucky.

Melvin jumped between the girls and the newcomer, as if to protect them, but Kristin shoved him aside.

"You're blocking my view."

"Don't be alarmed," said the stranger. "I won't hurt you." Oddly, he carried a briefcase and wore a crumpled jacket and tie. He extended one hand. "Kellerman's the name. Insurance is my game."

"What?" said Greg. "Who are you?"

"I just told you. Name's Kellerman." He smiled widely. "You can call me Bob, if you like. Now, you folks just relax. I'd be happy to handle all your insurance needs here in the Netherworld. Oh, you don't have an agent yet, do you?" His hand was still thrust out as if he expected Greg to shake. Greg and Lucky stared back blankly.

"What's going on here?" Greg demanded. "What do you want?"

"It's not what I want that matters, it's what you need. Like have you considered what's going to happen once that dragon swings back this way? Oh, look, here he comes now. No reason for you to concern yourselves with it, though. If you just let me lop off a few of your fingers, I believe I can help."

"What?" said Greg. "Get away."

The salesman's eyes diverted to a point above Greg's shoulder and grew disturbingly wide. "Perhaps we should discuss payment later," he said rather hurriedly, and with that he pushed Greg aside and stepped boldly into the path of the approaching dragon.

To Greg's horror, the beast released a scorching jet of fire that singed the ground in a wide swath that soared straight toward the helpless man. When the flames reached their target, they exploded with a fury beyond what even the dragon could deliver. The entire area flashed with blinding light. Greg felt himself lurched off his feet. For a moment he was completely disoriented, just as he had been when the magicians used their magic to send him here. The next thing he knew, he was lying on the ground with his cheek resting in the dirt. The field he had stood in moments before had been replaced by a lightly wooded area. The day was clear and bright, and there was no sign of the dragon or the flames and smoke that marked its passage.

Greg pushed himself up on one elbow. The strange man was lying face-down nearby, unmoving. The others were there as well, just now regaining their feet.

"What happened?" asked Kristin. "Where are we?"

"I don't know," said Greg. "Is everyone okay?"

All nodded to indicate they were. All, that is, except the odd man who had introduced himself as Bob, who continued to lie motionless in the dirt. Greg scurried over to check on him.

"Is he d-dead?" asked Kristin.

Greg studied the man's chest for any sign of movement. "I don't know."

"Looks dead to me," said Melvin.

Priscilla leaned over the body, curious, but clearly not wanting to get too close. "I'm going to have to agree with Melvin on this one."

"Me too," said Lucky.

But then Bob stirred and scrambled to his feet. The others jumped back.

"Whew, that hurts," Bob cried. "I'm afraid that's going to cost you."

"W-what?" said Greg. "We thought you were dead."

"Was for a moment," said the stranger, "but I'm feeling much better now. Anyway, we need to discuss payment. I was thinking one eye from each of you and a kidney from the healthiest of the lot. How does that sound?"

Kristin tugged on Greg's shoulder. "Greg, get away from him. He's creepy."

"Don't tell me you're going to refuse payment?" Bob said in a theatrical tone. "I'd hate to have to turn this over to a collection agency. Oh, by the way, I do sell collection agent insurance too, should you be interested."

"Come on, Greg," said Lucky. "Let's get out of here."

Greg would have liked nothing more, but when he tried to leave, Bob grabbed him by the tunic. Before Greg could so much as utter a scream, Bob yanked him off his feet and swung him around like a rag doll, warning the others to back off or get hurt.

"Put him down," screamed both Priscilla and Kristin as one. They charged at the man while Melvin and Lucky stood frozen in place, mouths agape.

Bob swung Greg around, fending off both girls with a single sweep. Tears came to Greg's eyes. He imagined his arm tearing from his shoulder. His legs flapped out behind him like a flag as Bob swished him back and forth, and Greg wasn't sure he was totally pleased that the girls wouldn't give up.

"I'm not going to hurt him," said Bob. "You can have him back just as soon as I collect his kidney."

"Let him go," insisted Kristin.

Priscilla tried to grab Bob's tie but got smacked in the cheek by Greg's foot for her effort.

Finally Melvin and Lucky snapped out of their trances and raced forward. Melvin tried to sneak past Greg's flailing feet, but fared no better than the girls had. Lucky yelled for the others to watch out, and with a single swing of his walking stick, swept Bob's ankles out from under him. Greg felt Bob's grip relax. He pulled free, scrambled to his feet and rushed to join the others.

Priscilla grabbed his hand. "Run."

But Greg shook loose and strode purposely forward. "Wait. Let's find out what this guy knows about Nathan."

Lucky tried to grab Greg's arm and pull him back, but again Greg shook free. Bob was just crawling back to his feet, clearly favoring his right ankle, when Lucky's hood slipped.

Bob's mouth dropped open. "Your hair . . ."

Lucky quickly pulled his hood up and raised his stick menacingly. "Get back."

"But your hair." Bob looked so excited, Greg was sure he'd be jumping for joy if he were able to use both ankles.

"What about it?" asked Lucky.

"Where did you . . . how is it possible?"

With one eye on Kristin, Melvin snatched the stick from Lucky's hands and threatened Bob with it, though if the truth were known, he was not nearly as skilled with its use as Lucky. "What's wrong with you, Mister?"

When Bob saw the stick, his enthusiasm faltered. Still, a smile returned to his face. He stared again at Lucky, looking much like a dog that has been told to wait while a meaty morsel sits within easy reach.

"Oh, this changes everything. Tell you what. Your friend can keep his kidney. I'll just take three locks of your hair instead. Quite a bargain, don't you think?"

"What?" said Lucky.

"Two then . . . okay, one. Do we have a deal?"

"I'm not giving you anything."

Bob's smile disappeared entirely. His neck reddened, and his eyes bored into Lucky. "But I just died for you. You owe me."

"I didn't ask you to—"

"What are you talking about?" Greg asked Bob.

"I offered you folks a premium before, remember? When the dragon swung back around, I assumed you were acting on good faith and went ahead and paid out on the policy I knew you intended to purchase."

When Greg did nothing but stare back at him stupidly, Bob elaborated.

"I diverted the dragon's attention so that I would die instead of you, causing us all to hyperspace out of danger. What's not to understand?"

"He's crazy," Lucky said, rather pleadingly. He backed away from

Bob, eyes wide. "You're not getting my hair."

"Oh, for crying out loud," said Melvin. In one quick movement, he flipped back Lucky's hood, snatched a fistful of hair, and lopped it off with a pocketknife. Lucky stared aghast, as if the boy had taken a kidney.

"Here's your silly hair," Melvin said, tossing the lock at Bob's feet.

Bob fell to the ground as if gravity had increased tenfold and snatched up the treasure. "Oh, my. Look how beautiful."

"It's just hair," said Priscilla.

Lucky mumbled an inaudible argument.

"But it's red." Bob closed his eyes and savored the feel of the hair against his cheek.

"Yeah, so?"

"Did I mention he was creepy before?" said Kristin.

Greg shot Priscilla a warning glance, but she was well ahead of him. Her hood was pulled so tightly over her own red tresses, she looked as if she had only half a head.

"What's the big deal?" asked Melvin. "So his hair's red?"

Bob shook himself out of his trance. "So? Have you ever seen red hair before? Oh, of course you have. You two are traveling together. Well, I haven't. And neither has anyone else I know. But I'm told it's essential to many dark spells. Why, this one lock alone should carry me into next fall, maybe even winter if I bargain wisely." His eyes narrowed, and his face broke into the same insincere grin he'd used when they first met. "You know, you're going to be needing a lot more protection than I first thought."

Greg frowned. "Have you ever heard of a man named Nathanial Caine?"

"Possibly," said Bob. He watched Lucky's hair with a carnivorous look in his eye.

Greg followed his gaze, and only then noticed Melvin stalking up behind Lucky. With a single swipe, the boy retrieved a clump of Lucky's hair by the roots and handed it to Bob.

"Ow!" Lucky yanked his hood back over his head.

Bob could hardly contain himself as he folded the hair into a kerchief and tucked it into the inner pocket of his jacket. "No, I don't know him."

"What?" said Lucky.

"How about a Dolzowt Deth?" asked Priscilla.

Bob just stared back at her.

Melvin distracted Lucky while Priscilla probed a finger under his hood and plucked out a pinch more hair.

"Ow! Stop it."

Priscilla handed the hair to Bob, who tucked it safely away with the rest. "Of course I know Dolzowt. He's a legend here in the Netherworld. They say he can travel in and out of the Styx at will, but I have my doubts. I know no other who's ever come to this place and managed to step foot back again."

"Huh?" said Lucky, forgetting the pain in his scalp. "Mordred never mentioned that."

Indeed, Greg remembered the magician had said only that they would need to figure out how to get back, not that it was impossible. It seemed an important detail to omit. But he would have to cross that bridge later.

"So, do you know where he lives then? Dolzowt Deth, I mean."

"Again, possibly . . ."

"You're not getting any more of my hair," insisted Lucky, pressing a hand over his hood.

"Suit yourself," said Bob. He crossed his arms over his chest and waited. The others waited too, with Lucky being the only point none of them focused upon.

"I can't believe I'm doing this," Lucky said, reaching under his own hood and plucking still more hair. His eyes watered as he handed the clump over to the creepy salesman.

"No," said Bob, "I have no idea where Dolzowt lives."

"What?" said Lucky. "But—"

"Sorcerers of his ilk tend to keep pretty much to themselves. Sorry."

"But he just gave you more of his hair," said Greg.

Bob smiled. "Yes, thank you. I appreciate that."

"Give me back that stick, Melvin," Lucky said.

"Now, hold on," said Bob. "Let's not do anything rash. If you expect to find your friend, you're going to need my help. Why, you lot wouldn't last an hour here in the Netherworld without my protection. Perhaps now would be a good time to discuss payment for my ongoing services."

"You're not getting any more of my hair," Lucky said, rubbing his scalp through his hood.

"Very well, perhaps one of you can give up an eye or a finger. I take all the standard forms of payment."

"Greg, do something," said Kristin.

"You help us find Nathan, and we'll give you one final lock of Lucky's hair," Greg bargained.

"Wait just a minute," said Lucky. "Who gave you the—"

Bob's eyes flashed, but he caught himself quickly and managed an insulted look. "Perhaps I could do it for three. I'd be cutting my own throat, you understand, but you seem like good kids."

"Two," said Greg, "and that's our final offer."

"But—" said Lucky.

Bob looked as if he might start hopping with glee, even on his bad ankle. Still, his voice was calm when he spoke. "Very well. You drive a hard bargain." He reached out toward Lucky's hood. "Now, let's have that hair."

Lucky ducked out of reach as Greg slapped down Bob's hand. Bob looked surprised by the quickness of both boys' movements.

"Nathan first," said Greg. "Then you get paid."

Bob frowned. He stooped to pick up his briefcase, then paused to brush himself off and straighten his tie. "Very well. The village of Edmonton is a short walk from here. There's a man there who is likely to have the answers you seek. I'll take you to him, but you need to promise me one thing."

"What might that be?" asked Lucky, frowning.

"I'm your insurance agent now. You won't talk to anyone else, right?"

"Sure, fine," said Greg. "Whatever. We're wasting time."

Bob offered the widest smile Greg had ever seen. "You've made a wise choice. I offer the best service for the price in this area."

"We're still wasting time."

"Does that really matter?" Melvin asked. The others looked at him curiously. "Mordred said when we left here we'd come back to the exact instant we left. We can spend as much time as we want, and it won't make a bit of difference."

Greg frowned. "Something happens to Nathan down here," he reminded them all. "If we don't reach him and warn him before it does, we won't *be* going home."

An awkward moment of silence followed.

"This way, then," said Bob, slipping an arm around Lucky's shoulder and pointing with his briefcase. "We better go find your friend Nathan."

The Dirty Flagon

Edmonton resembled a scrap yard more than a village, reminding Greg of his brief trip to Gyrth. His grip tightened around his walking stick as he recalled the large gang of boys who had attacked him there.

Most of the homes barely remained standing. In fact, many had fallen, left abandoned where they lay. But when a loose board shifted, and a man crawled out of one of the larger piles, Greg realized the ruins were less abandoned than he thought.

The haggard-looking man was wrapped in more bandages than most mummies. Two men wearing crumpled suits and carrying briefcases swarmed on him as he crawled from the rubble. He ducked his head low and waved to indicate he wasn't interested in what they were selling, but they continued to hound him all the same.

"If it's financing you need, I can help you there, too," one of them yelled, but Greg could hear little else.

Toward the center of the village, more people could be seen bustling about. They were similarly covered in bandages, and an unusual number were missing limbs. For each of those dressed in tattered tunics, two or three men in crumpled suits followed at their heels, pitching their services on deaf ears, or in some cases, no ears at all.

"What do these people do here?" Greg asked. "We're in the middle of nowhere."

"Maybe they're farmers," said Kristin.

"Hardly," said Bob. "Aside from some foul-tasting roots, nothing edible grows in the Netherworld. Even if it did, I sure wouldn't eat it."

"But then how do these people survive?" Priscilla asked. "Where do they get their food?"

Bob smiled. "There are plenty of sorcerers in the area who can provide everything they need, for a price."

"You'd think everyone here would be bald," observed Lucky.

"The demand for hair, other than red, is small," said Bob, "as it is so plentiful. But there are other parts of the body that are valuable. Fingernails and toenails are a popular item, though they must be whole and can be a bit painful to remove. Skin is useful in some spells, and of course, for those who are really hard up, a few parts come with spares."

Priscilla looked at him quizzically.

He waggled his fingers in front of her face for clarification.

"Gross!"

Bob smiled reassuringly. "Don't worry, miss. You're insured, remember?"

"How do we find Dolzowt Deth?" asked Greg. Aside from wanting to change the subject, he was anxious to finish his business in this disgusting place and get back home—assuming Nathan was with Dolzowt and had Ruuan's amulet *and* knew a way to cross back into the Styx.

"There's a little pub a bit farther up on the right," Bob said. "Believe me, if there's something to be known in these parts, the barkeep there will know it. Shorty's always had a . . . knack . . . for drawing information out of his patrons."

Kristin shrank back.

"It's okay," Bob told her. "I'll handle things for you. That's why you're paying me, remember?"

The pub looked in better shape than any other structure in the village, though it, too, was little more than a hovel. The weathered sign for the Dirty Flagon had broken loose from one of its hooks and now hung creaking in the breeze, so low Bob had to duck as he reached for the door handle. He pulled the heavy wood door wide and held it open, but Kristin refused to step inside.

"We can't go in there."

"Nonsense," said Bob. "You're still covered inside."

"No, I mean we're not old enough."

"Speak for yourself," said Melvin. "My brother Marvin's taken me into plenty of pubs."

"Well, if he's going in, I'm certainly going," Priscilla announced.

"Me too," said Lucky.

The group stepped past Bob into the dimly lit pub and blinked until they could once again make out their surroundings. The stench of stale smoke and even staler ale was nearly masked by the stench of more recent smoke and ale. Through the haze Greg could see that the furnishings perfectly matched the room in that they, too, looked about to collapse.

About twenty feet away sat two other patrons. Okay, *sat* was the wrong word. Both were slumped over their table, passed out drunk, or perhaps suffocated by the smoke.

Shorty, the barkeep, towered a full head taller than Bob, although at first glance Greg thought it was a weathered skull, not a head, resting atop the man's shoulders. His skin was the palest of whites, his eyes deeply sunken, his thin blond hair plastered to his scalp. At the moment he stood behind the bar wiping off glasses with a dirty rag. Something about the way he carried himself suggested he had already killed eleven patrons this morning and wouldn't mind making it an even dozen.

Bob led the group to the bar and asked Shorty if he knew where to find Dolzowt Death.

"I may," Shorty said, pivoting stiffly toward Bob. He smiled, revealing a mouth full of rotted teeth. "But it's gonna cost yeh."

"Here we go again," said Lucky, reaching for his hood.

Bob cleared his throat and motioned for Lucky to put his arms down. "What sort of payment were you thinking?" he asked Shorty in a businesslike tone.

Shorty set down his glass and sauntered around the bar. He paused to peruse each of the children in turn, taking an extra-long time to study the hump on Greg's back. When he got to Priscilla, he seemed taken aback, apparently only then realizing she was a girl. Priscilla flinched under the scrutiny. Her trembling hand reached up to secure her hood tighter about her face.

Even with her relatively worthless brown hair, Kristin looked uncomfortable with the inspection Shorty gave her. When it came his turn, Melvin glared back at the barkeep, as if daring him to start something. Shorty stared back disinterestedly a moment or two before moving on. Lucky refused to meet the barkeep's eye. He held his head low, so Shorty would have no chance of spotting what remained of the hair beneath his hood.

And then the focus was back on Greg. Shorty's gaze lingered a bit too long on Greg's fingers. Greg quickly moved his hands behind his back.

"Hmm," Shorty said. He returned behind the bar and picked up the glass he'd been drying. "Where'd you find this crew? Not an eye or limb missing in the lot. Strange. Quite strange indeed."

"They're new clients," explained Bob. "Just moved to the area. Just so you know, I'm waiving my usual fee because they seem like such nice folks."

Shorty regarded him suspiciously. "Well, sorry, but I'm not quite so altruistic. I was thinking a couple of fingers from each of the girls might do it. How 'bout it, ladies? Want to lend me a hand?"

Both girls backed up a quick step. "Get away from us," Priscilla threatened, though her voice barely managed to escape her lips.

"Um, look here now," said Bob, "you're frightening these good people." He lowered his voice and looked about the empty room, as if about to reveal a confidence. "I'll tell you what. Perhaps we could make a deal, just between you and me. How are you looking on insurance?"

"Step off," Shorty snarled. "No one here's interested in your *protection*."

"But the Netherworld is a dangerous place. I can offer you peace of mind . . ."

"I got plenty of mind already, thanks." He turned back to the children. "Now it don't have to be fingers. If one of you wants to give up an eye or an ear instead, I think we can work out a deal."

"Tell you what," Bob cut in when he witnessed the looks of horror on the children's faces. He glanced about the empty room again, as if to see if anyone was eavesdropping. One of the two patrons in the corner slid off his chair onto the floor with a thump, but did not wake.

Obviously intrigued, Shorty stopped wiping the glass he was holding and placed it back on the bar. "I'm listenin'."

"I came across an unusual find not long ago," Bob said in a low voice. "I may not know much about you or your situation here, but I'm sure it's something you could use."

Shorty's eyes darted toward the children. "Did I just see that hump of yours move?" he asked Greg.

"No, sir."

Even if he suspected Greg was lying, Shorty was not to be distracted from a deal. He turned back to Bob. "I'm still listening."

Bob reached inside his suit jacket and removed the folded kerchief from his pocket. Shorty leaned forward curiously, but Bob turned his back on the man. He carefully unfolded the material, removed a single hair, and folded the kerchief back again. His eyes darted around the shady establishment a second time. Then he regarded Shorty seriously and held out the hair.

"What's this, then?" Shorty asked. He leaned stiffly forward for a better look and reached across the bar with two elongated fingers.

Bob yanked the hair out of reach. "Careful, it's very valuable." His hand eased forward again, and Shorty's mouth lolled open as he accepted the proffered hair.

"Is this what I think it is?" Shorty asked, his voice barely above a whisper.

"Nothing less," boasted Bob. "Finest red hair this side of the Styx border. Red as the locks of the Pendegrass queen herself."

Priscilla made a grunting noise that was quickly stifled by Greg's palm.

Shorty offered a low whistle. He looked back to Greg and the others. The smile that split his face held all the warmth of an injured badger. "I may be just a simple country boy, but I'm thinking we might want to have us a look under them hoods."

The children drew back as one. Bob jumped between them and Shorty. That, plus the tall wooden bar between them, kept the situation nearly tolerable.

"Now, see," Bob said, "that's just the type of tone that frightened my clients before. I told you, they have nothing to give. I picked up that treasure weeks ago."

But Shorty didn't stop leering at the children. "Then these . . . clients of yours should have nothing to hide, should they?" He dipped his shoulder below the bar and straightened again, gripping a large wooden club in his massive fist.

Bob backed up a step. "Now you're just being rude. I have half a mind to take our business elsewhere . . . oh, ah . . . do you think I could have that hair back before I go?"

"Sure," Shorty said, grinning. He placed the hair temptingly on the bar between them and slapped his palm with the club. "Soon as we see what's under them hoods."

In blatant disregard for all the messages his body was desperately trying to send him, Greg willed himself forward and threw back his hood. "This is ridiculous. We don't have time to waste on this guy. We need to find Nathan and get back to the kingdom before Witch Hazel figures out how to use that amulet of hers."

Shorty grunted. "Just how're you planning to get to the kingdom, boy? No one can cross out of the Netherworld—except Dolzowt Deth, that is." He laughed, a hollow, humorless sound.

"That's not true," Melvin argued. He stepped forward and threw back his own hood. "My dad says he came over here to slay the dragon Tehrer and got back home again without any trouble at all."

The barkeep laughed again, even louder than before. "Your dad's a liar, boy. Tehrer still lives. I seen him just yesterday with my own eyes."

"He's got a point, Melvin," Lucky whispered.

"Now I see why you're so desperate to find the sorcerer," said

Shorty. "But what makes you think someone of Dolzowt Deth's ilk would help you?"

"We don't need Dolzowt Deth to get back home," Melvin told him. "We just want to reach him to find our friend. Nathan can provide all the magic we need."

Bob reached out a hand and pulled Melvin back by his hood. "I'm not sure your policy covers you if you go aggravating a man with a club. However, if you would like to purchase a rider to your policy . . ."

Shorty had not taken his eyes off of Melvin. "A sorcerer with friends? Not very likely."

"Nathan's not a sorcerer, exactly," said Greg, "but he *is* a powerful magician—the best in the kingdom."

"Yeah, and he's not going to be happy when he hears you tried to stop us from reaching him," said Kristin. Apparently she'd once again forgotten she didn't know Nathan.

Shorty was in no way intimidated by her outburst. Again he slapped his palm with the club. "Too bad you'll never reach your friend to let him know I stood in your way."

Lucky had been sidling around the others this entire conversation and had managed to position himself just a few feet from where Shorty stood on the other side of the bar. With a sudden lunge, he landed flat on his chest on the counter, thrust out one arm and snatched the hair off the counter. Shorty's eyes grew wide, but before the barkeep could do more, Lucky scurried out of the club's reach.

"I believe this is ours," Lucky said, and his indignant tone left Greg half expecting him to flip back his hood and replant the hair in his own scalp.

"Oh, please," said Priscilla. "This man doesn't know any more about Dolzowt Deth than I do. Let's get out of here."

"Wait." Shorty struggled to keep the hair Lucky had stolen in sight. "I do know where he lives, I swear."

"And where might that be?" Bob asked.

"It's rather hard to say," said Shorty.

Bob scowled. "Let's go, folks. We're wasting time here."

"No, wait. It's hard to describe, but I could show you."

Bob paused with his arms stretched wide as he corralled his clients toward the door. "Well, now, if you can get us safely there and back . . ."

"Oh, if you're talkin' about getting there *safely*, then that's another matter entirely. I can offer protection, but for that I'm afraid I'm going to need more of those pretty red hairs."

"What makes you think I'd have more?" asked Bob.

"Well, do yeh?"

Bob's arms dropped to his side. He looked reluctant to answer. "I believe I may have one other."

Shorty grinned. "And I have just the guide. Tom!"

Greg heard a rustling from within a small room behind the bar.

"What is it?" a voice replied.

"Get out here. I got a job for yeh."

"Sure thing, Mr. Short."

A chair scraped across a hard wood floor, followed by ever-strengthening footsteps as the owner of the voice approached the door. All eyes fixed on the doorway. Finally the man stepped from the tiny office and glanced around at the small party gathered there. Briefcase in hand, he straightened his tie.

"Well, now, Mr. Short. Something tells me we're looking at a rider to your policy."

Dual Indemnity

"Hold on," Bob told this newcomer with the briefcase. "I already have a standing agreement with these folks to offer all their insurance needs. They signed on with me exclusively. Isn't that right, sir?" he said, addressing Greg.

"Huh?" said Greg. "Oh, yeah, I guess so."

The man called Tom looked to Shorty and back again. "I'm confused. Do you folks want my help or not?"

Shorty picked up another glass from the bar and attempted to blow off the grime. "They do if they want to find their sorcerer friend."

"He's not a sorcerer," Melvin insisted.

"I don't trust him," Bob told Greg. "I don't think he has your best interests in mind."

"Oh, and you do, I suppose," said Tom.

Greg lowered his voice. "We need to reach Dolzowt Deth," he told Bob. "If you don't know the way, well, I think we have to go with him."

Bob's frown was equally wide as Tom's grin. "I'm sorry you feel that way. But you know, you've already paid me for a policy to cover the trip. I think I'll tag along anyway, make sure nothing bad happens along the way."

Tom laughed. "You folks are in the Netherworld now. Of course, something bad's going to happen along the way. The whole place is crawling with organ-hunters." He regarded Greg with an expression that made Greg want to run. "That's precisely why you'll be needing my protection."

Tom Olson led Greg and his party out of Edmonton and deep into the woods toward a destination only he knew. As Bob had promised, he walked at the back of the group, guarding them from behind. But after all of Mordred's warnings, Greg couldn't help but take it upon himself to scan the trail ahead and behind. Organ hunters or not, he wasn't all that comfortable letting his guard down around his two protectors, either.

Tom, on the other hand, was not the least bit tense. He had been Shorty's insurance agent for the past five years. With the type of clientele that frequented the Dirty Flagon, Tom had to pay out claims on a regular basis. He was so accustomed to dying, the thought of barging into the residence of the Netherworld's darkest sorcerer to rescue Nathan didn't concern him in the least. If anything, he seemed anxious to try it.

"Then last month these two sorcerers got in an argument over which was better for spells, livers or spleens," he boasted now. "And when they pushed back their chairs and jumped to their feet, electricity zapping between their splayed fingers, who do you think had to step in and take the full brunt of the blast?"

Greg walked just a step behind. "Say, where are we going, anyway?" he asked for the tenth time since they had left the Dirty Flagon. He had decided after the first dozen of the man's stories that attempting this trip without a guide might have been worth the loss of a few organs.

Tom offered the type of smile only a salesman could manage. "Dolzowt Deth lives on a secluded island just a few miles off the coast of New Haven." He observed Greg's blank expression. "It's a small town five miles north of Old Haven," he said, as if this would make everything clear. "We can rent a boat there and try to reach him. Just because everyone says it's impossible doesn't make it so." His grin widened. "I don't mind helping at all. Really, I don't."

Bob scowled. "As long as they're willing to pay, you mean."

Lucky pulled his hood tightly about his ears. "We already paid that creepy bartender."

"To have me take you where Dolzowt lives and protect you from common threats along the way," Tom said, "but I imagine you'll find plenty other, far more terrible threats between here and there, waiting at every turn."

"Wouldn't that make them common threats, too?" Lucky asked.

Tom scowled. "They're not covered under your current policy. If such a threat were to occur and my protective services were required, I'm afraid I would have to ask for additional payment."

"Wait, no one ever mentioned that." Greg looked to Bob for support, but Bob just shrugged.

"He's right. That's standard policy in the insurance business."

"Now," Tom continued, "Shorty said you would have no trouble covering any additional services that may be required—he mentioned something about a certain hair?"

Lucky's face blanched. "We don't know what you're talking about."

"Something about a certain . . . *red* . . . hair?"

"H-he must be confused."

"We have plenty of red hair," said Melvin. "Just get us to Dolzowt, and it's all yours."

"Melvin," Lucky hissed.

Greg was so intent on the conversation, he nearly missed a sudden rustling in the bushes.

"Organ hunters," Bob warned.

From all sides, men stepped from the woods. Each was heavily bandaged like the villagers back in Edmonton, and Greg didn't spot a single one who wasn't missing at least one appendage.

One raised a curved blade that glittered in the midday sun. A scar ran from the bridge of his nose, under one eye and across his cheek to his neck. If Greg had to guess, he'd say whoever tried to take an eye or an ear from this man was now known as "Lefty," or something equally gruesome. Worst of all, he appeared far less intimidated by magicians' robes than Mordred had theorized.

With a sneer that was probably his scarred face's best attempt at a grin, the man spoke in a raspy voice. "What's this I hear about red hair?"

Greg had spent years running from trouble on Earth. He was more than willing to draw on that experience now, but he worried for the others. Lucky was a fast sprinter, he knew, and Melvin must be too, to have lived through the type of excursions he claimed to have shared with his brother. Even Princess Priscilla had survived her share of scuffles. But what about Kristin?

Scar-Face waved his blade experimentally and sneered wider still. "We can do this the easy way, or my preferred way."

The bandits drew closer, tightening the circle. Each carried a blade. One used his as a distraction while another reached out and flicked back Lucky's hood. His booming laughter cut off abruptly, and everyone gasped—Lucky loudest of all. Tom was just as surprised as any. His eyes nearly bulged out of his head.

"Seize them!" shouted Scar-Face.

Lucky dodged aside but ran into Melvin, and both boys dropped to the ground. The man who had flipped back Lucky's hood grabbed him by the arm and yanked him to his feet. Another flipped back Melvin's hood and frowned.

Greg stood frozen in horror. Then one of the men reached for Priscilla's hood, and Greg let out a scream that might have been heard back at Pendegrass Castle. The man who'd tried for Priscilla stopped in mid-reach and spun, releasing a long dagger to meet Greg's charge.

Greg didn't have time to stop. He was flying forward, out of control. He clamped his eyes shut. But then someone screamed, and again his world shifted.

The knife never struck, but the ground was less kind. It smacked Greg so hard in the chest, he couldn't catch a breath to cough. Hard to imagine it could have felt worse if the blade had found its mark. The soft loamy trail had been replaced by solid rock, and Greg knew at once he had again been transported by magic.

He rolled over on his back and fought to breathe. "Ow."

Lucky stood over him, one hand clenching a walking stick, the other extended to help Greg to his feet. Greg glanced about the area. Apparently the organ hunters had not been transported with him, but everyone else was crowded around, all looking on with concern. All except Tom, of course. Having paid out a claim, the insurance salesmen now lay dead at Greg's feet.

Even Bob was there. He stared down at the fallen agent and prodded him with a toe.

"You okay, Greg?" Lucky asked. "That was close."

Priscilla and Kristin knelt and started fawning over him in a way that made him less comfortable than before. He felt somewhat relieved to find it was Rake's tongue probing his ear. He gently pushed the shadowcat away, then did the same with the two girls and slowly stood.

"I'm fine, I'm fine. But what about Tom? Is he . . . ?"

"Dead?" finished Melvin. "'Fraid so."

With a shriek, Tom jerked awake and scrambled to his feet. He jumped about, staring at his chest, until finally he shook off the effects of his payout and smiled Greg's way.

"I'm fine," he assured them. "Happy to assist. Though we do need to discuss an adjustment to your rate for the next few days."

"For what?" Kristin asked. "You were already paid to protect us."

"Against common threats, yes."

"But you said this whole place was crawling with organ hunters."

Tom tried quite unsuccessfully to offer a sympathetic expression. "Your policy does cover danger from organ hunters," he explained, "to a certain extent. But not when you walk carelessly into a group of them due to your own negligence. So, if you don't mind, I'll just be taking me a little more of that fine red hair of yours."

Bob handed a knife to Lucky and spoke to Greg in a low voice. "Don't say I didn't try to warn you."

One thing Greg liked about having Lucky with him on his previous adventures on Myrth was that trouble tended to remain at bay whenever the boy was around. Such was not the case in the Netherworld. By the end of the day the group had been attacked over a dozen more times, mostly by monsters of various sorts, twice by organ hunters, and once by the forest itself.

Tom reacted so quickly to the attacks that Greg and the others never had a chance to raise their walking sticks, even on a few occasions when Greg never felt he was in much danger. In each case, Tom insisted that the threat was not covered under a standard policy, and Bob sheepishly agreed. Lucky's head was starting to look like a patchwork quilt, and tensions were mounting. Who knew how far it was to New Haven? What if Lucky ran out of hair before they reached their destination?

"Well, I've always wondered what I would look like with short hair," Priscilla quipped. Both Bob and Tom were out of earshot, hunting firewood. It was the first time the two men had left the others alone since leaving the Dirty Flagon, and Greg absently wondered what would happen to their "protection" if someone or something were to attack them now.

"But your hair is so beautiful," Kristin said. She stroked Priscilla's hood softly. "I hope it doesn't come to that."

Priscilla smiled back at her. "Well, unless you have some organs you'd like to donate when the time comes, I'm afraid we'll have no choice."

Melvin slipped up beside Kristin and sniffed her. "If anyone around here has beautiful hair—"

"Not now."

"How do I look?" Lucky asked, throwing back his hood. "Honestly, is it bad?"

None of the others answered. Even Melvin had the sense to hold his tongue. Greg avoided Lucky's eye by removing his pack and loosening the straps so Rake could climb out and stretch his legs. But when Rake caught his first sight of Lucky's patchwork hair, he reared back, hissed and darted into the forest.

Lucky frowned. "I just don't understand it. I've never seen so many monsters in one place. Sure, Mordred said things were bad here, but this is unbelievable."

"Seems perfectly normal to me," said Melvin, who wasn't accustomed to having Lucky's good fortune to guide him when he traveled the forests of Myrth.

"Me too," said Priscilla. "Oh, except for all the insurance agents. They're really scary."

"I heard that," said Bob. He and Tom had just returned, each with a full armload of wood.

Priscilla smiled nervously. "Oh, I, er . . . was just kidding."

"By the way," said Tom, "you folks still owe me for saving you from that flock of harpies earlier."

"Oh, um . . . yeah, all right," Greg muttered uncertainly.

Lucky snugged his hood tightly around his head.

"Just how far is it to New Haven?" Greg asked Tom.

"Not far. Shouldn't take long at all if we continue the same run of good luck we've had today."

"Good luck?" said Lucky. "I'll be bald by this time tomorrow."

Both Bob and Tom nodded, as if in agreement with his estimate.

"Not a problem," said Tom. "I'm sure with the percentage Mr. Short's getting from his referral, he won't mind me waiting for your hair to grow out again."

"We don't have time to wait for his hair to grow back," Greg said. "We need to find Nathan and get back to the kingdom."

Neither Tom nor Bob offered an alternative. Both clung to their briefcases and tried to look sympathetic, and neither noticed the moisture in Priscilla's eyes, or the way Kristin threw an arm about her and stroked her hood consolingly.

Insurance Fraud

The next morning proved to be as perilous as the day before. By the time the group stopped to eat, Lucky was over two-thirds bald.

What little food Greg had packed was now gone, so Bob and Tom headed out to gather some roots for lunch.

"It's not really that bad," Priscilla said when Lucky pulled back his hood to get their opinion.

"Yeah, it's hardly noticeable at all," said Kristin.

"What are you talking about?" said Melvin. "He looks like a freak."

Both girls gasped, but Lucky looked at Melvin approvingly. "Thanks, Melvin. I knew I could count on you to tell me straight." He stooped forward. "How long do you think we have left?"

Melvin studied Lucky's head carefully. "An hour or two at the most. What do you think, Greg?"

Greg sighed. "I think we need to come up with a plan, quick."

Priscilla spoke softly, her eyes lowered to the ground. "Well, we always have my hair to fall back on. That should last us the rest of the trip, wouldn't you think?"

Lucky threw an arm around her shoulder and gave her a consoling hug.

"I'm not so sure that's a good idea," said Greg.

Kristin pushed Lucky out of the way and gave Priscilla a hug of her own. "Of course it's not."

"You saw how those two reacted when they saw Lucky's hair," Greg explained. "Imagine what they'd do if they saw Priscilla's. It may not have occurred to you, but we're in the middle of nowhere. I think we're in as much danger from our 'protection' as from any monster."

"Greg's right," said Lucky.

Melvin made a rude noise. "You just don't want to lose any more hair."

"No," said Kristin, "Greg *is* right. Except they're certainly not going to hurt Lucky. After all, you don't kill the goose that lays the golden eggs."

"What goose is that?" said Melvin.

"It's just an expression where we come from," said Greg. "She means as long as they keep Lucky alive, he'll keep growing more red hair for them to take. But that means they're never going to let him go. And why haven't they gotten rid of the rest of us?"

"Maybe they figure the more of us around, the more people they'll get to save," said Priscilla. "Maybe they're waiting to see what else they can get from us. I'm sure they'd be quite interested to know I was a princess."

"Right," said Lucky. "And about Greg being the Mighty Greghart, or that everyone back home is counting on us to return to save the kingdom."

"Absolutely," said Priscilla.

Greg noticed she and Lucky seemed awfully agreeable now that they shared a common bond. Maybe losing a bit of hair was the best thing that could have happened to the two of them.

An hour and a half later, Greg snipped off the last lock of Lucky's hair a full five hours before the sun was due to set. He handed it to Tom, who had just hyperspaced them into a small clearing after a group of boulders came to life for no reason and bounded toward them, shaking the ground with every weighty bounce.

"Looks like that's the last one," Tom observed with a neutral expression.

"What do we do now?" Kristin asked worriedly. Princess Priscilla glanced up at him, cautiously awaiting his reply with more at stake than any other.

"Don't worry. You're policy is paid in full until your next accident. Even if something else bad does happen, you'll be covered until the end of the grace period, as long as you make up the premium then."

"How long is that?" asked Greg.

"Till sunset."

"But how are we supposed to come up with more hair by then?" Kristin asked.

Tom's smile returned. "You don't have to. Remember, I take all standard forms of payment." His gaze came to rest somewhere in the vicinity of her fingers. She quickly moved her hands behind her back. "Of course, you might not need to worry. Maybe we won't see any more trouble today."

"Yeah, right," said Melvin under his breath.

But miraculously, Tom was right. They hiked the rest of the

afternoon and evening without another incident, and all five children were counting their blessings when the sun finally set, and Tom and Bob once again left to collect firewood.

Greg dropped to the ground with a groan. "I can't believe we made it through the day."

Lucky dropped beside him. "Yeah, well, I wouldn't count on our luck lasting forever."

The others froze in mid-drop and stared at Lucky, horrified. To hear him imply their luck couldn't last was a sure sign all hope was lost.

"Now, don't panic," said Priscilla, allowing herself to continue to the ground. Kristin and Melvin followed her lead and sat. "I still have a full head of hair, and we don't know for sure these guys won't keep honoring their agreement with us if we offer it to them. Only this time we put on a limit. They'll get all my hair if need be, but nothing more. No matter what we encounter from here on out, they'll take us all the way to Dolzowt Deth, and they don't get a single strand until we do."

Lucky took her hand. "Even so, I'd hate to see you end up looking like me."

"That's for sure," Melvin said, snickering.

"Shut up, Melvin," Lucky warned.

"Well, I'm not crazy about the idea either," said Priscilla, choking up.

"You okay?" Greg asked. "I know it's your hair and all, but . . . well, it'll grow back."

"Yeah," Lucky said, trying his best to sound as if he agreed, though it was clear he didn't. "It's really not so bad."

"Men," Priscilla huffed, and before Greg or Lucky could say another word, she jumped to her feet and ran, sobbing, into the woods.

"What's her problem?" Melvin asked.

"She has such beautiful hair," said Kristin. "You couldn't possibly understand. You're a man. Sort of."

Greg frowned. "She shouldn't be wandering around alone," he said, attempting to stand with the ease of a boneless corpse. "I better go find her."

Kristin stopped him with a hand to his shoulder. "I'll go."

"Oh, now I feel better."

"We'll be fine," Kristin assured him. She rose and wandered off in the direction Priscilla had gone. The boys remained quiet for a time, until Melvin finally spoke.

"Priscilla's sure gonna look funny bald."

"Shut up, Melvin," both Greg and Lucky told him.

When the two girls came running back, they looked about to explode with excitement, but then a sudden rustling caught their attention, and when they saw Bob and Tom emerge from the woods carrying firewood, they quickly shut up.

"What's with you two?" Greg asked.

"Yeah," said Lucky, "you look like you just found Nathan strolling in the woods or something. Hey, you didn't, did you?"

"I don't know what you're talking about," Priscilla said a bit louder than necessary. She caught Greg's eye and motioned with her head for him to follow her to one side, away from the others. Greg picked up the hint and did as she asked, though it probably would have looked less conspicuous if Lucky, Melvin and Kristin hadn't tagged along. Fortunately the two insurance agents were too busy stacking logs to notice.

"Why all the secrecy?" Greg asked, once they were out of earshot.

"Ssh. You won't believe what we just heard."

"Yeah," said Kristin, "you're not going to believe it."

"You want to try us?" asked Lucky.

"We overheard Bob and Tom talking in the woods," Priscilla explained.

"Arguing, to be more exact," said Kristin.

"About what?" all three boys asked at once.

"You're not going to believe it."

"Would you just tell us what they said?" Greg demanded a little too loudly. Everyone looked quickly back to the fire, but Tom and Bob were still busy, arguing now over whether or not a person could be seriously injured stacking logs.

Priscilla poked Greg to recapture his attention. "All this terrible stuff that's been happening to us . . . it hasn't been by accident."

"Yes," said Kristin. "Tom's been using spells to cause it all on purpose."

"He's been what?" Lucky shouted.

This time Tom and Bob did look up. "You call me?" Bob asked.

"No, no," said Kristin, "we were just . . . goofing around."

"Well, you folks probably shouldn't stray too far. No telling what kind of danger's lurking about."

Greg felt his anger rising. "Yeah, no telling."

The cords in Lucky's neck fought to escape from beneath his skin. "You mean I cut off all my hair for nothing?" Suddenly he was storming toward the two agents, clenching his walking stick.

"Wait," Greg called after him.

But Lucky didn't stop. He walked straight up to Tom and threw back his hood. "Do you want to explain this?" he said, pointing at his own prickly scalp.

Tom stared curiously. He looked to Bob for an explanation, but Bob avoided his eye.

"Don't bother denying it," said Lucky. "We're wise to your tricks."

"I'm not following," Tom said.

"You've been summoning all these monsters we've been seeing just to get your stinking hands on my hair."

"That's preposterous. Why, that would be a terrible violation of the sacred agent-client trust." He looked again to Bob for support, but Bob's gaze was fixed on Lucky.

"I didn't know, I swear. Of all the hair-brained—er, sorry," he told Lucky. "Of all the stupid schemes . . ."

"Then it's true?" Greg asked.

"It's not what you think," said Tom. "Well, I guess it is . . . but you don't understand. I didn't do it for his hair."

"Then why?" asked Priscilla.

"Yeah," argued Lucky, "why else?"

Tom stood with his shoulders slumped and his head held low, looking as if his briefcase held the weight of the world. "It's rather embarrassing to say."

"More embarrassing than what we think now?" said Greg.

Tom's head popped up. "You have a point."

"Well?" said Lucky.

"Now before you go judging me, I work hard at my job, I really do."

Lucky moved his stick into sensen position. Even though it was not likely Tom recognized the exact significance of the stance, he caught the general drift.

"Wait. People always seem so grateful when I pay out a claim," he quickly explained. "I truly believe they respect the way I selflessly help them through what would otherwise be a disastrous situation."

"Are you saying you did it because you wanted to feel important?" asked Priscilla incredulously.

"Of course not. Well, not *just* that. It also makes them feel good about buying a policy. People don't like to feel taken advantage of. They need an occasional disaster to feel good about paying for my services."

"I'm gonna kill him," Lucky informed them all.

"But don't you see?" Tom pleaded. "It's a win-win situation. This way everybody goes home happy."

"That's it," said Lucky, hoisting his stick. He launched it through a wide arc that looked as though it was intended to cleanly remove Tom's head from his shoulders.

Greg had to admit it might have done just that, had Tom not disappeared in a flash the instant the stick contacted his neck.

"Where'd he go?" Melvin asked.

"Apparently he was self-insured," Bob said. "He could be anywhere."

"Oh no," cried Priscilla. "Now how are we going to find Dolzowt Deth?"

"Don't panic," said Bob. "Tom told us he lives off the coast of New Haven. I've never heard of it myself, but he claims that it's just five miles north of Old Haven. Of course, Shorty could have just come right out and told us that back at the Dirty Flagon, but apparently he and his agent were in cahoots."

"No," said Melvin, "they were right there in the Dirty Flagon."

"You know where Old Haven is?" Greg asked Bob.

"Oh, sure. Everyone knows Old Haven. It's just the other side of Dragon Horns Pass."

"But will you take us there?" Greg swallowed hard. "I'm afraid we can't pay."

Bob looked uncomfortable at the thought of not being paid for his services. Still, he surprised Greg by speaking in an uncharacteristically genuine tone. "I feel bad for you folks, I really do. Tell you what. I'll take you to New Haven free of charge and offer you protection the entire way. After all, you've paid more than enough to cover that distance already, and it shouldn't be nearly as dangerous now that Tom's not around to conjure up monsters every few minutes."

"That would be great," said Greg, and even Lucky seemed happier knowing his sacrifice had not been given in vain.

Bob straightened his tie and smiled widely. "Glad to help. Have I mentioned you seem like nice folks?"

The image of that smile implanted itself in Greg's mind as a dagger soared over Greg's shoulder, straight toward Bob's forehead.

And then the image lingered there, long after Bob disappeared with a flash.

Lapse in Protection

"Organ hunters!" cried Melvin, and four walking sticks whirled up in a flash.

Kristin screamed hysterically, but then must have realized her time could be better spent ducking in between the others, where they could form a circle of protection around her with their weapons.

Another attacker released his blade.

"Watch out," Lucky warned Kristin, even though the knife was soaring straight toward his own head. In a move befitting his name, he managed to slap it out of mid-air and into the chest of a one-armed man who possessed little more than half an ear if you totaled up the bits on both sides.

Nearby, a one-legged man hopped left and right repeatedly, dodging Greg's thrusts. *Amazing,* Greg thought, but then the man's blade snagged Greg's tunic, and Greg cried out. He spun through a move he hadn't tried since he last traveled with Nathan, and smiled when the man's dagger was knocked away.

Defenseless, the one-legged attacker still managed to hop about, ducking Greg's thrusts, until he accidentally jumped into Greg's path and was launched head over heels—well, over heel anyway—into another of his gang, stealing that man's attention just long enough for Priscilla to connect with her stick.

"Gotcha."

Behind her, Melvin had backed his opponent up to the roaring bonfire. He should have had no trouble finishing off the contest but was too busy watching Kristin out of the corner of his eye—nothing new for Melvin, only Greg knew he was watching because she'd entered into a fight of her own.

"Careful," Greg warned.

The stick Kristin had picked up was far too short to be useful, and she had no clue how to wield it, but she was holding her own, mostly because the man she faced had no eyes or ears. He seemed to sense her coming just the same, and managed to dodge all but one of her swings.

One was all Kristin needed.

She'd never needed to fight before, and certainly not under the unspoken agreement that a loss would be paid for with the donation of her organs. Adrenaline racing, she sent the man reeling backward as effectively as if she'd hit him with a medium-sized tree.

Melvin cheered and turned back to easily dispatch his own opponent.

"Retreat," Greg yelled, and all five children darted into the darkness, sprinting blindly between the trees.

Greg prayed no one would trip, or run over a cliff, or worse. The way looked nothing but black, but after a few seconds, a hint of moonlight helped him avoid the trees. He fixed his gaze ahead, searched for any sign of motion. Even so, he nearly ran down Kristin before he spotted her.

He grabbed her hand as he passed and helped her run faster than she'd ever run in her life. Fueled by jealousy, Melvin ran even faster. He managed to catch up and took Kristin's other hand in his own.

"Come on," Greg cried, and Melvin, one arm now looped about Kristin's waist, struggled to keep up.

"Let go of me."

Soon they emerged into a clearing. Greg could just make out Priscilla running a few steps ahead.

A faint movement beyond her, Lucky led the pack. "Hurry," he called without slowing down.

When a huge black wall rushed up to meet them, Greg nearly called for the others to stop, but then Lucky reached the wall and ran straight into it, disappearing in an instant, so Greg continued to run, with less enthusiasm, toward the same fate.

To his relief, the "wall" turned out to be nothing more than dense woods, the far side of the clearing. Again they were running blindly between the trees. Suddenly more concerned about the danger ahead than behind, Greg called the group to a halt.

Kristin broke free of Melvin's grasp. The two were shuffling around, panting and wheezing, when Lucky approached Greg, not the least bit winded. He raised his voice above the noise. "You think we lost them?"

"I think so," Greg gasped, "but we should probably keep moving, just in case."

"Moving where?" Priscilla asked. "We don't know which way to go."

Greg looked to the sky to guide him, but the trees were too thick to see more than the occasional star, and Greg knew he'd have had no idea which way to go even with a clearer view.

Lucky pointed in the direction they had been running. "I say we go that way."

Greg shrugged. "I'm willing to go with one of Lucky's hunches."

"Not a hunch," said Lucky. "Those organ hunters may still be chasing us."

The others agreed and started off into the dark. Eventually they reached another clearing and stopped to rest. They decided against lighting a fire. Why provide a beacon to guide every organ hunter within miles straight to their camp?

The night passed slowly. Every time a twig snapped or a bush rustled, Greg was sure he was about to lose a kidney. He knew nothing about the forests of the Netherworld, but he desperately hoped they were teeming with harmless monkeydogs, just like those in the kingdom.

"What do we do now?" Kristin asked the next morning. "We still don't know which way to go."

Lucky pointed again. "We go that way."

Greg realized that was the direction they had been going the night before. "You think those organ hunters are still chasing us?"

"No, look," said Lucky. "That peak in the distance. See how the one section looks like two dragon horns jutting up into the sky? Bob said Old Haven was just the other side of Dragon Horns Pass."

Kristin studied the mountains in the distance. "You don't think they are, do you? Dragon's horns, I mean?"

"Not unless the dragon's a half mile long," quipped Melvin. No one laughed. For all they knew, running afoul of a half-mile-long dragon was perfectly normal in the Netherworld.

"Okay, we head for the peak," said Priscilla. "Do you think we'll run into Tom or Bob again?"

"I wouldn't count on it," said Greg. "Tom won't exactly want to be found, and Bob could be anywhere by now."

"Well, not anywhere," said Melvin. "He's not here."

"Thanks, Melvin. That's helpful."

The group marched all morning. When the sun was high in the sky, they took their first break.

Greg's stomach growled. "I'm starving."

"Uh-oh," said Lucky.

Greg winced. "What now?"

"It's just, Tom and Bob have been providing our meals. Now that we don't have any monsters 'accidentally' crossing our path, what are we going to do for food?"

"Well, we didn't always have regular meals," Kristin reminded them. "Remember those roots they fed us?"

Melvin grimaced. "Who could forget?"

Certainly not Greg. But even if they did taste like the leather sole of a worn-out sandal fished from a landfill, roots were better than nothing. He only wished he'd paid closer attention when the two insurance agents were collecting them. None of the group could identify which plants had edible roots and which did not.

"What about this one?" Melvin asked. He held up a yellow-orange root that resembled a twisted voodoo doll.

The root suddenly opened its eyes, spotted Melvin holding it up by its ears, and clawed Melvin's arm. With a howl, Melvin dropped it and watched the root scurry away on four of its points.

"I'm guessing no," said Lucky.

"I found one," said Kristin. She held up a tan root that she'd plucked from an area where Rake had been digging, and while to Greg it looked in no way different from any other, she seemed deliriously happy.

"How do you know?" Greg asked.

"What do you mean? Don't you remember Bob giving us some like this?"

Not surprisingly, Melvin had been digging just a few feet away. He took the root from Kristin and shrugged. "They all look the same to me."

"Let me see," said Lucky, but Melvin pulled it out of reach. He wiped it off with his dirty hands, inspected it carefully from every angle, sniffed it, and finally took a bite. The others leaned in close to observe his reaction.

"Auuugh!" Melvin screamed, and began thrashing about on the ground, clenching his throat.

"What's wrong?" Greg shouted. "What's happening?"

Melvin stopped thrashing and smiled. "Nothing. Tastes just as bad as the ones Bob fed us."

"That's not funny," Greg said, emphasizing the fact with a punch to Melvin's shoulder.

Melvin's natural dragon-slaying abilities allowed him to escape the blow unharmed. "I know," he said, grimacing as he took another bite of the root. "It's just plain awful."

In spite of Melvin's warning, Lucky and Greg dug up a dozen more roots and distributed them to the others. That night after dinner they debated starting a fire, but since they didn't know what bandits might be lurking about, and since here they were with all their organs after sleeping the previous night in the dark, they decided against it.

"You think Nathan's okay?" Priscilla asked through the darkness.

Greg was trying to lure Rake up onto his chest so he could get some sleep. "I hope so. I mean, I'm sure he is."

"Do you think he'll have all his organs?" came Melvin's voice.

"Nathan can take care of himself," Lucky reassured them. "He's a powerful magician, remember?"

"But what about Dolzowt Deth?" said Kristin. "Mordred said he was powerful too. What if he's cast some spell that keeps Nathan from being able to use his powers?"

"I'm sure he's fine," Greg lied.

"But then why didn't he return to the kingdom?" Priscilla asked, voicing Greg's silent concern.

"Maybe he doesn't know how," said Lucky. "Remember Bob told us that nobody but Dolzowt Deth could leave the Netherworld. What if Nathan came down here not knowing he couldn't get back again?"

"That's crazy," said Melvin. "Dad said he came here and back, and he doesn't know the first thing about magic."

"But your dad lied about slaying Tehrer," Lucky reminded him. "Maybe he lied about his whole trip down here."

Melvin dropped into silence. Despite the fact the boy had been annoying her ever since they met, Kristin spoke up on his behalf.

"Not necessarily. If Melvin's dad did make a deal with this dragon, then the dragon could have taken him back to the Styx. After all, we already know it can go in and out of here. That's why Mr. Greatheart said he got called in to help in the first place."

Melvin smiled at her, and even though he always grinned whenever she was near, this time the expression looked different. "Thanks."

"Well, then there's no problem," said Lucky. "If your dad did make a deal with Tehrer, then we just need to make a deal with him too."

"Yeah, no problem," Greg muttered. "After we rescue Nathan from a legendary master of the Dark Arts, we just need to find a dragon that hates all of mankind and could be living anywhere in the Netherworld, and talk him into giving us a ride out of this inescapable world. Oh, and all so we can, assuming Nathan is alive and actually has the Amulet of Ruuan with him, battle an evil witch who's bent on destroying us and all of the kingdom. Why would there be a problem?"

Non-Troll Bridge

Shortly after noon the following day, the group crossed a small rise that permitted a clear view of the mountains ahead. Encouraged by the sight, they shuffled down a sandy slope that led about a mile to a bridge spanning a narrow river.

"Odd place for a bridge, here in the middle of nowhere," Lucky observed.

"After you," said Melvin, motioning for him to cross.

The bridge looked plenty sturdy, and even if it didn't, Lucky probably wouldn't have hesitated. The others followed just as confidently, until a hairy man, covered from head to toe with black dirt, crawled up from under the bridge and vaulted over the rail. He landed in the center of the span, blocking their way.

"Halt. Who goes there?"

"Troll!" screamed Kristin. No one who'd ever seen a troll could have possibly made the same mistake.

"Who you calling a troll?" the man shouted. "Why, do I look like a troll to you?"

Kristin studied him a good while.

"No, I don't," the man answered for her. "Why, I've never been so insulted in all my . . . hey, you lot don't have none of them nasty insurance agents with you, do you?"

"Insurance agents?" said Greg. "No, why?"

The man scowled. "I don't take too kindly to insurance agents." He motioned sideways with his head, as if one glance to the right would make everything perfectly clear.

Greg peered over the railing and felt his stomach churn.

A half-dozen men in crumpled business suits hung upside down by ropes tied to the rail, swinging with their heads hovering just inches above the water. Greg couldn't tell if any were alive or not, nor if Bob or Tom was among them, as all insurance agents tended to look pretty much the same from this angle.

"No, I don't care much for salesmen at all," the man elaborated.

"Are they . . . dead?" Greg asked.

"Ah, heavens no," said the man. "If they was, do you think they'd still be hanging there? Nope, soon as one of them dies, they pops off to who knows where to bother some other fella, and then I don't need to worry about them no more. Until then, well, this is fun too, don't you think?"

"But what did they ever do to you?" Priscilla asked.

"They didn't need to do nothin'. They're salesmen. That's bad enough." His eyes darted about. The wild look behind them would have proved he was mad, even if the sight of six swinging insurance agents hadn't already done the trick.

"My daddy was a salesman," he told them. "Always on the trail. Never had time for Mum or me at all. Well, I showed him now, didn't I?" His wild eyes nearly bore into Greg. "I said, didn't I?"

"Okay . . . sure."

Kristin looked over the rail. "That's horrible . . ."

"Yeah, I know," said the man. "You can't get a decent view at all from up here, but there's nothing higher up I could tie 'em to."

"No, I mean—oh, never mind. Let's get out of here," she whispered to Greg.

The man stepped into her way, his look of madness increasing. "Not so fast, little lady. I can't let you pass. No, no, that wouldn't do at all. What then would I eat for supper?"

Kristin flinched back. "I thought you said you weren't a troll."

"'Course. Do I look like a troll?"

"Then why would you want to eat us?" Greg asked, hoping to reason with the man.

"Well, I've got to eat something. These insurance agents don't get it. Soon's you roast one, he up and disappears on you."

Priscilla stepped bravely forward. "Okay, look. We're perfectly willing to pay to cross your bridge."

"Pay?" he said, incredulous. "I don't have no use for organs. Unless they's tasty, of course."

Greg noticed Priscilla's legs shaking—or maybe it was just his vision, as his own legs were trembling plenty.

"I was referring to . . . hair," said Priscilla. "Red hair."

The man grimaced as if she'd suggested they pay with insurance agents. "You can't eat hair. It just balls up in your stomach and makes you all sick. Believe me, I've tried."

"No," Lucky said, "you don't eat it. You trade it for the things you need."

"Like food?" said the man.

"Exactly."

"You see anybody around here to trade with?"

A muffled groan emanated up from below the bridge.

"Ah, no."

"'Course not," said the man. "If there was, I'd've eaten 'em." He raised his eyes to the sky and shook his head, as if tired of dealing with fools. "Okay, let's get to it. It ain't getting any less hungry around here, is it?"

"Wait, aren't you going to ask us a riddle or something?" asked Kristin.

"Shh," said Melvin. "Trolls don't do that."

"But he said he wasn't a troll."

"Quiet." The man studied her curiously. "Why would I ask you a riddle?"

"It's just something non-trolls do," said Lucky, and then, being someone who'd spent his entire life beating the odds, he added, "It gives us a fighting chance of getting across the bridge alive."

"Why would I want to do that?"

"Because it will prove to us you're not a troll," Greg said quickly.

"But I'm not," the man insisted.

"Yes, and this will prove it."

The man thought about this a while, raking his fingers through his matted hair, a pained expression across his face. "I don't know any riddles."

"I could give you one," suggested Kristin.

The man thought a moment longer, then spun toward her, enraged. "What do I look like, an idiot?"

Kristin, who'd judged incorrectly on him looking like a troll, apparently knew to remain silent.

"Well, then we'll ask *you* one," said Melvin. "If you answer right, you can eat us. If not, you let us pass."

"Melvin!" shouted the others.

"Don't worry," Melvin whispered behind his hand. "This guy's obviously out of his mind."

While the man was distracted, Priscilla tried to sidle past him, but he jumped into her way. "You didn't ask me no riddle," he reminded her.

"Okay," said Melvin, "how did the dragonslayer lose his job?"

"He got fired," said the man without a moment's thought. "I guess

I'll just be eating you now, then."

"No wait," said Melvin. "That was just practice. How about this? Why did the dragon lose his taste for young maidens?"

This time the man considered for a full second. "I suppose because his food kept disagreeing with him."

Melvin's face blanched.

"These are too easy," said the man, licking his beard.

"Yeah, but here comes the real one, all right?"

"Melvin," Priscilla scolded. "This is serious. You're gambling with our lives."

"Yeah, well, he's just been lucky so far. Wait till he hears this next one."

"No, hold on," said Priscilla. "Ask me first."

Melvin scowled, but before he said anything out loud again he whispered something into Priscilla's ear.

"You've got to be kidding," the princess said, frowning. "He used his scales."

Melvin frowned too, and whispered something else.

Priscilla rolled her eyes. "Because he'd never live to tell the tail. Come on, Melvin. This is important."

"You think you could do better?"

"No, I'm not the one who goes around asking stupid riddles every five minutes. Greg, what about you? Do you know any good Earth riddles?"

Greg frowned. "No. The only one I know is, 'Why did the chicken cross the road?'"

"Why did the chicken cross the road?" the man repeated. "Yes, why indeed, why indeed?"

"What? No, that wasn't the riddle. We were just discussing . . ."

But the man started pacing back and forth determinedly, his eyes cast to the ground, trying to think. "This one doesn't involve dragons at all, does it? No, I should think not. Chickens, of all things. Who ever heard of a riddle involving chickens?"

"Do you give up then?" asked Melvin.

"Hold on, give me time to think. There must be an answer."

"Okay, *now* do you give up?"

The man stopped abruptly and looked to Greg. "How about a hint?"

"We're talking about our lives here."

"But, can't you just . . . ?" He tugged on his hair and looked around, as if the others might help. "Not even one hint . . . any of you?"

Silence.

"Tell you what," he finally said. "I'll let you pass whether I get it or not. Just give me the hint."

"Promise?" said Kristin.

"What do you take me for—some sort of troll?"

"No, of course not," she said quickly. "So you'll let us go then?"

"Yes, yes, just give me the hint."

She glanced at Greg, who nodded to let her know it was okay.

"All right. It might have been asked, 'Why did *we* cross the *bridge?*'"

The man thought a moment longer, raking his fingers through his hair again. "Still nothing to do with dragons. How should I know why you want to cross this bridge? I suppose to get to the other side. Why else?"

"That's it exactly," said Kristin. "To get to the other side."

"You're kidding?" he said, slapping his knee. "Really? You mean I got it? No, wait, what was it again?"

Greg could hardly believe the man was going to let them escape over such a stupid riddle, but he knew better than to hesitate too long. "Er . . . we need to get moving. You understand, right?"

"Huh? Oh sure," the man said, waving them along.

Priscilla glanced at Greg, not believing either, but he motioned for her to go, and she wasted no time herding the others past the man and off the other end of the bridge.

"Hey," the man called out to Greg. "You're not thinkin' of going through Dragon Horns Pass, are you?"

Greg stopped on the edge of the bridge and turned back to face him. "I think we are."

"Well, either you is or you ain't, which is it?"

"Okay, yes, we are."

"Well, then it really didn't matter whether I et you now or not, did it?" And with that he crawled back over the railing and disappeared beneath his bridge.

Friendly Faces in Ghastly Places

"What do you think he meant?" Melvin asked as they quickly put some distance between themselves and the bridge.

"He was crazy," said Greg. "I'm sure he didn't know what he was talking about."

"But it sounded like he didn't think we'd survive our trip through the pass. Do you think he knows something we don't?"

Of course, Greg thought. *We don't know anything.*

"Greg just said he was crazy," Lucky told Melvin. "He didn't know a thing."

"But what if he did?"

"He didn't."

"Yeah, but what if he did?"

"We'll cross that bridge when we come to it," Greg said.

"This another one of your riddles?" Melvin asked. "Because that chicken thing was lame."

"It got us over the bridge, didn't it?" said Kristin. "Besides, how would a lame chicken cross a road?"

Melvin groaned and picked up the pace. As they left the danger of the non-troll behind, the tension began to ease. Soon the two girls started whispering and giggling. Apparently they'd forgotten that even if they did manage to cross the pass, and even if they were able to rescue Nathan, retrieve the Amulet of Ruuan, get back to the Styx *and* reach Pendegrass Castle in time to stop Witch Hazel, Greg was still destined to die.

At least, Greg hoped they'd forgotten.

"I'm hungry," Melvin announced.

"Me too," Greg admitted, "but we don't have anything to eat, so try not to think about it."

"We're going to have to think about it soon," Priscilla said. "I wonder if there are any more towns out here."

"Don't know," said Greg. And he also didn't know where they were going to find food if there weren't. He was still contemplating the matter when the bushes rustled, and four men stepped from the brush, weapons drawn.

"Organ hunters," Lucky warned, though in Greg's opinion, far too casually.

One of the men was a full head taller than the rest. He waved away the thought. "No, no, we're not hunting organs. We thought *you* were."

"Us?" said Priscilla. "Why would you think that?"

"Your robes," said another of the men. "You are sorcerers, aren't you?"

"That's right," said Melvin, strutting forward. "What're you gonna do about it?"

"Shut up, Melvin," said Greg. "No, we're not sorcerers," he told the men. "We're just dressed this way to keep away trouble."

The tall man nodded uncertainly. "How's that been working for you?"

"Hard to say," said Lucky. "Who knows how much we'd have been attacked without them?"

The man chuckled. "I suppose you've got a point." His face turned serious. "Lucky we stumbled upon you. Five youths like yourselves, wandering around lost in the these woods . . ."

"Who says we're lost?" asked Melvin.

"You're headed toward Dragon Horns Pass. You're either lost, or you've lost your minds. No matter which, you're lucky we found you. We can show you the proper way to Edmonton."

"But we've just come from Edmonton," said Greg. "We need to get to New Haven."

"New Haven? Where on Myrth is that?"

Priscilla stepped forward. "It's supposed to be five miles north of Old Haven."

The man scoffed. "You can't go to Old Haven. Why, to get there you'd have to go straight through Dragon Horns Pass."

A brief murmuring broke out among the men.

"Apparently that's a bad thing," Kristin noted.

"Come," said the second man. "We live not far from here. Perhaps after a good meal you'll be thinking more clearly, and we can set you on a proper course."

"But we need to rescue our friend," Priscilla told him.

"Did he say a good meal?" Melvin whispered to Greg.

"I am really hungry," said Kristin. The others agreed. Even Rake let out a growl from inside Greg's pack, earning several concerned looks from the strangers.

It appeared they had reached an unspoken agreement, but Greg had seen enough of the Netherworld to be cautious.

"How do we know we can trust you?" he asked the men.

"You don't," the tall man answered. "But you've got to eat somewhere, and you won't find any other food between here and Dragon Horns Pass."

"Maybe they could ask some of the folks there to give them some organs to eat," another said, and several of the men chuckled.

"Quiet," said the tall man. "These fools have forgotten what it's like to walk alone in an unfamiliar woods. They didn't mean to scare you. I know you have no reason to trust us, but I give you my word, we mean you no harm."

Seeing as Greg and his group really had no choice, they followed the men from a reasonable distance back to a small village called Edward's Demise, a short march away. The whole way Greg worried they may be walking into a trap, but the men made no move against them, and Edward's Demise appeared no more threatening than Edmonton had been. Most of the homes there barely managed to stand upright, just like those they'd seen in Edmonton. Also, just like in Edmonton, everyone living there was grossly disfigured in one way or another.

At least they were friendly. A one-eyed woman named Erin invited them into her home and offered them food. She offered to put them up for the night, too, which sounded wonderful to Greg. It had been a long time since he could sleep without needing to keep one eye open. Then again, when he saw how Erin had but one eye to keep open, he started to question just how safe they were in the small town of Edward's Demise. Probably just as safe as Edward had been.

"We can't stay," he told her. "We need to reach our friend Nathan."

"Why do they call it Dragon Horns Pass?" Kristin asked.

Erin placed a steaming bowl of gruel in front of her, observed Kristin's frightened look and spoke in a soothing tone. "Don't worry, child. They just call it that because of its shape. It has nothing to do with real dragons. We're perfectly safe here."

"Well, that's a relief," said Greg.

"'Course, if you was planning on headin' up that way, you'd have plenty to worry about," said her husband Sean. "Like about a hundred organ hunters on any given day. Good spot for 'em, you understand, what with the pass being the only route to the east. Why go out to hunt when you can just hang around in one spot and let your prey come to you?"

"Prey?" said Greg.

Erin laughed teasingly. "Organ hunters don't scare me as much as all those creepy insurance agents." She witnessed their worried expressions and adopted a similar one herself. "What's wrong?"

"We need to get through that pass," Greg told her.

Erin's mouth dropped open. "What on Myrth for?"

"We want to get to New Haven."

"Where?"

"They say it's five miles north of Old Haven," Priscilla told her.

Sean offered a skeptical look. He swallowed a large spoonful of gruel. "And what business do you have in this . . . New Haven, then?"

"We're trying to find a man named Dolzowt Deth," Priscilla answered.

Sean's gruel sprayed all over the table. Erin gasped, nearly taking out her one good eye with her spoon when she raised a hand to cover her mouth.

"Who?" Sean asked.

"Dolzowt Deth," Priscilla repeated, and both spoons hit the table.

"Why on Myrth would you want to look for a man like that?" Erin asked, her voice trembling between two octaves.

"We think he's got our friend," said Greg.

If Erin hadn't already dropped her spoon, she'd have surely dropped it now. "If so, then it's too late for your friend."

"Yes, Dolzowt is not particularly kind to his prisoners," Sean told them. "At least that's what they say. I don't know that any have ever lived to tell the tale."

"Nathan's different," said Kristin. "He can do magic."

Sean's eyes grew wide. He retrieved his spoon and thrust it out before him for protection, though Greg could tell he held little confidence it would do the job. "You consort with sorcerers?"

"No, Nathan's not a sorcerer," Priscilla said. "He's a magician."

"Sorcerer? Magician? A robe by any other name."

"That's rose," Kristin corrected.

"*Who's* Rose?" asked Erin.

"Wait," said Sean, "I thought you said you were going to some New Haven place. Dolzowt Deth lives on Deth's End, a small island off the east coast about five miles north of . . . oh."

"You mustn't go there," Erin warned. "You'll die if you do."

And if I don't, Greg thought to himself, but he thanked her for her concern and assured her they had no choice.

She spoke very little to them after that. Probably didn't want to get too attached to anyone who was sure to be dead before the day was up.

"Uh, one other thing," said Greg.

Erin looked at him reluctantly, as if she really had no choice.

"You wouldn't know where we could find Tehrer, would you?"

Erin didn't answer, but Greg could tell from her expression that the thought of finding Tehrer was not one she entertained often.

"Nathan will know," said Priscilla.

"All the more reason we need to find him," said Greg. He finished his gruel about the same time as the others and thanked the strangers for their kindness.

"You're sure you don't want to go to Edmonton?" Erin asked as they were preparing to leave. "Aside from this one nasty man who guards the bridge down that way, it's quite lovely this time of year."

"No, we really need to get to New Haven," answered Greg.

It wasn't hard to read the concern on her face. "Oh . . . well, suit yourselves then. I'd say we'll be seeing you, but . . . well, my momma taught me not to lie."

Dragon Horns Pass

"Look," said Lucky. They were no more than a hundred yards from the cut through the mountain, the tall rock formations that gave Dragon Horns Pass its name looming too high overhead to recognize from this angle.

Greg looked into the gap where Lucky was pointing. More than two dozen men camped at the edge of the gap, barring the way to travelers, and that was just those they could see. Who knew how many more were camped within the gap, or on the other side?

"We can't go through there," said Kristin. Greg was glad he brought her along. For once he didn't feel like the only one capable of seeing the obvious.

"We have to," said Lucky, "if we don't find Nathan and the amulet before whatever happens to him happens, we're never leaving this place."

"Maybe we can go around," suggested Priscilla.

"I don't think so," Greg said. "Usually a mountain pass is called a pass because it's the only way through. We don't have time to look for a different route that may not even exist."

Earlier Kristin had helped Priscilla neatly trim a few locks of hair that they could use for payment, but Greg worried what sort of riot they might incite if they were to show such a treasure to anyone in this world.

From within the pack on Greg's shoulders came a warning growl.

"Shh," said Melvin. "Did you hear something?"

"Yeah," said Greg. "Rake."

A head appeared in the field directly between them and the pass. When the head quickly grew into a head and shoulders and then into a full-sized man, dressed in a crumpled suit and carrying a briefcase, Greg realized the ground dipped ahead, and the insurance agent was hurrying toward them.

He was not alone, either. Several more heads appeared, and soon a half dozen insurance agents were rushing straight toward them. Greg was reminded of a time when his dad had taken him car shopping. The salesmen had swarmed on them there, too, and the experience had been no less terrifying.

"Insurance agents," said Priscilla.

Greg nodded. "Be careful," he told her, and then stepped forward to meet the first of the men halfway.

The salesman manufactured a grin. "Morning, sir. Might I ask how you're set on insurance?" The other salesmen stopped and watched uneasily, much the way the car salesmen had done back home.

"I need someone to take me and my friends through Dragon Horns Pass," Greg told him.

The salesman glanced at the group. He took particular interest in the two girls and grinned even wider.

"Well now, I think we can help you. But Dragon Horns Pass is a dangerous place. I'm afraid it could get quite expensive."

"We can pay," said Greg, feeling guilty over preparing to bargain with Priscilla's hair.

The salesman stared at Kristin, his teeth flashing brightly. "I'll bet you can."

Greg didn't care for the man's expression, but there was no way they were getting through the pass ahead without his help.

"I'll be needing payment up front, of course," the man told him.

"No," Greg told him. "We'll pay once we're standing safely on the other side."

The salesman's expression turned less cordial. "That's not how it works."

Priscilla stepped forward. "Fine. We'll give you part now and the rest when we reach the other side. Take it or leave it."

The man stared at her a long moment. "I'll take it."

Greg removed his pack and fought to keep Rake from escaping as he withdrew a few neatly trimmed strands of Priscilla's hair. "Here," he said, handing over the treasure. "There's a full lock for you once we're safely on the other side. That should more than cover it."

The man's eyes nearly sprang from his head. He took the strands and examined them closely, smiled and turned back to his associates. "Seize them."

Walking sticks and briefcases started swinging everywhere. Then several of the insurance agents opened their briefcases and produced knifes and hatchets. Suddenly Greg's walking stick felt very small in his hand.

He had defeated much worse opponents than these on Myrth, but again he worried for the others. As if to validate his concern, one of the salesmen grabbed Kristin around the neck. She thrashed around violently until she slipped free, then broke away from the group and sprinted through the field ahead.

"Run," Greg called out, and he, Melvin, Priscilla and Lucky tore off after her, a dozen insurance agents in close pursuit.

It was only then Greg realized they were running toward the heavily guarded pass.

"Wait," he shouted, but even he knew they dare not stop. Little did it matter, because just then the men guarding the pass spotted the charge and jumped to their feet. Within seconds, dozens of men were charging toward them from both sides.

"We're going to have to fight," he warned as the distance closed between those charging from the pass.

But then the oddest thing happened. The first of the men from the pass reached them and ran straight past Greg to tackle one of the pursuing salesmen. Others from the pass reached them as well but did not stop. They, too, sought out the salesmen and took up the battle behind.

"They're making sure we can't be protected," Greg realized, but before he could do more, one of the men from the pass grabbed him and pulled him to the ground.

Greg struggled to break free as Kristin had done, but the man's grip was too strong. His face buried in the deep grass of the field, Greg could hear fighting, but he couldn't see a bit of it. Then finally the day turned silent. The man's grip relaxed, and Greg scrambled to his feet. They were completely surrounded by rough-looking men, not a single briefcase in sight.

"What are you going to do with us?" Greg asked.

"Yeah," cried Melvin. "I'm too young to lose my kidneys."

"Lose your kidneys?" said one of the men. "You think we're here to hurt you? Why would we do that after we just saved you from all these dang insurance agents?"

"Saved us?" said Greg.

"Well, sure." The man motioned at the surroundings, where a dozen insurance salesmen lay strewn about the field.

"I thought the agents were here to protect us against you."

The man laughed. "Hardly. There ain't nothing up here to protect people from except insurance agents."

"But we were told hundreds of organ hunters guarded the pass because it's the only way to New Haven."

"Where?"

"I mean Old Haven."

"Oh, it is. And they used to, but there was so many of them up this way that people stopped going to Old Haven after a time, and then there weren't no one for the organ hunters to hunt."

"Then why does everyone think the pass is so dangerous?"

"Oh, them dern insurance agents have kept the rumors alive, so they could charge folks a fortune to go through here, but there really ain't much to worry about anymore."

"Then what are you all doing camped out here?"

"Oh, we heard them insurance agents had turned more aggressive and was actually attacking folks up this way, so we came to put a stop to it."

"So then there's no one guarding the pass?" asked Melvin.

"A few men," said the man. "Volunteers, making sure folks make it safely through."

"Do you know how to get to Old Haven?" Priscilla asked him.

"Sure. Just head through the pass and turn left a mile before where the old oak used to be."

She stared at him, along with the others.

"It's the first trail on the left."

Haven on Myrth

Old Haven was exactly where the man had told them, and just like he had said, the occasional man they saw within Dragon Horns Pass had been there to protect them, not to harm them.

For the first time since entering the Netherworld, they had to pay for their dinners, but they managed to do so with a single strand of Priscilla's hair.

"How far to New Haven?" Melvin asked their server.

The wrinkled woman wiped her hands on a filthy napkin. "Where?"

"New Haven," Priscilla answered. "It's supposed to be about five miles north of here."

"Oh, really? Well, if so, then I'd say it's probably around five miles."

"Thanks," said Greg.

At most there were two hours of daylight left. The five finished their dinners and debated whether to stop for the night, but in the end all agreed to go on. Nathan might not have one more night left.

Using another of Priscilla's hairs, they bought extra food for Greg's pack. The shopkeeper seemed quite interested to know where they'd come across such a find, but when asked, Greg simply pointed to his ears and pretended he couldn't hear. He could only hope the shopkeeper wouldn't remember they'd been carrying on a conversation not one minute earlier.

New Haven was less dilapidated than other towns the group had witnessed. An unusually high number of villagers still had all their eyes, ears and limbs. Even the professionally clad insurance agents were conspicuously absent, and Greg had to wonder if that was the real reason for the town's name.

A one-legged man hopped around outside the first shop they passed, rushing to beat the darkness as he hammered on loose boards in the wood siding.

"Ahem," said Priscilla.

The man ignored her and continued hammering.

"Ahem," Priscilla tried again, a little louder.

With a frown the man lowered his hammer and looked her way. "Yeh need a glass o' water?"

"No, we need help."

"Hmph. I don't remember seeing you kids around here before. Where'd you come from?"

"Old Haven," she told him.

"Where?"

"Do you know how we might reach the docks?" Greg asked.

"Most likely you'll reach 'em dead," said the man. He plucked a nail from the corner of his mouth, set it against the wood, and tapped it home with two strokes of his hammer. "I guess if you're not from around these parts I ought to warn you. Ain't safe to be walking anywhere near the docks alone, even in the middle of the day. But with darkness settling in, well . . . big market for little girls and boys down that way, you know."

"Who you calling little?" Melvin asked, stretching up to his full height.

The man squinted right past him, trying to peer under Lucky's hood. Fortunately Lucky's hair was too short to identify the color.

"Still got both your ears, don't you? Nope, I wouldn't recommend going down to them docks at all." He plucked a second nail from between his teeth and proceeded to secure another board.

"But we need a boat," said Kristin. "We're trying to reach Deth's End."

"Ow!" The man dropped his hammer and hopped about on his one leg, interrupting his thumb-sucking only long enough to curse in words Greg had never heard before.

"You're going *where?*"

"Deth's End," Kristin repeated. "It's an island."

"I know what Deth's End is. I just don't believe it. No one would be foolish enough to go there, not even a child. Do you have any idea what Dolzowt Deth would do to you there?" The man shuddered and returned to sucking his throbbing thumb.

"But we need to rescue our friend," said Kristin. "Can you at least tell us how to get to the docks?"

"No. Even if you had the best of intentions, I wouldn't feel right sending you down there—I'd have to take you myself—but I sure ain't doing that. What's the point of helping you if you're just gonna go off and get yourselves killed after?"

"Please?" pleaded Kristin. She batted her eyes at him, which Greg figured just made him all the more reluctant to help her.

"I'll take yeh to the docks," said an unshaven man who happened to be passing by. Even through the stubble, Greg could see that his cheeks were badly scarred. His one ear was missing, as were most of his teeth. This last was probably what made his grin appear so diabolical.

"Er," said Greg, "I don't think so."

"That's it," said the one-legged man. "I'm taking you myself. Move along," he told the other. "They won't be goin' nowhere with the likes of you."

The toothless grin faded, much to Greg's relief, and the man ambled off, glancing back over his shoulder a few times and laughing.

"Creepy," said Priscilla.

The one-legged man shoved his hammer into a holster on his belt. "Yeah, well, get used to it. He was one of the better ones."

Sudden Departures

Even before the sun set, the docks somehow managed to appear dark as night. The shop where they had chosen to stop was even more decrepit than the Dirty Flagon. The stench of rotted fish hung cloying in the air, and the sound of breaking waves was interrupted only by the occasional call of a distant gull—and the more frequent screams of un-escorted travelers.

"Six eyes is ridiculous," argued the one-legged man, who on the way to the docks had confided to the children that his name was Pete. "We'll give you three fingers and a pinch of skin, not a bit more."

"Uh, but—" said Greg.

"Ha," said the shop owner. "I wouldn't throw you in the water for twice that. Look at these fine crafts. They's more than just seaworthy, you know. They's works of art."

Pete scowled. "We're not asking to buy it, just rent it for a time."

"Very amusing," said the shop owner. "Just how long exactly will you be needing it?"

"How long does it take to get to Deth's End?" Melvin asked innocently enough.

"Deth's End? In one of my boats? That's it. Negotiation's over."

Priscilla motioned for Pete to stoop so she could whisper into his ear. She handed him something the others couldn't see. Pete glanced into his palm, and his eyes bulged.

"Er—wait," he told the shop owner. "I . . . uh . . . I think we may be able to buy that boat outright."

"I'm not gonna ask where you got that, mind," Pete told Priscilla after the shop owner turned over his best vessel to them. (He was so happy he even threw in a spell that would keep the sails trimmed, the wind strong, and the course straight.) "But if you got it where I think you did, it don't matter whether you're going to Deth's End or not. There ain't no place safe for you in the Netherworld."

"We'll be safe if we can just reach our friend," Greg told him.

Pete shrugged. "Deth's End is due east about two miles. With that spell you got, you shouldn't have no problem catchin' the wind and staying on track. 'Course, there's other dangers . . . but I expect you'll find that out yourselves."

"Thanks for all your help," said Priscilla, holding out her hand to reveal a second lock of flowing red hair.

Pete stared at her hand and emitted a low whistle. "I . . . uh . . . that's more wealth than I've seen in my entire lifetime, missy. I don't know what to say."

"Take it," she said. "You deserve it."

Pete reached out with shaking fingers and removed the lock of hair from Priscilla's hand, buffing her palm with all his trembling. "Thank you. Thank you all. I wish there was more I could do."

"You could tell us what you meant by 'other dangers,'" Lucky suggested.

Pete nodded, frowning. "Ah, I wish I could."

"Why can't you?"

"Because no one can, really. Far as I know, no man's ever returned from Deth's End alive."

Whether a result of the spell the shop owner provided or not, the wind blew strong at their backs as the group set sail to the east. They talked very little. Greg could see nothing but blackness outside the boat. He listened to the splash of the water cut by the bow, worried over what they'd find when they reached Deth's End. Had he known better, he would have used the time to worry over what they'd find *before* they reached Deth's End.

Rake crawled out from Greg's pack and stared ahead with the others. All eyes were fixed upon the dark horizon when a loud crash astern caused everyone to spin.

"What was that?" said Kristin.

"Don't know," Lucky said. "Melvin, check it out."

"Me? You check it out."

Lucky scowled. "Stop being such a baby."

A second crash broke the night. In spite of all of his years of good fortune, Lucky edged closer to the bow.

Greg spotted a gigantic tentacle slithering off the deck, slipping away into the darkness. Kristin screamed, but only half as loudly as Melvin.

Like a huge roll of carpet dropping from the sky, the tentacle flopped onto the deck again, splintering boards and scattering debris in all directions.

Kristin pushed Greg forward. "Do something."

He stared at the tiny walking stick in his hand. *Do what?* he asked himself, but even so, he launched himself forward, brought his walking stick up and around with all the force he could muster, and planted the tip deep into the fleshy tentacle. The resulting flinch catapulted him back to the bow. Fortunately Lucky was there to pad his fall, surely reconsidering the benefit of his talent in that moment.

"Watch out, Greg," Kristin warned, a little too late.

The tentacle flopped about the deck, as if searching out the passengers. Melvin and the girls scattered. Greg and Lucky still lay in a heap, separated from the others. Lucky jumped to his feet and risked a leap that sent him safely up and over the probing tentacle.

"C'mon, Greg. It's gonna find you there."

Greg was slower to rise. When the tentacle rolled his direction, he had nowhere to retreat. He timed the motion and jumped at the last possible second, just as Lucky did, but without Lucky's fortune to keep him from harm. The tip of the tentacle jerked around and caught his ankle. Greg landed face first on the deck with a loud splat and an even louder groan.

"Watch out!" Kristin shouted helpfully.

Once again the tentacle began its slow-motion slide off the deck, this time dragging Greg with it. The others stood frozen in horror, but Rake at least thought to help. The shadowcat charged and pounced with a shriek, sinking its claws deep into the monster's flesh.

With a jerk the tentacle released Greg's ankle. But the effort was not a total success. Greg watched in horror as Rake was flung over the rail. The tiny shadowcat soared away like a Frisbee and disappeared into the darkness.

"Rake!"

With a sickening slurp, the tentacle resumed its slide off the deck and faded into the night. Greg rushed over to the rail and scanned the surface of the water, but . . . nothing. Another crash sounded, and the boat lurched sideways.

"Look," Priscilla shouted, pointing straight ahead. "Land."

Greg tore his eyes from the dark spot where he had last seen Rake spinning away into oblivion. His stomach hurt so much he could barely stand. Ahead he could make out a mass of black, slightly darker than the night sky. Deth's End. As they drew slowly nearer, he could make out something tall jutting from the surface. Very tall. And blacker than the blackest of nights.

Lucky, too, was staring at the sight. "It's a spire. Just like Ruuan's."

The image of Rake flying to his doom left Greg too confused to debate the full significance of the sight.

Priscilla debated for him. "Do you think it belongs to another dragon?"

A sudden rush of movement at the base of the spire revealed an enormous creature, three-hundred-foot long, unfurling its wings and taking to the sky.

Lucky gulped. "I guarantee it."

Dolzowt Deth

"Tehrer?" guessed Kristin.

Greg gulped. "Yep. He's coming right at us."

Enormous leather wings dominated the horizon, even with the dragon a good mile distant. Seconds later, when it was just ahead of the bow, its wings blocked out the entire sky. Sea monster or not, Greg tried to jump overboard.

Again the boat lurched. A huge tentacle landed with a crash on the deck in Greg's way. Melvin, who'd been slightly quicker at deciding to jump, banged into Greg's back, knocking him down. Greg looked up to witness a huge set of jaws sweeping down from the sky.

"Watch out!" said Melvin.

Greg tried to stand, but the tentacle rolled into him, knocked him flat on his back. He had but one instant to observe the dragon's mouth rushing up like a cave to engulf him, a cave that sported ten-foot-long stalagmites and stalactites from floor and ceiling, razor sharp and stained with blood.

Greg didn't have time to scream. He heard the sudden crunch of wood, and the little bit of moonlight he had been using to see with cut off in an instant. As dark as it had been outside, it was hard to believe it could be even darker inside the dragon's mouth.

Greg felt a disturbing sensation in his stomach, as if he were inside a suddenly rising elevator, and then he was pitched into Lucky, and a six-foot section of tentacle rolled into the two of them, oozing green slime, competing with the stench of dragon spit as the most putrid odor imaginable.

The dragon wasn't going to eat them just yet, he realized. It was taking them back to Deth's End, which at first Greg thought was a blatant misnomer for a spot halfway up an infinitely tall spire and therefore not even close to an end, but now he realized this was "End" with a capital "E," which held a much more ominous meaning.

Seconds had barely passed before Greg was strewn, amidst a pile of flopping fish and splintered deck wood, across the floor of a cool storage chamber nearly identical to the one found in Ruuan's lair. He was relieved to at least see the others had been scooped up with him.

"Ow," he said.

The others agreed.

While not all of them had ridden inside a dragon's mouth before today, all but Melvin had at least some experience inside the storage locker within Ruuan's lair. Everyone was glad for the respite from the searing heat outside, but Greg suspected even Melvin recognized their good fortune as temporary at best.

"That was disgusting," said Priscilla. Her hood had fallen back, and she raised a hand to her hacked-up haircut and pulled away a long trail of yellowish goo.

"Ugh," Kristin added. "What is that smell?"

"I still say it's a lot better riding inside than underneath," said Lucky. He glanced around the chamber, where streaks of light from the white-hot lair outside cut the gloom. "Hey, this is just like the storage locker in the Infinite Spire."

Kristin used her bare hands to wipe her face, sniffed her palms, and grimaced. "Except Ruuan wasn't around to eat us when we were there."

"He was when I was there," Lucky informed her. "Fortunately Greg talked him out of it."

Greg could see Kristin's eyes light up through the dark. "You did that, Greg? That's great. Think you can do it again?"

"I don't know. That was Ruuan. They say Tehrer's not as friendly. I doubt he's going to care about me fulfilling a prophecy."

"Maybe not," said Melvin, "but you heard what Dad said. He made a deal with Tehrer once."

"That's true," said Greg. "Maybe we do have a chance."

"Say no more," said Lucky. "If we have even a slight chance, my talent should pull us through."

"Not likely," said a woman's voice from the shadows.

Greg spun toward the sound.

"Who's there?" Somewhere during the dragon attack, he'd lost his walking stick, and his hands felt very empty.

The darkness rustled, something darkness ought not do. All eyes fixed on the shadows. A woman's head shifted into one of the beams of moonlight cast from outside the chamber.

"Who are you?" Greg asked, backing up along with the others.

"Oh, it's not me you have to worry about," said the woman, "or the dragon. Dolzowt Deth knows you're here. He'll be along for you soon.

He likes children."

Melvin gulped. "How does he know we're here?"

"And why hasn't he come for you?" Greg asked.

"Dolzowt knows everything that happens on or around Deth's End. He's the one who sent the dragon to pick you up. As for me, I'm afraid I'm too old to be of much use to a sorcerer. Soon he'll come and take whatever parts he needs, and after . . . well, the dragon has to eat . . ."

"That's terrible," said Priscilla.

"Think how I feel."

"We've got to get you out of here," said Greg.

The woman laughed. It was a sad sound. "If only it were that easy. At least you kids will get to stay in the passageway. I hear it's nice in there. Not like this place. You're young and healthy. It could be years before you have to worry about Dolzowt taking anything you can't live without."

"That's a comforting thought," said Lucky.

"What's that?" Greg asked.

"What's what?"

"That weird prickly feeling in the air."

"Uh-oh, he's coming," said the woman, and no sooner had she said it before the air flashed a brilliant blue, and the pure white form of a man appeared, glowing brightly in the center of the room.

The man's robe fluttered as if caught up by a strong wind, though the air stood perfectly still, and his hair hung full below his shoulders—or at least it would have, if it weren't being blown about so fiercely. Equally long as the hair on his head, his misshapen beard fluttered from his chin like eels in a feeding frenzy.

But his glowing red eyes were what concerned Greg most. The way they peered out from the otherwise white image put Greg in mind of a short-tempered rat he'd had as a pet back in grade school. Every time Greg tried to feed it, the rat had lunged for his finger, and while it only bit him twice, Greg knew this was largely due to his own keen reactions. Still, at the moment he would have welcomed Mr. Binky back in place of this.

The others stood frozen in place, as if pinned to the spot by the light cast their way.

"All right, let's have it," said the glowing man, surveying the small gathering of robed figures before him. The calmness of his voice sounded more terrifying than if he'd shouted. "Who dares set foot on my island?"

"Actually, I'm not sure we ever set foot on the island," said Melvin. "We were on a boat, then inside a dragon, and now we're up here."

"Shut up, Melvin," warned Lucky.

Greg realized any negotiations with the dragon Tehrer were going to have to start with this man. "You're Dolzowt Deth, I assume?"

"You will find I ask the questions here. You are?"

"Greg Hart," Greg said. "You may have heard of the prophecies involving me."

Dolzowt smiled, his mouth forming a sliver of black within his glimmering face. "I'm afraid not. We don't get much news here in the Netherworld. But there was a time when I enjoyed interfering with a good prophecy. What is it you said you were called?"

"Greg Hart."

"He's *the* Greg Hart," said Melvin, "so you better do as he says."

Dolzowt laughed, a haunting sound that echoed throughout the chamber. "The name means nothing to me. It matters little anyway, as he will do fine for my purposes. I have an urgent need for a femur for a spell I'm working on."

"What's a femur?" asked Melvin.

"Just a bone in your leg. Don't worry," he said to Greg. "You have two."

Greg's face paled. "But . . . the prophecy . . ."

Dolzowt waved him to silence. "I have little time or interest in prophecies today. As I said, I'm working on a most important spell."

"Well, we don't want to keep you," said Lucky. "If you could just show us the way out . . ."

Dolzowt fixed him with a stare that made Lucky's voice trail off to nothing. "Step forward, boy. Let me see your legs."

"Oh, Nathan," Priscilla said in a low voice. "If there was ever a time when we needed you . . ."

Dolzowt's glowing eyes turned her way. "You wouldn't be referring to Nathaniel Caine, by chance? Because if you are, you'll be disappointed to know he can't rescue you. He's in one of my many cells. Such a good find. You'd be amazed at the power to be unleashed from even the expendable bits of a sorcerer of Mr. Caine's merit."

"What are you going to do with us?" Greg asked.

"Have you already forgotten I ask the questions?" Dolzowt said, fixing his horrible red eyes on Greg. Mr. Binky never stared like that, even when he was about to bite. "From those robes, I am guessing you, too, are sorcerers? Am I right?"

Greg didn't answer.

"I might be inclined to relate your size and youth to your abilities," continued Dolzowt, "but I have been fooled in the past. It is of little matter anyway, for regardless of how powerful you are in your own domain, you are no match for me here. As I said, I will need one of your femurs right away, but don't worry. You will all get to donate to my cause in time. I can always find a use for your . . . assets."

"What a horrible man," said Kristin.

"That's hardly fair. I was just about to say I would let you decide which of you donates first. And I was going to move the rest of you out of this dreadful place and into a cell. I would think you'd be grateful. Just moments ago my dragon made it quite clear he was tired of waiting for his supper."

A whimper from one corner of the chamber reminded Greg of the old woman who shared Tehrer's storage locker.

"Come along, all of you. I must get back to my work." Dolzowt's glowing form glided toward the opening to the lair and stopped just ahead of the crack in the rock. He turned back to observe them all still frozen in place. "It was not a suggestion."

The children exchanged concerned glances, but otherwise, no one moved. Finally Greg took a few jerky steps toward the lair, and the others followed.

A door just like the one leading to the Passageway of Shifting Dimensions opened as they approached. Dolzowt led them through it and down a set of stone steps that eventually melded into a gradual slope, threading itself between the rough stone walls. Everything about the place reminded Greg of the similar passageway within Ruuan's spire. But just about the time Greg expected to see the alcove where the spirelings stored their section of the Amulet of Ruuan, he found something else entirely.

The only light in the tunnel radiated from Dolzowt himself, so it was difficult to see much, but that didn't keep Greg from seeing more than he wanted. Cut into the face of the rock was a shallow cave, empty but for a small boy seated on a worn rock. The child was clothed in soiled rags, his face black with filth, his eyes cast toward his feet—or in this case foot, as he had but one.

"Greg," Kristin said, squeezing Greg's arm.

But the boy never looked up, and Dolzowt kept leading them silently past dozens more cells cut into the rock, each home to a child mutilated in one fashion or another. None of the imprisoned children seemed to notice their presence, even those with two good eyes and ears.

"What is this place?" Greg gasped.

"Aup, I ask the questions, remember?" Dolzowt turned a corner and led them down a side passage lined with cells. Again he turned, and again, revealing a catacomb of passageways filled with hundreds of compartments, each home to another desolate soul.

About halfway through the trip, they reached a cell that held not a child but a man. Although his face was shadowed by an unshaven beard, he wasn't dirty like the others. He wore a magician's robe, similar to the one Greg wore now, and sat not on the rock that had been provided for him, but cross-legged on the floor in meditation.

"Nathan?" Priscilla moaned.

"Your friend cannot hear you," Dolzowt said matter-of-factly. "Come, we have far to go to find an empty cell."

Reluctantly, Greg left Nathan behind, and with him, all hope of ever leaving the Netherworld alive. They seemed to walk forever. Finally they reached an empty cell. Dolzowt motioned them inside, and with very little enthusiasm, Greg stepped forward. He turned to argue with Dolzowt, but to his horror, ran face-first into stone. Much like the shifting trails through the Enchanted Forest, the opening he'd just passed through was already gone.

The wall looked solid, but then the other children shuffled through the rock to stand before him, and Greg had doubts. He touched the surface of the stone. It was just as solid as it appeared.

"Whoa," said Melvin. "What happened to the passage?"

A brilliant white light squeezed through the wall, and Dolzowt Deth's glowing form once again took up a spot at the center of their group.

"I hope you find these accommodations satisfactory. Sorry I don't have more room, but it's been a very good year for careless children. Now, I'll only be gone a short while. I suggest you not waste the time. You need to decide among yourselves who should be first to contribute to my work."

He turned then without waiting for a response and disappeared through the wall in an instant, along with all light. Greg tried ineffectually to blink away the blackness that pressed against his eyes.

"I'm scared," he heard Kristin say.

"Me too," Greg admitted, but the full extent of his fear didn't hit him until he heard Lucky say, "Ditto."

"How are we supposed to get out of here?" asked Melvin. His tone suggested that nothing in his dragonslayer training had trained him for this.

"I'm not even sure how we got in," said Greg. He began to shuffle about the floor, feeling along the walls for any means of escape. Nothing, not even a hairline crack in the surface of the stone.

"Anything's possible with magic," said Kristin. Greg stared at the blackness where the sound originated, remembering how a few weeks ago Kristin thought he was crazy just insinuating there could be a world other than Earth.

"What are we going to do?" asked Priscilla.

"There's nothing we *can* do," said Greg, "but wait."

"That's not true," said Melvin. "Remember what Dolzowt said? We have a decision to make."

Welcome Party

"No," Greg insisted. "We are not going to vote on which of us offers up a leg for Dolzowt's spell."

"But we should at least have someone in mind," Melvin insisted, "just in case we can't escape."

Greg frowned at him. "We're not voting."

"I say we do."

"If so, we'll probably weigh the votes higher in accordance with our ages," Lucky joined in.

Melvin's brow creased. "What does that mean?"

"You'll lose."

"Oh," said Melvin. "I say we don't."

As he suffered the agonizing wait, Greg thought about all the horrors they'd faced so far: the countless griffins and harpies and basilisks that attacked them along the trail, the scattered bands of organ-hunters determined to relieve them of their limbs, the mad non-troll who guarded the bridge near Edmonton. And those poor insurance agents swinging by their ankles. No one deserved such a fate.

What about when Tehrer nearly incinerated them when they first stepped over the border from the Styx? Or when that probing tentacle crashed into their boat and seized Greg by the ankle?

Poor Rake. Launched up and over the edge of the boat into blackness. For what? So they could all end up locked in a cell waiting for Dolzowt Deth to come and take them away in pieces?

Time barely dragged by, until Greg could hardly believe a day had not yet passed. He knew, as did the others, that any second now Dolzowt would reappear to claim his first victim, which is why they all moaned when they heard what sounded like scratching at the door. Of course, this would have been impossible, since there was no door to be scratched, but perhaps that fact alone made it all the more terrifying.

Greg froze and listened to the silence, hoping he'd imagined the sound. He groped in the dark for the others, and they all waited in a huddle, staring wide-eyed into the blackness.

The tension mounted, and Greg was not ashamed to scream when something soft brushed against his leg. He recognized a familiar chatter.

"Rake?"

"What on Myrth are you kids doing here?"

Greg's head jerked up just as a bright light flashed, leaving huge dots in front of his vision no matter which way he looked. For a moment he thought Dolzowt Deth had returned to claim his first donor, but then he recognized the face bathed in the light cast by the glowing staff.

"Nathan?"

The man's blue eyes smiled back at him. "Don't even try to say you weren't expecting me."

As if a drain had been opened, Greg felt his anxiety wash away. The others must have felt it too. With a cry, they rushed forward to greet the magician, and Nathan graciously accepted hugs from each of them, though he did seem a bit confused about the one he received from Kristin.

"Who's that?" he asked as he hugged Greg.

"Kristin Wenslow," Kristin answered for herself. "I'm a friend of Greg's from Earth."

Rake looked on impatiently at first, but then spotted an opening and managed to jump into Greg's arms and bang his cheek into Greg's chest, crushing back his whiskers. Greg was so happy he couldn't speak. Perhaps he'd have found it easier if he'd remembered that no matter whether he escaped this room or not, the prophecy clearly spelled out his doom—or at least it did until Brandon wrote it down.

"We thought Dolzowt was holding you captive," Greg finally said. "We saw you in a cell when he was leading us here."

"Well, I'm sure Dolzowt thought he was holding me captive too, but when this little shadowcat of yours came wandering past my cell a short time ago, I had an idea you wouldn't be far off, and I thought I better come find you."

"But why were you here in the first place?" Lucky asked.

"To see the dragon Tehrer. We can't hope to win against Hazel without him."

"So did you see him?"

"Oh, yes. And negotiations have been going quite well—at least now that he's quit shooting flames at me so much. Why, the last time I tried talking to him, he hit me with just three or four half-hearted blasts."

"Oh, Nathan," said Priscilla. "We were so worried. We thought Dolzowt was using you for spare parts."

Nathan grinned faintly. "You needn't have concerned yourselves over me. I've dealt with far worse sorcerers than Dolzowt Deth." He observed her doubtful expression. "Don't get me wrong. Dolzowt's not someone to be taken lightly, but as powerful as he is, he's not studied magic to nearly the depths I have. He couldn't possibly hold me here against my will."

"But then why didn't you come home?" asked Priscilla. "Brandon's note said you'd be back before nightfall."

"What's this?" said Nathan. "I didn't come back?"

"According to Brandon you were only supposed to be gone a day," Greg said. "We waited as long as we could, but when we got back from the Greathearts' and you still weren't home . . . well, we thought we better come find you."

"Yeah, the spirelings were due any time," added Lucky, "and we didn't think it would be easy to convince Queen Gnarla to sit around and wait when there was a good fight to be had."

Nathan's smile had vanished, and the eyes that had so easily reassured Greg a moment ago looked truly worried. Greg couldn't say he liked the change. "What's wrong, Nathan?"

"If what you say is true, then Dolzowt must have found a way to restrain me. This is serious. We must get out of here right away."

He motioned for the kids to gather round, urged them to take up hands, and waved his staff through an intricate pattern only he understood. Greg felt a familiar charge of electricity, but that was all. Nathan's eyes went from worried to disbelieving.

"What's wrong?" Greg asked again. "Why are we still here?"

"The spell failed," said Nathan. "I've never encountered such resistance. It's as if my own power is working against me."

"Does this mean . . . ?" Kristin asked.

Nathan's face glowed eerily in the light cast from his staff. "Yes, young lady, it does. It's true. Now I understand why you claim I never returned from here."

"This is terrible," said Greg.

"I thought you said Dolzowt Deth couldn't possibly hold you," Melvin said. "What was all that? Just boasting?"

"I don't know how he's managed it, but he has," said Nathan, and before he'd even finished his sentence the air began to prickle and hum. All eyes jumped to the wall where Nathan had appeared as Dolzowt Deth's image slowly slipped into view.

The sorcerer barely glanced at them when he first arrived, deep in thought on some unrelated matter. "You're in luck. I found a femur in my cupboard and was able to complete my spell without you. Odd, that's been happening a lot lately." But then his eye caught sight of someone taller than expected in the room, and his glowing red eyes shot toward Nathan. "You escaped."

Nathan nodded. "You didn't seriously think you could hold me."

The fear on Dolzowt's face lasted only a second. Then it changed to doubt, and finally transformed into a confidence equal to Nathan's own. "Something doesn't add up. If I can't hold you, then why are you still here?"

Nathan simply stared back with a confident smile he had no business using. Dolzowt smiled too. Greg might have even said he was glowing, but that seemed redundant.

"You've already tried, haven't you?" said Dolzowt. "I'm betting you escaped your own cell some time ago. But now you find you cannot escape from here. My spell must have worked."

Nathan waved his staff again. Greg felt his hair stand on end, but little else happened. Yet to Greg's surprise, Nathan didn't look disappointed. His smile relaxed, and he stared at Dolzowt as if expecting him to make the next move.

"What was that about?" Dolzowt asked.

Perhaps it was just Greg's imagination, but he could swear the sorcerer's glow weakened. Dolzowt noticed too. His glowing red eyes faded to black like cooling embers and took on a worried look. He watched his own radiance diminish, until his image had turned completely solid, and the only light in the room was the soft glow cast by the tip of Nathan's staff.

"What manner of magic is this?" Dolzowt stammered. "What have you done to me, wizard?"

"Thank you for joining us," Nathan told him. "I hope for your sake your spell is not so powerful that even you cannot escape it."

Dolzowt's eyes filled with rage. "What have you done?" He thrust out one hand, and a ball of blue fire erupted in his palm.

"Ah, ah, think about what you're about to do," Nathan warned. "If anything happens to me, I suspect you'll find yourself here for a very long time."

Dolzowt stared helplessly for but a moment. His gaze settled on the children cowering by the wall. "Then I'll kill them, one by one, until you release the spell you hold over me."

He made as if to throw the ball of fire Kristin's way, but Nathan's staff came up just as quickly, and the flame never left Dolzowt's palm. The sorcerer shrieked as the ball increased in brilliance. He shook and shook his hand, but couldn't release the fire.

"Enough," said Nathan, waving his staff again.

The flame Dolzowt held disappeared in a flash, and Dolzowt clenched his hand to his chest, tears in his eyes. "You will die for this, wizard."

"No one will die here today, Dolzowt, as long as you cooperate with me. After all, we'll need to work together to overcome this spell of yours."

"Work together? Are you mad?" He inspected his palm briefly and moved it back to his chest. "Why would I help you after what you've done?"

"Because it's the only way you'll leave this room alive."

Dolzowt looked like he desperately wanted to throw something at Nathan, but Greg had an idea the magician would think twice before summoning another fireball. He settled for a burning glare that Greg found nearly as threatening.

"What will it be?" Nathan asked. "Don't feel too rushed. We have nothing but time."

Dolzowt scowled, his contempt for Nathan obvious. "What makes you think working together will help?"

"I assume when you entered this cell you intended to leave again. That means there exists some flaw in the spell that I can leverage. You simply need to explain how you managed to accomplish such a feat, and then, if luck is with us, I should be able to set us all free."

"Oh, luck is with us," Melvin said, shoving Lucky forward.

"Oh, no, no, no," said Dolzowt. "That spell is mine and mine alone. Why would I let you in on how I cast it? You and your little friends will just disappear and leave me here to rot."

"No, you have my word," said Nathan. "I have no reason to leave you behind. You pose no threat to me."

Dolzowt looked highly offended by this last, but the poorly concealed fear in his eye also suggested he knew Nathan spoke the truth. "Very well," he said through clenched teeth, "but if this is a trick, I will hunt you down and make you rue the day—"

"If this is a trick, you will die in this cell," Nathan corrected him. "But you need not fear. I would not lie to you."

Though far from happy about it, Dolzowt revealed to Nathan the details of his latest work. Nathan listened intently to all of it, until

Dolzowt finished his explanation and eased himself to the floor, defeated.

"Ah, yes, I see," said Nathan after a time. "Now I must think." He separated himself from the others as much as possible for the small space and dropped into silence.

Rake swatted Greg to let him know the level of attention he was receiving didn't match his expectations. Greg didn't mind. He hugged the shadowcat to him and buried his nose in Rake's fur. "Oh, Rake, I still can't believe it's you. But how? I saw you disappear into the night. Whatever that thing was in the water threw you hard enough to send you all the way back to the shore at New Haven."

Nathan looked up from his thoughts. "Apparently he was flung hard enough to reach shore, all right, but the shore of Deth's End, not the one in New Haven. Now if you don't mind, I'm trying to think."

"But," insisted Greg, "even if he did reach land, we're in an infinitely tall spire . . ."

"Yes, but only half way up," Lucky reminded him.

"How did he get here?"

Nathan snapped out of his thoughts again, looking annoyed over the distraction.

Dolzowt crawled back to his feet and pulled Greg aside. "Shadowcats are quite mysterious creatures," he told Greg, "far smarter than people give them credit. You must be a powerful magician, for I have never seen one take to a man before . . . or a boy, as the case may be. And this one seems special, even for a shadowcat."

"He did summon all his friends to help us get into Ruuan's spire that one time," Lucky reminded Greg.

"And he's constantly warning us of trouble," said Melvin.

"And helping you out of jams, like on the boat," added Priscilla.

Kristin, who had no stories to share about Rake, stared at the furry creature in Greg's arms and offered all she could. "And look how cute he is."

Greg didn't really see what that had to do with anything, but Rake seemed to like her comment best. The shadowcat struggled in his grasp until Greg had no choice but to let go. Rake shook off the humility of falling and wandered over to Kristin's feet, where he rubbed against her legs until she picked him up and cuddled him.

Greg frowned. If Rake was going to be sharing a bond with someone, that someone ought to be Greg. And whether he was ready to admit it or not, Greg wished Kristin would say *he* was cute and offer to hold *him* that way.

"I think I've got it," Nathan suddenly announced, his face beaming with excitement.

"You've figured out a way to escape?" said Dolzowt.

"Yes, but first we have other business to discuss."

Dolzowt's face turned nearly the same shade of red his eyes had held before Nathan turned him solid. "I knew this was a trick. You lied to me. You never intended to let me out of this cell."

"Quiet," said Nathan. "I didn't lie. We'll go in a moment."

"Then what are we waiting for?"

Nathan removed an object from beneath his robe. Circular and roughly half the size of his fist, it gleamed even brighter than the tip of Nathan's staff, engulfing the room in an eerie green glow.

"There's still the matter of the dragon," he said, and Greg now recognized the object in Nathan's hand as the legendary Amulet of Ruuan, which Nathan once described as the most powerful artifact ever borne of this world.

Greg wasn't sure exactly what that meant, but he had no doubt of the power resting in Nathan's palm. On his last trip to Myrth he had held all four of the pie-shaped center pieces in his own hand. He couldn't imagine what it would feel like to hold them as they were now, nestled within the center of the fifth and most essential piece, an outer ring used to keep the others in place.

Dolzowt thrust out his chin defiantly. "No. I won't help you there."

Nathan offered a sympathetic frown. "With this amulet I can take Tehrer with or without your help, Dolzowt. But you're the only one he'll listen to of his own free will. Those on the side of Good were given the edge in the Dragon Wars because the dragon controlled by this amulet did not resist the magicians who sought to control him. Without Tehrer's cooperation, I'm afraid he'll be no match for Ruuan. As fierce as he was in his day, his anger and hatred for men has taken a heavy toll on him. He has not aged well."

"Is he talking about the dragon that bit our boat in half?" Kristin whispered to Priscilla.

Greg could swear he saw the red return to Dolzowt's eyes. "I told you before, I won't help you," the sorcerer said with a hiss.

Nathan frowned. "Then Witch Hazel will most surely win her battle against the kingdom."

"I care nothing about your witch, or your kingdom."

"Did I mention that once she controls the kingdom, she will

certainly extend her power to the Netherworld as well?"

Dolzowt scowled. "Let her come."

"But your dragon will be dead. And perhaps I failed to mention that with the amulet Hazel now holds, she is more powerful than I."

Dolzowt looked less certain.

"And that while I am forgiving to those who stand in my way, she is not."

"No," said Dolzowt. "Tehrer will not let you control him. You don't know him like I do. He's bitter about his past. He hates everything about men and the kingdom."

"He must like you," said Nathan. "You're still breathing."

"Tehrer and I have an agreement. I guard the passageway to his lair, and he . . . well, he doesn't eat me. It's a good arrangement from both our points of view. But that's something special between us. He's not much for cooperating with other humans."

"The dragon has made agreements with others in the past," said Nathan, and Greg wondered if the magician knew about Norman Greatheart letting Tehrer live, or vice versa. He supposed Nathan must. He knew Tehrer was alive, which was only possible if Norman had lied.

"That was years ago," claimed Dolzowt. "But as you said yourself, age has been hard on him. He's not as reasonable as he once was. He listens to me only out of respect for my power."

"If that were true, he'd surely listen to me," said Nathan, "but I think it more likely he listens to you because you are kindred spirits. You share similar views of morality, and he is not alone in losing his race against age."

"Are you calling me old?" Dolzowt said, his voice rising.

"Not old, exactly. Just too old to take on an opponent like Hazel."

Dolzowt searched the room with his eyes, as if he might have overlooked a means of escape.

"What will it be then?" Nathan asked. "Should I be making myself comfortable?"

"I will see you die for this, magician."

"Yes, given what I'm about to attempt and what I know of Hazel, you quite possibly will. But we're doing it just the same. Now, do we have a deal?"

"Yes, yes, just let us out."

The tip of Nathan's staff brightened, and one of the walls that had appeared perfectly solid a moment before melted away to nothing, revealing the open passageway behind.

Nathan bowed slightly to Dolzowt Deth and motioned toward the opening. "After you."

Dolzowt growled to himself and stormed from the cell. Nathan winked at Greg and stepped out after him, and the children followed. They'd made only a few turns before Greg felt a tug on his robe and realized Rake was scampering along behind, trying to get his attention.

"Rake, I almost forgot you."

He stooped to pick up the shadowcat and noticed movement in the tunnel behind. To his astonishment, several children were milling about the corridor, peering cautiously in all directions.

Greg glanced ahead, to where Nathan and Dolzowt led the others up the corridor. Each cell they passed shimmered, a nearly undetectable shifting of the rock, and within moments a child emerged on shaky legs—or at least leg—to join the others.

In some cases, those in the hall had to rush in and offer a shoulder of support, because the newcomers could not stand on their own. Other children walked with their hands on another's shoulder to guide them, as they had no eyes to see. But slowly they amassed—dozens in all, slowly banding together, searching for a way out of the catacomb of tunnels.

Kristin noticed Greg missing and turned. Her eyes nearly sprang from her head, but for once she didn't scream. Instead, she tugged on Lucky's robe and let him in on the secret. Within moments Priscilla and Melvin knew too. When Melvin saw the sight he nearly shouted, but Lucky happened to be pointing past the boy's nose when Melvin spotted them, and he managed to clamp a hand over Melvin's mouth before Dolzowt was alerted. Once again Greg realized how glad he was to have brought Lucky and his good fortune along.

Knowing no other way, the gathering children followed Greg and the others through the tunnels as Dolzowt negotiated turn after turn, each identical to the last. From every cross-passageway, more joined in, until hundreds walked behind them, their pounding footsteps impossible to ignore. Yet Dolzowt never noticed. The sorcerer floated along ahead of Nathan, still griping to himself, oblivious of the activity behind.

Eventually they stepped into a wider passage, where the floor sloped noticeably to the left, and Greg knew that they had reached the Netherworld's equivalent of the Passageway of Shifted Dimensions that bore through Ruuan's spire. Dolzowt turned right and started up the incline toward the dragon's lair, but Greg dropped behind to talk without being overheard. He pointed toward what he hoped was the main tunnel.

"Gather everyone and go that way, down the incline," he whispered to one girl who looked remarkably whole. "If I guess right, it will take you to a wider tunnel that leads out of the spire."

The young girl simply stared, tears in her eyes, and pushed back her hair to reveal two holes in her head where her ears should have been. Greg recoiled from the sight, but caught himself and fought hard not to add to the girl's fear.

An older boy stepped up and placed his hands on her shoulders.

"I'll help her," he whispered, and to Greg's relief, guided the girl away.

Greg ran after the others. When he caught up to Priscilla and Kristin, they were looking even more worried than he felt.

"What's wrong?" Greg asked, though he could think of very little that was right.

"How are they going to travel the main passage?" she said. "Once we leave, they'll have nothing to protect them from the heat."

Greg's stomach lurched. He'd just sent all those children to their doom. The passages they traveled before were cooled by magic, but if the outer tunnel resembled the one in Ruuan's spire, those children couldn't possibly step into it without melting into the rock. The best they could do would be to wander the catacombs looking for a way out until Dolzowt returned and herded them up again.

"But your friend Nathan's obviously using magic to free them," Kristin argued. "Maybe he'll protect them from the heat, too."

Greg looked ahead to where Nathan led the pack. As if hearing her words, Nathan glanced back at Greg and nodded, and Greg knew that at least the children would be safe.

With Nathan in control, Greg was nearly willing to believe the same about himself, but then he remembered Simon's warnings. Even if they did get back to the kingdom safely, all Greg had to look forward to was his "rather unfortunate demise."

"WHY SHOULD I COOPERATE WITH *YOU*, MAGICIAN?"

Greg stood cowering with the other children near the wall of Tehrer's lair, as Nathan and Dolzowt presented their proposal to the dragon. Since befriending Ruuan, Greg had forgotten how much bigger a dragon could look when it was angry.

"It's the only way the kingdom stands a chance of survival," Nathan told him.

Tehrer's head dropped to Nathan's level so quickly, Greg thought the walls were caving in. The dragon's jet black coloring contrasted so much with the glowing white walls, it looked as if there were a dragon-shaped hole in the center of the immense cavern.

"I'M NOT SEEING YOUR POINT." The look in the dragon's eye could only be described as challenging, especially given Tehrer's eye was taller than Greg himself.

"It is not just the kingdom that will suffer," Nathan said. "Without anyone holding the reins on Witch Hazel's power, it is only a matter of time before she comes to stake her claim here."

"LET HER COME," Tehrer said. "I WELCOME THE CHALLENGE."

"That is only because you do not fully understand it."

"IT IS YOU WHO DOES NOT UNDERSTAND. THE WITCH WILL DIE IF SHE STEPS FOOT INTO THE NETHERWORLD. THIS IS MY PLACE. SHE HOLDS NO POWER HERE."

"That is where *you* are wrong," Nathan told him, "and why you will surely die. When she comes, she will come riding the dragon Ruuan, and she'll wield more power than you can imagine, for she will hold both the ancient Amulet of Ruuan and the Amulet of Tehrer."

Greg wouldn't have thought Tehrer's eyes could have grown bigger.

"Ah, yes," said Nathan. "You of all dragons should understand the danger. With them she can bend your will, control you like a puppet. You will perish, and then Hazel will force Ruuan to destroy himself, and all of your kind will be remembered as weak, mindless creatures, little more than livestock."

"LIVESTOCK! I WILL SEE THIS WITCH HAZEL DIE A LONG AND LINGERING DEATH."

"No. On the contrary, you will do whatever she asks, cater to her every whim."

The dragon released a jet of searing steam that would have surely disintegrated Nathan if not for his protective magic.

"Do it for Dolzowt," Kristin tried from behind Nathan's shoulder.

"HA! I CARE NOTHING FOR HIM," Tehrer shouted, his blazing red eyes darting Dolzowt Deth's way. And to illustrate his point he directed a second jet of steam, equally as hard as the first, straight at the sorcerer.

Dolzowt's magic must have been weaker than Nathan's, because he ended up standing about five feet shorter, as nothing above his calves remained.

The screams of all five children echoed about the lair.

"You killed him," Kristin said, horrified.

"DO NOT TELL ME WHAT TO DO," the dragon advised her.

Sound advice, Greg silently decided. He could hardly believe his ears when he heard Kristin say, "But what about your anger? Dolzowt told us you grow more ornery every year."

The dragon's gaze locked on Kristin, and Greg could only hope Nathan wasn't going to be stingy with his spell of protection just because he didn't know the girl.

"YOU'RE LUCKY I DO NOT CONSIDER THAT AN INSULT, OR YOU WOULD SHARE DOLZOWT'S FATE."

Greg very slowly released his breath, but Kristin refused to learn from her mistake.

"I just mean, there's a reason why you're angry. I'd be angry too if someone killed my father."

"NO ONE KILLED MY FATHER. HE DIED HERE IN THE NETHERWORLD SEVERAL CENTURIES AFTER THE DRAGON WARS."

"Okay, then, I'd be mad if someone forced my dad into hiding for the rest of his life."

"DRAGONS DO NOT HIDE."

Tehrer unleashed a third jet of steam straight at Kristin, and for a change it was Greg who screamed for *her* safety. Kristin opened her eyes again, and if Greg could interpret her expression correctly, she was quite surprised to see she still had eyes to open, or a head to support them. Again Greg released a nervous breath.

Nathan gave him a nod to indicate he might want to help Kristin. With caution, of course.

"Okay, maybe your dad wasn't down here hiding," Greg said. "Maybe he wasn't afraid of the amulets that were used on him and his kind during the Dragon Wars."

"OF COURSE HE WASN'T."

"Then why does everyone think he was?" said Kristin.

"WHAT? WHO THINKS THAT?"

"Everyone," Kristin repeated. "At least that's what it seems like to me. Of course, I've only been here a few days. It could just be everyone I've met—you know, a matter of coincidence—but I'm betting it's really *everyone* everyone."

"THEN EVERYONE DESERVES TO DIE. LET THE WITCH HAVE HER DESTRUCTION. THE WORLD WILL BE A BETTER PLACE FOR IT."

Not the result Greg had been hoping for. "But they'll die thinking your father was a coward."

"A COWARD? MY FATHER?"

"I'm not saying he was," Greg said, backing away. "I'm just saying that's what people will think."

"But if you fought Witch Hazel and showed you weren't afraid of the amulet," said Kristin, "everyone would assume your father didn't feel threatened enough to bother."

"HMMM. DO PEOPLE REALLY THINK MY FATHER WAS A COWARD?"

"Well, not any of us, of course . . ." Greg said, to which all of the children hastily agreed, "but other people . . ."

"THIS WILL NOT DO." The dragon's head turned swiftly toward Nathan, causing all five children to shriek. "VERY WELL, MAGICIAN, THIS ONCE I SHALL HELP. WHAT IS IT YOU NEED?"

Unwelcome Greeting

Mordred's arms were still raised when Greg felt the hard stone floor of Pendegrass Castle rise up to meet his feet. It was an especially welcome feel, since not an instant earlier he'd been seated just behind Tehrer's neck, clutching on for dear life as the dragon soared across the border between the Netherworld and the Styx.

The other children were there too, at his side.

Nathan? Greg thought. A minute ago the magician had been seated directly in front of Greg on the dragon. Where was he now? The last thing Greg wanted to do was mount another rescue inside Dolzowt's spire, even if Dolzowt's boot-clad shins possessed far less threat than the entire sorcerer.

"Ah, here at last," came a familiar voice, and only then did Greg spot Nathan standing next to Mordred, dressed not in a black magician's robe but in his more familiar white shirt and loose pants cinched at the waist by a heavy cord.

"Huh?" said Greg. "We were just with you in the Netherworld."

"Ah yes, but when I returned it was to a time two evenings ago, just after I left. Good thing, too, as I have my doubts that without my prompting, Mordred would have thought to bring you back here once you crossed out of the Netherworld. Best not to think about it," he said winking. "It'll just make your head hurt."

"But what about the dragon?" said Greg. "Where's Tehrer?"

"Let's hope he's on his way here," Nathan answered. "He did agree to help. Anyway, we should know in a few minutes."

"Let's hope he eats before he gets here," said Lucky.

Nathan's face took on a more concerned quality. "Perhaps I should be outside to oversee his arrival."

Greg and the other children followed Nathan and Mordred out into the late afternoon sun to greet Tehrer, but too late. The three-hundred-foot long dragon already lay, munching peacefully, on the castle lawn. From the hundreds of thousands of furious shouting spirelings, Greg had a bad feeling about what Tehrer was munching on.

"What's going on here?" Nathan asked.

Greg caught a blur to his right, one that seemed to originate behind the dragon and sweep around it in a wide arc, racing toward them with the speed of a cannonball. The blur seized to a stop, revealing the gruesome face of an enraged spireling. Actually Greg was just guessing it was enraged, as spireling faces tended to always look pretty much the same, but the tone of the spireling's voice fit his suspicions.

"What is the meaning of this? You summon us for assistance, and this is how you welcome us?"

"I'm afraid I don't know what you're talking about," said Nathan. "Did something happen?"

"Did something happen?" the spireling shrieked. "Did something happen?"

"I'm guessing it did."

"We come to you in good faith, generously offer our assistance, and how do you repay us? By having this dragon sentry of yours sweep up our lead with a single swipe of its tongue. Look, it's still chomping on the last of him now."

Greg cringed as Tehrer slurped up a tiny leg that had been dangling from the corner of his mouth. The two girls gasped.

"Ugh," added Lucky.

"Oh, dear," said King Peter, who'd stepped from the castle gate just in time to witness the sight. "Please accept our sincerest apologies, sir. We had no—"

"Sir? My name is Gnag, and I am no more male than that one," she said, pointing at Melvin.

"But I *am* male," insisted Melvin.

"Again I apologize," King Peter said. "As I started to say, we had no way of knowing you would be here so soon."

"Soon? We would have been here yesterday had we not stopped to pick up the wyverns."

"Ah," Mordred said, "hence the wailing. What do you plan to do with those?" His face indicated he held little regard for wyverns. Or spirelings, for that matter. He probably wasn't the best person to have around while King Peter was trying to console this spireling over her loss.

"Queen Gnarla wants to know what you have to say for yourself," said the spireling. "Are you declaring war against us, or what?"

"War?" said King Peter. "Heavens no. This has just been a most unfortunate accident, I can assure you. A small oversight gone horribly awry . . ."

Nathan withdrew the amulet he wore on a chain about his neck. He held it up before him and called out across the lawn in a commanding tone.

"Tehrer, back."

Although the dragon stood nearly fifty yards away, Tehrer's neck swept around so that his head rushed up like a speeding car. Hatred for Nathan and the object he carried was written in every facet of Tehrer's features. It was the same kind of look Ruuan once gave Greg after Greg hit him with a heavy sleigh at the bottom of the Infinite Spire, not an expression he wanted to see on any dragon's face, then or now.

Begrudgingly Tehrer sidled to the north, shaking the castle lawn as he moved. To the east was revealed the start of the King's Highway and the first hundred of what was sure to be the entire race of spirelings, screaming and shaking their fists at the dragon.

"Oh, dear," said King Peter.

As if an inaudible signal had been given, the spirelings parted. Up through their ranks marched three angry wyverns, snapping at the air and tugging against frighteningly thin chains secured about their necks. Fixed to the other end of each of those chains were four spirelings, who despite being hurled first one way, then the other, managed to maintain a firm grasp on the chains.

Each time one of the spireling-laden chains swung too close, the surrounding spirelings dodged nimbly out of the way, their incredible speed keeping them from harm. As quick as they were, Greg couldn't imagine how Tehrer ever managed to snatch up one of them. He could only assume that with an entire army pressing from behind, the luckless leader simply had nowhere to retreat once the dragon spotted him.

Queen Gnarla was among the first to cross the castle lawn. Greg knew this not because he could distinguish her from any other spireling, but because she was being carried on a litter atop the shoulders of four of her tallest warriors. The litter-bearers stopped directly in front of Greg, their mouths full of gruesome teeth aligned roughly even with Greg's throat, and lowered the litter to the ground.

Queen Gnarla stepped off with the grace of an injured rhinoceros. She tried to speak, but King Peter interrupted, pleading for her forgiveness. The queen's anger over the death of her warrior paled in comparison to her rage over being interrupted. Fortunately King Peter picked up on her expression and quickly quieted, even before she waved him to silence.

"We do not care about the loss of one of Our kind," she yelled. "We are more concerned that you have been so careless in preparing for Our arrival. We are, after all, your only hope of survival in this newest development. We believe you should be more grateful for Our willingness to help."

Melvin, who had twice before been in the presence of the spireling queen, should have known to keep his mouth shut, but no. "It's Greg who's going to defeat Hazel, not you. Simon's latest prophecy says so."

"Why is this child speaking in Our presence?" Queen Gnarla demanded.

"I'm not a child. Has everyone forgotten my role in the last prophecy?"

"Ah, he is the Mighty Greghart. Forgive Us. We did not realize."

"Greatheart, not Greghart! Melvin, remember? I slayed the dragon Ruuan."

If Queen Gnarla was at all embarrassed, it was impossible to tell. She continued to address King Peter when she spoke. "By making the dragon laugh. Yes, We remember him now. You must understand all you humans look the same to Us. But We are still confused. Why is this child speaking in Our presence?"

"I'm very sorry, Majesty," said King Peter. "The boy fails to understand the intricacies of events to come."

"I understand enough to know Greg's going to be the hero," said Melvin. "Personally I think it should have been me or Marvin, but . . . well, we can't argue with Simon."

"That's enough, son," King Peter told him. "Queen Gnarla and I were talking."

Melvin was about to say more when Princess Priscilla clasped a hand over his mouth and dragged him away. Her father offered her a grateful nod and returned his attention to the spireling queen.

"Was he talking about the hero Greghart?" Queen Gnarla asked. King Peter acknowledged he was. "So it is true, what the dark magician said? He has been named in another prophecy?"

"I'm afraid so." The king leaned in close, so he could speak to her without being overheard, but Greg had a pretty good idea what he'd said after every spireling in sight gasped, turned to stare at him and muttered, "Demise?"

The closest spirelings pressed forward for a better look, and Greg could hear the murmur from hundreds of thousands more lined up to the east. Queen Gnarla pushed past King Peter to see for herself. She looked first at Lucky and then, to Greg's annoyance, Kristin and Priscilla, before zeroing in on Greg. She studied him up and down, took a second, longer look at Kristin, and finally met Greg's eye. "This is highly upsetting."

While Greg would be the first to admit King Peter's words were upsetting, staring eye to eye with Queen Gnarla seemed nearly as bad.

"You are the Mighty Greghart, are you not?" she asked him.

Greg nodded. A murmur throughout the crowd revealed that the others were impressed by her attention to detail. Queen Gnarla basked in the praise for a moment before issuing a wordless command for silence.

"You have become a living legend to Us," she told Greg, "as your many heroic deeds are beyond even Our measure. We know you will fight bravely in the coming trial, and We will be honored to fight by your side. Rest assured that after you die, your name will carry on for generations to come. Our ancestors will know that We fought with the greatest warrior the land of Myrth has ever known."

"Great," said Greg.

"Why the wyverns?" King Peter asked the queen.

"We heard that We would be fighting the dragon Ruuan. As skilled as We warriors are, We find Ourselves at a serious disadvantage when it comes to attacks from the sky. The wyverns should even up the sides a bit. We have always recognized what magnificent fighting beasts they are, but not until recently have We tried to control them. Under the right hand they can make most formidable steeds."

Just then one of the wyverns threw back its head and wailed to shake the trees. The eight warriors who maintained a death-grip on the chains about its neck were lofted high into the air. Annoyed by their weight, the beast shrugged, swinging the spirelings into the ground with eight sickening thumps. When the wyvern raised its head again, there were two empty spots on one of the chains. Two more spirelings dove in to take the fallen warriors' places.

"I guess none of them had the right hand," observed Melvin.

"Quiet, son." King Peter dabbed at his brow with a handkerchief. "Yes," he told Queen Gnarla, "I'm sure you'll have no trouble controlling them."

Kristin leaned over to whisper in Melvin's ear again, and Greg thought it was more than coincidence that Melvin's cheek moved suddenly into the path of her lips.

"Ow!"

"Oops, sorry," said Melvin. "Were you about to tell me something?"

Kristin put a hand to her lips and checked for blood. "I was just thinking that those hideous dragons are going to get somebody killed. They'll help Hazel's side more than ours."

"They're not dragons. They're wyverns," Melvin corrected. "Hey, did I ever tell you how Greghart and I once—?" He noticed the concern in her eye and dropped the sentence in mid-thought. "Yeah, I think you may be right."

Preparations

King Peter continued to appease the queen for what seemed an eternity. Finally Queen Gnarla gave orders for her warriors to stake down the wyverns in the eastern section of the yard. It looked to be a lengthy procedure, so the kids tagged along behind Nathan while he took Tehrer around back.

Nathan knew no restraints would be able to hold the dragon. He raised his amulet for Tehrer to see. "You will not snack on the wyverns before morning—or any more spirelings—or people." The dragon seemed a little too thoughtful over his wording. "Let's make it, you will not snack on, or stomp on, or flame, or harm in any way, *anything* before morning, or *in* the morning, or after noon, or anytime at all. If Hazel doesn't attack before long, I'll bring something suitable to eat."

The dragon agreed, no doubt because Nathan was commanding him with the amulet, and he really had no choice.

Instead of returning the way they had come, Nathan led them behind the castle, where no less than fifty men in black robes stood huddled on the castle lawn. The king's magicians had their part to play in the upcoming battle, and they too needed to prepare. Nathan stopped and talked to Mordred for a time, the two of them nodding and pointing at the surrounding treetops, but try as he might, Greg was unable to hear any of the conversation.

To the west, the lawn was mostly hidden beneath the many blue uniforms of the Army of the Crown. Greg had traveled with Ryder Hawkins and his five hundred or so troops on his first visit to Myrth, and then with General Talbout and his thousand men on his second visit. Now it looked as if all those men had joined with another thousand or more to practice for the upcoming battle. The entire western perimeter had been lined with practice targets, and the men had divided into no less than a hundred lines, where they each stood awaiting their turn with a bow and arrow.

"I didn't know King Peter's men were archers," Greg said to

Nathan as they ambled past. "They all carried swords when we were on the trail together."

"Most of them aren't," said Nathan, "but they will need to be soon. You don't want to get close enough to use a sword against a beast like Ruuan."

Or a bow and arrow, Greg thought. In truth he hated to use any weapon against Ruuan. It wasn't the dragon's fault Hazel was controlling him.

Greg spotted General Hawkins giving personal instructions to one of his men. He called and waved, and Ryder stopped long enough to offer him a salute before returning to his teachings. Ahead General Talbout was consulting a third man in officer's attire, who Greg had to assume was General Stephanopolis, the only other general in King Peter's army.

"Why so many?" Greg asked. "I mean, it's not like the Dragon Wars, when there were lots of dragons to worry about. Now there're just two."

Nathan grimaced. "The Dragon Wars were fought two dragons at a time, as well. I don't know about you, but two dragons is more of a fight than I want to be around."

"But you're a magician. The Greathearts have been slaying dragons for centuries, and you have way more abilities than they do."

"Hey," said Melvin.

"Maybe so," Nathan said, "but what you don't realize is, there's only one way to slay a dragon. Catch it while it's sleeping. No mortal has ever stood a chance against one of the beasts when it was awake. And believe me, when Ruuan comes, he'll be awake. To answer your question, the rest of us are here to make it possible for this to be a two dragon fight."

"What do you mean?"

"You'll see. Anyway, we'll do what we can, but I'm afraid the outcome will be up to you. Either you will win and the kingdom will survive, or . . . you will lose."

"Oh," said Greg. "Well, no pressure."

The children watched the practice until dark, then retired to the castle for a meal and on to their chambers for an early night's rest. Priscilla had shared her room with Kristin while Greg was in Gyrth and continued to do so now. She arranged for the boys to sleep in the quarters adjoining hers, so they would be close during the tense hours that followed. For all they knew, Hazel would attack at any moment, and from what Greg knew of Ruuan, he could imagine the entire castle being burned to the ground before the sentries outside could so much as shout out a warning.

He plopped down on the edge of the bed he would be sharing with Melvin. Earlier they'd drawn straws to see who got the second bed for himself, although Greg didn't know why they had bothered. Lucky hid a smirk as he shooed Rake off his pillow and pulled back the covers to his own bed.

How will it happen? Greg wondered about his upcoming demise. He eyed Melvin while he fluffed up his pillow. Not that long ago the boy had tried to kill Greg. The thought was still playing in Greg's mind when a knock sounded upon the door.

"It's us," Greg heard Priscilla say. "Open up."

Melvin walked over and unlatched the door. Priscilla entered, pushing Kristin along ahead of her. While annoyed over the manhandling, Kristin put up little fight, though her cheeks did redden slightly when Priscilla tipped her over onto the bed next to Greg.

"You have to go home now," the princess told the two of them.

"What?" said Greg. "But we haven't done anything yet."

"What are you talking about? You figured out why Nathan was missing when you first got here, didn't you? And you went back in time to make sure he came here years ago from Gyrth and again now with the amulet. Now you've even gone and rescued him from the Netherworld. Well, I say you're done. Everything is as it should be. Time for you to go home."

"But we haven't fought Witch Hazel yet."

"Of course not," said Priscilla. "If you fight Hazel, you're going to die."

Greg didn't need to be reminded of the obvious. He glanced at Kristin. She looked as if she wanted to hug him but was too embarrassed.

"But if you believe the prophecy, then you know I can't go home," Greg said. "I'm supposed to ride Tehrer when Hazel attacks. It's the only way she can be defeated."

"Who says it's the only way?" said Kristin. She was sitting so close he could feel her breath on his ear. In spite of the severity of his situation, he couldn't say he was displeased by the sensation. "If the prophecy is broken, couldn't Hazel be defeated some other way? Couldn't Nathan ride the dragon alone? Aside from that one incident with the spireling, he seems to be controlling it fairly well."

"You can't change a prophecy," Lucky called out from the other bed, where he lay snug beneath his covers. "Greg ought to know that by now. Oh, sorry, Greg. I don't like it any better than you do, but you know I'm right."

"Who says?" said Priscilla. "Just because no prophecy has ever been changed before doesn't mean we can't change one now."

Melvin walked over to his own bed and squeezed under the covers, nudging Kristin closer to Greg, to which she reddened further still. "Lucky's right. Even if you could change a prophecy, you wouldn't want to. People would stop believing in them, and then what good would they be?"

Priscilla looked nearly as flustered as Kristin. "But Greg's going to die if we don't change this one."

"Yeah, I know," said Melvin. "That's tough luck." He nudged Greg with his foot from beneath the covers. "And I mean that, Greg. I really do."

Greg didn't answer. He was thinking about what Priscilla had said. Could he change the prophecy? Or were Melvin and Lucky right? Did he have to go along with it as written, even if he could find a way to change it?

"I think Priscilla's right," said Kristin. "You've done enough. More than enough. We should go home now, before you get hurt."

"No," said Greg, "I think I need to at least ride the dragon. It says so in the prophecy, and it sounds like that part is crucial to us defeating Witch Hazel."

"But the part about you dying is in there too," Priscilla reminded him, "and I can't think of a better way to get killed than by riding Tehrer in a fight against Witch Hazel."

The others agreed, and Greg knew they were right. But he could think of no other options.

"Look, if we're going to break the prophecy at some point, I don't think it matters when we do it," Priscilla told him. "I say we let Nathan ride Tehrer against Hazel. After all, he's the most powerful magician I know. Who better to fight a witch?"

"She's got a point, Greg," said Kristin.

Lucky nodded, though with little conviction, and Melvin wasn't talking, as he was clearly not happy with the idea of breaking a prophecy under any circumstances.

"You don't even have to go home," said Priscilla. "You can stay and watch the fight. If Nathan can't handle it . . . well, maybe then you can step in and do what you think is best. But if the prophecy is unchangeable, as you seem to believe, waiting won't be an issue."

Greg's mind raced. He remembered Nathan telling him that the reason prophecies always came true is because the heroes in them were not the type to let them fail. Somehow, waiting at a distance to see how things turned out didn't seem overly heroic.

Still, this was his life they were talking about. Why discard any options?

"Okay," he finally agreed. "I'll let Nathan ride Tehrer first. If he fails . . ." *What chance do I have?* For the benefit of the others, he left the sentence unfinished.

Priscilla exhaled deeply. "Good. Now, finally, I'll be able to get some sleep."

Greg wished he could say the same.

Priscilla strode over to the door and pulled it wide. She paused and stared at the bed where Greg was seated. "You coming?"

Greg nearly got up and left, but then Kristin answered. "What? Oh, yes, of course." She stood rather uncertainly and meandered toward the door, then turned and ran back to the bed to give Greg that hug she had stopped herself from giving him earlier. "Good night. Everything's going to be fine. You'll see."

Melvin shifted uneasily beneath the covers. "I wouldn't count on it."

Greg lay awake for hours. Halfway through the night he jotted down a few of his adventures and stuffed them into his journal. It was the first he had picked up the book since he loaned it to Kristin, and the feel of its worn leather binding helped calm him.

He awoke what seemed an instant later to the feel of Rake's rough tongue exploring his chin. Why the shadowcat picked today of all days to make sure Greg didn't sleep through the activities irked Greg to no end. But then he thought of what Dolzowt Deth had said about shadowcats being far smarter than people thought, and about all that Rake had done to protect him so far. He couldn't help but wonder if Rake didn't have some inside knowledge about events to come.

"Okay, Rake, enough. I'm up."

Rake chattered and hopped off of Greg's chest, only to land on Melvin's cheek. Melvin bolted upright out of a dead sleep and gasped, effectively waking up Lucky in the other bed.

"What's going on?" said Lucky.

"It's morning," said Melvin, feeling his cheek for blood. "I guess Hazel didn't attack last night. Maybe it's today Greg's supposed to die."

Greg shot the boy a glare that Melvin totally missed.

Outside in the brisk air, every sound echoed brilliantly across the castle lawn. As Greg marched across the frost-covered grass, he wondered if the day really was this clear, or if he was just cherishing it more because it was the last he would ever see.

He glanced over at Lucky, who was striding along beside him, avoiding his eye. For the first time Greg could remember, the boy seemed anxious, and in spite of the fact Greg was the one about to die, he felt the need to console his friend.

"You look worried," Greg told him.

"I am, a little," Lucky said. "I don't like the idea of you starting off watching the fight today. You shouldn't be messing with the prophecy like that."

Greg's spirits sank lower than they already were. "I thought you might actually be concerned about me."

Lucky looked embarrassed. "Oh, sorry. I am. But I'm not kidding myself either. As much as I'd like it to be different, the prophecy says you're going to be killed in this battle. I hate the idea as much as you do—"

"I doubt it."

"—but I've watched too many of the Sezxqrthm's prophecies come true to believe it could be otherwise."

Greg's feet grew heavier. The crunching of frost beneath his feet echoed through his head like someone swinging a hammer inside his skull. "Yeah, well, if you're that sure the prophecy can't be wrong, then there's no reason for you to be anxious about me not fighting in time, is there?"

Lucky glanced sideways at his friend. "I'm sorry, Greg, I really am. I wish there was something I could do."

"You could ride on Tehrer with him," said Melvin, who was strolling closely behind.

"Huh?"

"That's a great idea," said Priscilla. She and Kristin were just now catching up to Melvin.

Lucky, whose lifetime of confidence must have been broken by his repeated misfortune in the Netherworld, stopped so abruptly he had to sidestep to keep Melvin from running into him. "How is that possibly a great idea?"

Priscilla and Kristin both carried pastries they'd taken from the kitchens inside. They doled them out to the boys, but Greg waved his away. He didn't feel much like eating.

"Isn't it obvious?" Priscilla said to Lucky. "With you out there in the battle, there's no way Tehrer can lose. It's the only way we can hope Greg will come back to us alive."

Melvin wolfed down his pastry greedily, but Lucky waited, regarding Priscilla unhappily. "Just because I'm safe doesn't mean Greg will be. He could fall off, or Hazel could hit him with a lightning bolt, or who knows?"

"But at least his odds would be improved, don't you think?"

Lucky, who clearly didn't want to ride a dragon into battle against Hazel, was the only one who didn't nod.

"Then it's settled," stated Priscilla with a finality only someone of royal heritage could manage.

"What?" said Lucky. "Who says anything's been settled?"

Greg said nothing throughout the discussion. He had to admit he liked the thought of Lucky being at his side. Amazing things tended to happen whenever the boy was around. But he also remembered Nathan saying he didn't think Lucky was as fortunate as everyone believed. Nathan attributed Lucky's talent to nothing more than optimism. No matter what harm came his way, Lucky always claimed how fortunate he was it hadn't been worse.

Like the time he'd managed to get himself pinned to a tree in the path of an angry ogre. That hardly seemed lucky at all. And what about the time he was dragged out of Ruuan's spire, crushed beneath the dragon's belly? How crumpled and beaten he had looked. Lucky was so sore he'd wanted to die, yet he still considered himself lucky to be alive.

Yes, Lucky's optimism was amazing, and a great thing to have, but Nathan claimed it could also cause him to be overconfident and might one day get him killed. If so, today seemed more likely to be that day than any other—especially if Lucky was stupid enough to climb on top of a murderous dragon to battle an angry witch. Just because the prophecy didn't mention Lucky's death didn't mean it wasn't a possibility. A lot of men and spirelings had died battling trolls the last time Greg was here, and Simon's prophecy never mentioned any of them specifically.

"No," Greg finally said, "I don't want him to come. It's not safe."

"But Greg," both Priscilla and Kristin said at once.

"I mean it," Greg said. "There's no sense both of us getting killed."

"Yeah, like that's going to happen," said Lucky, but Greg could see he was relieved.

A grating screech broke the chill air, and the children all turned toward the eastern edge of the lawn. Near the trees, a wyvern reared. The eight spirelings who attempted to hold it were whipped around like ornaments on a chain. Another had attempted to crawl upon the creature's back. He was hurled a good thirty feet, where he landed in the crackling lawn on hands and knees. After a moment to regain his composure, he jumped to his feet and climbed back aboard the wyvern. Less than a second later he landed hard on his back. This time he was slower getting up.

"Are they seriously thinking of riding those things?" Kristin asked.

"My brother Marvin rides wyverns all the time," claimed Melvin.

"Your brother never," said Lucky.

"Does too," insisted Melvin, "and someday he's going to teach me, soon as I'm old enough."

"Have you ever seen him ride a wyvern?" Lucky asked, not bothering to hide a chuckle.

"I didn't have to," Melvin said, growing furious. "He wouldn't lie to me."

Greg had spent some time traveling with Marvin Greatheart. It was hard to think Melvin didn't question every word that came out of his brother's mouth, let alone an entire string of them.

"Well, we'll find out soon enough," said Lucky. "Marvin should be up any time now, and I'm sure when he sees how much trouble the spirelings are having, he'll want to go over there and show them how it's done."

"He will," insisted Melvin. "You'll see."

Crunching footsteps approached rapidly from behind Greg. He turned to find Nathan striding purposefully his way.

"There you are, Greg. I've been looking all over. I think it best we get in some riding practice before breakfast."

"Too late," said Melvin as he slurped up the last of the pastries.

Greg frowned. "Please tell me you're not talking about *dragon* riding?"

Nathan regarded him sympathetically. "Well, you don't want to go up against Hazel without a bit of practice, do you?"

"I don't want to go up against Hazel at all."

Nathan nodded. "Believe me, if there were any other way . . ."

"There is," said Kristin. "You can ride alone."

Nathan's eyebrows arched upward. "What about the prophecy?"

"Prophecy, schmophecy."

"I don't believe I'm familiar with that term."

"Look," she said frowning, "just because this Simon guy predicted something doesn't make it so."

"It pretty much does."

"I don't believe it. Why should Greg need to ride against Hazel? Everyone says you and Mordred are the only two who can match her powers."

"That may be so, but after our experience with those last two prophecies, I'm beginning to place more stock in Simon's ramblings. Just because we don't understand him doesn't mean we know what is best. Never has he failed before."

"Yeah," said Kristin, "well, never has he predicted Greg was going to die, either. If you ask me, even if this prophecy succeeds, it's already failed."

The others chimed in their agreement. Only Greg remained silent. Inside he was begging to lift Kristin onto his shoulders so she could be heard more clearly.

Nathan studied the girl's face, observing her desperate concern for her friend. "I guess I hadn't looked at it that way. Maybe Simon's prediction is but one way we can succeed. Perhaps there are others. Who's to say?"

"Then you'll do it? You'll ride Tehrer alone?"

"I will think on it."

Kristin squealed, and afterward Greg wasn't sure if he had also.

"But in the meantime," continued Nathan, "we should be getting in all the practice we can. After all, Greg may be our only hope yet."

Riding Practice

Nathan held out an object on a chain—the Amulet of Ruuan.

Greg was so excited he nearly forgot the horror of why he needed it. Any metal object would have gleamed brightly in the morning sunlight, but the amulet possessed a radiance of its own, an eerie glow that managed to wash out the sun. Greg could only imagine what it felt like to hold such power in his hand.

Then Nathan forced it into Greg's palm, and Greg knew exactly how it felt.

Awful.

He quickly slipped the chain over his head. An unpleasant tingling surged through his entire body, as if all his limbs had fallen asleep at once. He found he could barely stand, but that mattered little, since Nathan had no more than given him the amulet before he levitated Greg into position on Tehrer's back.

Greg settled into a relatively flat spot between the dragon's shoulders at the base of its neck. The Amulet of Ruuan radiated so much power, Greg wondered if it would burn right through his chest. He took it in his hand the same way one might touch two electrical wires to see if they were live, and held it out before him, exactly as Nathan had instructed. The muscles in his arm danced under his skin, beyond his control, but he did his best to ignore the sensation.

"Fly," he commanded.

Tehrer's head swiveled back on his reptilian neck to stare Greg in the face. Greg waited, breathless, for a jet of steam to blast him off his perch, but none came.

Tehrer's jaws opened slightly, a mere Greg-width apart. "YOU'VE GOT TO BE KIDDING."

"But I need to learn how to control you," Greg pleaded. "How else am I supposed to defeat Hazel?"

"NO HUMAN WILL EVER CONTROL ME," Tehrer told him with such certainty, Greg was convinced it could never be otherwise. "I OFFER MY ASSISTANCE OF MY OWN FREE WILL, ONLY

BECAUSE I FEEL IT IS NECESSARY. NOW I AM TRYING TO REST. DO NOT FEAR. WHEN THE TIME COMES, I WILL FIGHT WELL FOR YOU."

"But don't you think we should practice?"

"I ALREADY KNOW HOW TO FIGHT, THANK YOU."

"But I need to at least learn how to hold on," Greg tried to reason. "You want me to get killed out there?" Even as he said it, Greg realized the dragon's desires toward Greg's fate mattered little. Still, it would at least make him feel better to know the dragon was on his side. "Well, do you?"

"MY MAGIC WILL KEEP YOU FROM FALLING. NOW, THE WITCH MAY BLAST YOUR HEAD FROM YOUR SHOULDERS, OR TURN YOU INTO A NEWT. THAT I CANNOT SAY. BUT IT IS OF LITTLE CONCERN TO ME, AS I DO NOT NEED A HUMAN WITH ME TO BATTLE ANOTHER DRAGON—OR EVER, FOR THAT MATTER."

"What's the holdup, Greg?" Nathan called from below.

"He doesn't want to practice," Greg called back.

"You have the amulet," Nathan reminded him. "Remind him who's in charge."

Greg seriously doubted Tehrer needed to be reminded he was in charge. The dragon's head swung down like a carnival ride to stop in front of Nathan. Nathan stared back at him, chin held high, though he would have been hard-pressed to hold it as high as Tehrer's.

"I HAVE ALREADY TOLD THE BOY I WILL FIGHT WHEN THE TIME COMES AND NOT A MOMENT BEFORE. DID YOU HAVE AN OBJECTION YOU WANTED TO VOICE?" He allowed a waft of steam to drift out one nostril, causing the frost to sweep back from around Nathan's feet.

Nathan continued to stare back at him through the steam. "So that's how you want to play it."

"Can I get down now?" Greg yelled. "It's not very comfortable up here, and I think this amulet may be killing me."

"Stay where you are, Greg," Nathan called up to him. "Tehrer and I have more to discuss."

"YOU ARE FOOLING YOURSELF, MAGICIAN."

Greg tried his best to ignore the discussion after that. He felt as if his own fate were completely out of his hands, and all he could do was wait for the inevitable to happen.

Off to his right, he could see the entire spireling race, several hundred thousand in all, sharpening their axes. To his left, Mordred was coaching the king's magicians in some last minute strategies. Behind, wrapped in a warm robe of magenta velvet, Queen Pauline sat in an elegant chair that had been placed awkwardly on the lawn for her. Princess Penelope was seated by her side, as were Princess Priscilla and Kristin. The four of them had come to watch Greg's practice, but as of yet they'd witnessed nothing more exciting than Greg's violent protests as he was being levitated to Tehrer's shoulders.

All heads pivoted toward the castle, where Marvin and Norman Greatheart stepped out onto the lawn. Both looked equally excited about the opportunity to pontificate about their extraordinary dragonslaying skills.

Marvin glanced up at Greg, then over to Tehrer's face, and must have gleaned from the expression there that nothing interesting was likely to happen soon. He spotted the spirelings trying to tame the wyverns at the east end of the grounds and smiled.

Melvin nudged Lucky, and the boys followed Marvin and Mr. Greatheart across the lawn—or at least they would have, if Norman had been making any noticeable progress. Instead, they followed Marvin, while Norman courageously continued his trek alone, his crackling bones echoing across the yard with every step.

A shriek echoed from the east. Greg looked up just in time to see one of the wyverns break free of the dozen spirelings that fought to hold its restraining chains. With a single bound, the beast spread its wings and took to the air. One lone rider still held fast to a chain behind its neck, digging in with his knees and struggling to control the flight, and Greg had to admit he was doing a remarkable job, at least until the wyvern bucked him loose and swung its head around to swallow him in a single bite.

Apparently there was no such thing as an experienced wyvern rider.

Marvin Greatheart stopped dead in his tracks, looked around the area as if he were just out to enjoy the day, then veered about and returned rather quickly to the castle.

Melvin watched with a look of utter confusion as his brother passed. Lucky tried not to smile.

"Where are you going?" Norman asked as Marvin passed, still just steps from the castle. Marvin didn't stop. Norman looked ahead to the spirelings and back again. With a scowl he turned around and began the long journey inside.

To the east, the wyvern banked around and swooped low, forcing the other spirelings to dodge out of the way or be flogged by the chains swinging wildly from its neck. It then took to the clouds and disappeared over the Enchanted Forest. Greg was still staring that direction when he spotted a sight that made his body quiver.

"Something huge is flying this way." He pointed over the forest to the south. "She's coming. Witch Hazel is coming."

The Second Dragon Wars

Greg couldn't tell much about the blob in the distance, just that it was large and winged and, worst of all, headed his way. It dipped and climbed as it flew, moving in and out of view below the treetops, and if Greg hadn't been perched atop a dragon's shoulders, he'd have stood no chance of seeing it. This was just one more reason he wished he were not perched atop a dragon's shoulders.

As much as Greg hated that vantage point, he liked his next even less, for just then Tehrer reared up and took to the sky.

"No!" Priscilla jumped out of her chair. "Greg, watch out. Get off of there."

Greg would have liked nothing more, but he wouldn't have considered jumping even before Tehrer seized the wind beneath his enormous wings and pulled himself and Greg into the air.

"Nathan, do something," King Peter ordered. Only without the amulet Greg carried, Nathan had no way of controlling the beast.

Below, the army of spirelings jumped to attention. They growled and waved their axes determinedly, but could do little else from the ground.

In a single leap, a lone spireling landed on the back of one of the two remaining wyverns and used his axe to sever its bindings. With a ferocious cry, the wyvern took to the sky, full of spirit, gnashing at the air. Unfortunately, instead of coming to Greg's rescue, it chose to sail off to the east and dump its rider over the surrounding farmland.

Mordred and his group of magicians raced to the center of the lawn and formed a large circle that looked barely bigger than a point. Greg heard a screech and focused on the approaching form ahead. At least he would have, if it weren't soaring toward him so unbelievably fast.

When they'd closed within a mere mile of each other, the two dragons released warning cries that shook the kingdom. And above it all came Hazel's cackle, amplified by magic. Greg slammed his eyes shut. An instant later he heard a rush of flames and felt a soothing warmth as both dragons unleashed searing jets of fire.

His eyes popped open. Nothing but clear blue sky ahead. Behind, no less than ten miles distant, Ruuan began the slow arc that would bring the dragons together again.

Greg exhaled deeply. Good to know Tehrer's magic would protect him from the flames, but he had to assume Ruuan's magic would do the same for Hazel. Perhaps this fly-by had just been a test, or maybe it was part of some bizarre dragon-fighting ritual. Either way, the real battle was sure to start soon, and that's when Greg feared he could expect to live out the prophecy—or in this case, the prophecy could be expected to outlive him.

Tehrer banked hard to his right. Greg's stomach banked left. After traversing an arc that seemed to cover half the kingdom, the dragon pulled out of his turn. A distant speck, barely visible on the horizon, Ruuan pulled out of his. Suddenly the two dragons were soaring toward each other again, closing the distance like a pair of speeding missiles. Greg barely had time to think. Fortunately Nathan was doing most of his thinking for him.

The castle, Greg. Order Tehrer toward the castle.

Greg heard the sound like a whisper trapped between his eardrums. He shook his head, but again it came, a nagging buzzing inside his skull.

Use the amulet, Greg. Take control.

Again Greg heard Hazel cackle followed by the shriek of dragons and a resounding clash. Launched up and away from his perch between Tehrer's shoulders, he barely managed to latch onto one of the horns running along Tehrer's spine. For the first time in his life he truly understood the meaning of the term *death grip*.

The last time Greg fought a battle on Myrth, Queen Gnarla had given him a potion that lent him the strength of ten men. That seemed a weak moment in comparison. His fingers clamped viselike. His biceps clenched. Gradually he drew himself to safety.

And then the dragons were apart again.

As Ruuan and Tehrer circled each other like two boxers, each looking for an opening in the other's defenses, Greg heard a nearly imperceptible gasp. A tiny speck, nearly lost amidst the brilliant blue of Ruuan's back, Witch Hazel was just regaining her feet, too. Her black dress fluttered behind her as Ruuan dove first one way then the other. The look on her face suggested she'd been no more prepared for the last impact than Greg had.

Greg!

The sound bounced around inside Greg's head.

Use the amulet!

Finally he allowed himself to hear the words. He recalled Nathan's instructions on how to control the dragon.

"Order Tehrer to stay over the castle grounds," Nathan had said.

"But won't Witch Hazel attack the castle?" Greg asked.

"She might try, but I have a spell of protection in mind. And Mordred has a spell of his own he's been working on with the rest of the king's magicians. You just get Ruuan to follow you to the castle where we can help. But remember, you'll have to take control. If you don't, Tehrer will think of nothing more than the fight. And he will lose. He does not know the strength of Hazel's magic."

Greg!

A bolt of blue fire shot by above, nearly frying him, and then Ruuan soared past, grazing Tehrer with a claw that was easily two Gregs long. Greg groped for the amulet beneath his tunic and thrust it out nearly hard enough to sever his own head with the chain.

"Fly to the castle!" he screamed, just as Ruuan thrust downward, his jaws wide and eager, his jagged teeth gleaming.

Instead of dodging the attack, Tehrer stiffened at Greg's command. For an instant Greg relived the sight of Tehrer's jaws cutting through his boat off Deth's End, but this time it was Ruuan's jaws clamping shut, and the vessel Greg was riding was soaring hundreds of feet above the ground.

Tehrer wailed and pulled free with a jerk. Blood sprang from the wound, splashing over Greg's face with a smell rivaling dragon spit as the most putrid stench imaginable.

What have I done? Greg's mind screamed. "Get to the castle," he shouted, thrusting the amulet out again. "Now, while you still can."

Again Tehrer resisted.

Ruuan launched a second attack, and Tehrer dodged aside, barely escaping with a nip to his foreleg.

"You'll die if you don't," said Greg.

The two dragons circled again, and this time Greg saw Hazel form a ball of green fire in her palm.

"And you'll be remembered as the dragon who was defeated by a witch."

Hazel raised her arm. Her face split into a maniacal grin. Without even stepping into the pitch, she unleashed her flame.

"And no one will be left to tell the world your father wasn't a coward."

Tehrer stopped so suddenly, Hazel's fireball missed by a full thirty feet.

"MY FATHER WAS NO COWARD."

"And if I survive this, I'll make sure everyone knows." Greg thrust out the amulet a third time. "But you have to get back to the castle!"

"OH, ALL RIGHT."

After one quick blast of fire at Ruuan, Tehrer turned north and retreated at jet speed toward the tiny speck of a castle. Seconds later, Greg spotted Mordred and the rest of the king's magicians, still joined in a circle, chanting. Kingdom soldiers and spirelings alike were waving their arms and shouting up at him, but Greg couldn't hear a word. He glanced back to find Ruuan's jaws gnashing the air just feet behind Tehrer's tail.

Tehrer dipped and whirled and let out a wail that buzzed Greg's spine. The two dragons clashed together in battle, shaking the walls of the castle below, or maybe it was just that Greg's eyes were shaking too badly to see. He nearly fainted when a head the size of a truck opened its jaws and sank its fangs between the scales in Tehrer's neck, just feet from the previous wound.

With a shriek, Tehrer whipped around and sank his teeth into Ruuan's head, just behind the ridges above Ruuan's enormous eyes. For one hysterical moment, Greg remembered a picture he had once seen of two snakes swallowing each other by their tails. Maybe the two dragons would swallow each other, and this whole problem would go away. Then he looked at the ground so far below. This seemed a bad time to be left to his own fate.

The two dragons remained locked that way for only a moment. Then Ruuan released his grip and shook free, and they were apart again just as quickly as they'd joined.

Tehrer shot off to the south, toward the Enchanted Forest. He banked upward at the edge of the lawn so abruptly, Greg felt his own body would have pierced Tehrer like a cannon shot if not for the impervious scales lining the dragon's back.

"I told you to go toward the castle," Greg shouted.

To the north, Ruuan shot upward too, and when Greg saw an eerie fog seeping between the trees of the surrounding forest, he realized the magicians gathered below must somehow be preventing the dragons from flying outside the boundaries of the castle grounds. But to what end?

Below, the kingdom soldiers raised their bows and released their arrows, an impressive sight that might have been effective if Ruuan had been soaring at half the height. Instead, the arrows fell short of their target and dropped harmlessly to the ground.

To the east, the spireling warriors organized into dozens of groups. Perhaps they thought to surround the enemy, but what possible threat could they pose from so far below?

Another shriek caused Greg to spin. Ruuan was circling again. Greg looked for any sign of recognition in the dragon's eye, some glimmer of hope that Ruuan remembered the friendship, or at least tolerance, he held for Greg. But Ruuan's eye burned with nothing but rage, and Greg turned away rather than dwell on the sight too long.

His gaze moved from bad to worse. Hazel had regained her composure and stood just like Greg remembered her, not the frail old woman who once greeted him at the door of her shack at the center of the Shrieking Scrub, but as she'd been later, when she thought he'd betrayed her, with her back defiantly straight, her body youthful and full of power. She'd been terrifying then, but nothing like now. In one hand she held the Amulet of Tehrer. In the other, a ball of emerald green fire.

This is it, Greg realized. This was when the prophecy would be fulfilled. He had but one instant to live.

With deadly accuracy, Hazel released the fire. It soared toward him, picked up speed as it flew . . .

Had it not occurred to Greg that he had yet to save the kingdom, he might not have dodged out of the way in time. Instead, he ducked and rolled, and the flames rocketed off into the woods. He was still staring that direction when the barbs of Ruuan's tail crossed his vision and met Tehrer's back with a crash.

Tehrer jerked hard to the left, sending Greg sprawling in spite of the dragon's magic. Escape to the south was impossible. The eerie fog at the edge of the lawn forced Tehrer to cut left again before the woods and race to the east. Ruuan chased hard on his tail, and Greg watched as Hazel, shouting words lost behind the rush of air, opened her palm and formed another fireball.

Again Hazel unleashed her magic, too fast for Greg to duck. Fortunately Tehrer banked north, out of the line of fire, and then west again.

Unable to fly far in any one direction, the dragons were forced to continually cut and weave to stay above the castle grounds. Perhaps that's what Mordred planned when he organized his spell. With Ruuan never able to fly too long in any one direction, Hazel had little chance to aim her throws.

Wait, this was Mordred. More likely he was just keeping the battle nearby so he wouldn't miss the moment when Greg got himself killed.

Greg's eyes watered from the rushing air, but he could still make out activity on the castle lawn. To his dismay, the splinter groups of spireling warriors seemed to be shrinking.

Only then did he realize the groups were growing smaller because they were also rising taller. The thousands of spirelings were climbing on top of one another, quickly forming living pillars that rose high into the air. Within seconds, dozens of blurry stacks rose up all across the yard, barely a dragon's width apart, providing obstacles to slow the dragons' flight.

Tehrer tried rising above the spireling pillars, but the mysterious fog was forming above as well, preventing escape from the sky. The dragon's climb leveled off abruptly, like a suddenly stopping elevator, leaving Greg's stomach floors behind. There Greg got his first close-up view of the topmost spirelings shouting and waving their double-bladed axes.

Hazel commanded her steed forward, and Ruuan matched Tehrer's path exactly, but while the warriors permitted Tehrer to pass unharmed, they took blurry swings at Ruuan. For the most part the blades kicked off the dragon's scales to no effect, but Ruuan was clearly annoyed all the same. He aimed a jet of fire at the nearest stack, one that would have surely incinerated the spirelings in an instant, had Mordred's spell not been protecting them. Instead the flames splattered backward, obstructing Ruuan's view, and the dragon nearly collided into one of the spireling stacks before he could regain his bearings.

Why even bother to avoid them? Greg wondered. Surely Ruuan could have sliced off the top of any of those stacks without ruffling a scale, or chomped off a dozen or more warriors with a single snap of his jaws, but Ruuan didn't even try. Greg had to wonder if the dragon somehow knew Mordred's spell would protect them.

Below, Greg saw the kingdom soldiers organize into stacks of their own, but each time the pillars grew more than three men tall, they toppled and fell. One of the generals shouted out an order, and as one the soldiers abandoned their efforts and scattered among the lawn, each climbing atop a spireling pillar. Now they could get close enough to the dragon to use their bows effectively, but that just meant Greg had a constant volley of arrows to dodge along with the spireling axes.

The chase may have slowed, but Tehrer was growing more familiar with the course with each pass. He dove and weaved between the stacks of spirelings so quickly and so often, Greg could no longer focus. In the back of his mind he thought how ironic it was that he was here, and the spirelings were out there in their stationary pillars, when it was the spirelings who were so accustomed to moving at these speeds.

Hazel sent a bolt of electricity soaring toward the nearest stack, but her power failed to penetrate the magicians' spell. As Ruuan flew close to the stack, two uppermost spirelings leapt onto his back. Ruuan, having to concentrate hard on avoiding the dozens of scattered towers, could do nothing to dislodge them.

A simple wave of Hazel's hand sent them flying backward. But they were not the only ones to try. One after another, spirelings jumped aboard and dropped helplessly to the ground, but still they came, offering their lives as a distraction to keep Hazel from using her power against Greg.

Why don't they stop? Greg's mind screamed. *I'm just going to die anyway. Because you haven't saved the kingdom yet,* he reminded himself.

Before long, with so many spirelings sprawled out on the lawn between them, the bases of the stacks became hard to distinguish. As the stacks grew shorter, Mordred adjusted his spell accordingly, and the fog dipped lower, preventing the dragons from escaping above the flailing spireling axes.

"Watch out, Greg!"

With so much screaming and rushing wind, Greg wasn't even sure he heard the sound, but he could swear it was Nathan's voice calling out to him. No matter who said it, Greg guessed it was good advice.

He dodged to one side just as a ball of green fire struck Tehrer's scales. With a shriek, the dragon cut sharply right. Greg tried to see where the warning had come from, but his eyes were watering, and he was moving so fast . . .

As if his wings had been torn from his body, Tehrer suddenly dropped from the sky. He pulled up just feet from the ground and whipped through the crowd, Ruuan hot on his tail.

Greg held his breath as the surrounding spirelings began their swings before he'd even passed, sweeping their axes through arcs that just narrowly missed his head. Pendegrass Castle soared straight at him. Tehrer had to slow and swerve to avoid crashing through the castle gate.

Greg had just enough time to make out the screaming faces of Princess Priscilla and Kristin below. Beside them stood Melvin and Lucky, and any hope Greg had of surviving the next few minutes were dashed as he recalled how Lucky was supposed to be up here by his side, spreading the good fortune that Nathan insisted the boy didn't have.

It was not until after his friends faded from view that Greg thought about what they'd said. They hadn't shouted the expected "Watch out!" or the totally unnecessary "Be careful!" or even an encouraging "We're all pulling for you." Instead, they were all yelling something about Nathan and using the amulet.

While in the vicinity, Ruuan took the opportunity to shoot a jet of fire at Pendegrass Castle. Nathan's protective spell did its job. The flames bounced off the stone and shot across the lawn, scattering Melvin and Lucky and what looked like Brandon Alexander in three different directions, and then Ruuan was off again, chasing Tehrer toward the woods to the west.

Tehrer turned at the edge of the grounds and unleashed a jet of fire at Ruuan, who dodged out of reflex, even though the flames probably couldn't hurt him. The motion sent Hazel reeling. She dropped a fireball by her own feet and then screamed and hopped about frantically until Ruuan banked, and the fireball rolled clear. Then Ruuan was charging at Greg again, and Tehrer was once more winding between the pillars of spirelings.

Greg watched Ruuan's gaping cavern of a mouth swoop up from behind and slam shut around Tehrer's tail with a boom. Tehrer shrieked like nothing on Earth—not all that surprising, since everything he did was like nothing on Earth—but somehow pulled free.

Why is he always fleeing? Greg's mind screamed out. *Why doesn't Tehrer turn and fight?*

But Greg already knew the answer. Even before his injury, Tehrer was the weaker of the two dragons. Maybe that was still stronger than anything else Greg could imagine, but Nathan was right. Age had caught up with Tehrer.

But where Nathan had also thought Tehrer would stand a chance if he fought of his own free will rather than struggle against the power of the amulet, he'd underestimated Hazel's ability to control Ruuan. Greg might delay the inevitable, but in the end the prophecy would win out. If only Nathan had fought this battle like they'd planned.

As if in answer to his thoughts, Greg heard Nathan's voice again. *Here, Greg.*

By the time Greg turned toward the sound it was gone. He could see nothing but thousands of spirelings shouting and waving their axes. *The amulet!*

Finally Greg realized what he must do. Ever since they returned to the castle, he'd left Tehrer to his own free will, but he still held the Amulet of Ruuan. He was in control, even if what he wanted more than anything was to hand over that control to someone else.

"Tehrer," he shouted into the wind, stretching the amulet out before him. "Can you see Nathan?"

"LITTLE BUSY RIGHT NOW."

"This is important."

Tehrer jerked hard to one side, separating from Ruuan for an instant of flight without the constant threat of Ruuan's jaws clamping on his tail.

"THE SORCERER IS BEHIND US TO THE EAST, ATOP ONE OF THE TOWERS OF CANARAZAS."

"Can you get to him?" Greg shouted. His arm drooped under the weight of the amulet, and he fought hard to lift it up again. "I mean, *go find him!*"

Tehrer jerked suddenly downward, and whether he was dodging Ruuan or avoiding spirelings or actually following Greg's order, Greg couldn't tell. The dragon wound through the spirelings and headed east again as Ruuan slipped in behind him and gained, his jaws opening wide.

From over Greg's head, a brilliant blue flame soared through the air and struck Ruuan in the ridge above one eye. Ruuan cringed and veered so abruptly Hazel would have surely been thrown to the center of the Enchanted Forest if not for her own magic.

Ruuan was dissuaded for only a second. Already he was banking back around when Tehrer glided to a sudden stop.

"GOOD SHOT. HERE HE IS," the dragon announced, "YOUR HUMAN FRIEND."

Greg searched the closest tower of spirelings, and there, amidst all the tangled Canaraza warriors, was Nathan, waving his arms and screaming right along with the rest of them.

"Closer, Greg. Bring him closer."

Comprehension finally struck. Greg again thrust out the amulet. "Move closer!"

Tehrer did as he was ordered. In fact, the dragon moved so close, its tail swept over the top of the tower, forcing the uppermost spirelings to dive off or be sliced in two. Nathan took the opportunity to leap aboard. He was still scrambling between the spikes running along Tehrer's spine when Tehrer took off again, narrowly avoiding a charge by Ruuan.

"The amulet, Greg," Nathan cried. "Give me the amulet." He

reached out as he climbed, and a ball of green fire soared by so close, it nearly severed his fingers.

Greg slipped the chain over his head and reached out toward Nathan. With a jerk, Tehrer dodged aside, and Greg felt the amulet slip.

No!

But Nathan had looped the chain with one finger. He tugged it from Greg's grasp. No sooner was the amulet in his grip before the magician shouted to Tehrer.

"To the ground. Now!"

Tehrer dropped as if his wings had been clipped. Once again Greg felt his stomach rise as he watched the ground soar up to meet him.

"Up!" Nathan shouted, far too late in Greg's opinion for Tehrer to pull out of his dive.

"What are you do—?" Greg shouted, but that was all he could get out before Nathan unexpectedly grabbed him by his tunic and tossed him overboard.

Greg's Unfortunate Demise

Tehrer missed the ground by inches. He was already soaring up and out of sight before Greg rolled to a stop next to a fallen spireling.

"Ow."

He might have spent more time complaining had he not landed just feet from the one remaining wyvern. The beast surged forward, lashing out with its jaws, and snapped its chains tight, inches from Greg's leg. Greg scrambled back. He counted his limbs.

A sudden thought struck him. Hadn't he just ridden the magnificent flying beast into battle and fought the witch? Now Nathan was taking his turn, and as long as he finished up the one little matter of saving the kingdom, the prophecy would be fulfilled—well, all except the part about Greg dying. But that was a small part, really. Hardly worth bothering with, if you stopped to think about it . . .

Now, with Nathan in command, Tehrer became the aggressor. He turned and met Ruuan's charge head on, and the dragons clashed like two colliding freight trains.

Nathan shouted out orders, extending the amulet with one hand while he used the other to weave his powerful magic. Electricity shot from his fingertips, straight at Hazel, who held out the Amulet of Tehrer and met the threat with a motion of her own. With a zap, the sizzling died away. Hazel yelled something indiscernible, and Ruuan backed off of his attack to swing back toward the castle.

"She's on the run," Greg called out, even though the wyvern was the only one close enough to hear.

Hazel didn't run long. When Ruuan passed over the spot where Mordred and the other magicians were gathered, the witch held out her amulet and ordered the dragon to unleash a jet of fire at the chanting magicians. Fortunately, just as when Ruuan tried to blast the tower of spirelings, the flames bounced harmlessly aside and scattered through the grass, lighting small fires that continued to burn long after he was gone.

The magicians kept chanting, oblivious of the threat from above.

The two dragons circled back. They were headed Greg's way.

Ruuan spun to face his attacker, and the two dragons slammed heads together, their teeth ringing out like clashing swords across all the land. Never had Greg heard such an impact. The dragons' magic faltered, and Nathan and Hazel were both jolted off their feet.

And then the unthinkable happened. The chain holding the Amulet of Ruuan snapped. Nathan scrambled across Tehrer's back and slapped a hand over it before it slid to the ground. "Gotcha!"

But then both dragons collided into towers of spirelings on either side of Greg, and just as Greg suspected, the towers remained strong while the dragons were thrown hard to the side. The sudden lurch caused Nathan to lose his grasp on the amulet.

For a moment all sound died away. Greg watched the tiny object slide across Tehrer's back and fall in slow motion, glittering in the soft morning light, spinning end over end, from the top of the closest tower all the way to its base.

In an instant the noise of the battle returned.

Free of the controlling magic, Tehrer tried to shoot past Ruuan toward the castle, but Ruuan anticipated the move. He lunged out at Tehrer's soft underbelly and clamped his jaws tight. Tehrer wailed like nothing Greg had ever heard before, nor ever wanted to hear again.

Mortally wounded, the dragon tore free of Ruuan's grip and made one last desperate attempt to flee. Ruuan lashed out a claw and sent the dying dragon spinning out of control. Greg watched in horror as Tehrer spun straight for the castle.

Ruuan veered sharply to the west, Greg could swear he heard Hazel cackle, and then Tehrer was crashing through the castle wall, scattering boulders the size of men in all directions.

"Nathan!"

"Here, Greg."

Greg spotted a disturbance in one of the towers of spirelings closest to the castle. There was Nathan, being passed hand-to-hand down to the ground. At the last he'd been able to free himself of the dragon's protective magic and leap off. Greg could hardly believe his eyes. Nathan was safe. Too bad when he was planning his spell he hadn't thought to protect the castle from Tehrer as well as from Ruuan.

"Ruuan," Greg gasped.

Under Hazel's orders, the dragon banked around and headed back toward the castle, scattering people the way Tehrer had just scattered boulders.

Those who'd thought to hide within the castle were having second thoughts, now that there was an enormous dragon-shaped hole in one of its walls. Greg wondered if Kristin and Priscilla were among them—or Lucky and Melvin. No, what was he thinking? As confident as Lucky was in his talent, he was probably standing atop one of the stacks of spirelings, calling out to Hazel to come back and fight like a man.

Ruuan's victory cry rang out so long and so loud, Greg could have sworn it was stuck inside his head. Then he realized the dragon's cry had died away, and what he was hearing was the alarmingly similar sound of an upset shadowcat.

Among all of the fallen soldiers and spireling warriors, Rake had managed to find him and was screaming for reasons only a shadowcat could understand. Rake scampered across the lawn, hopping over fallen spirelings, to where the amulet fell. He rummaged around for a moment. Then his head popped up, the Amulet of Ruuan clenched between his jaws.

"You found it!" said Greg. "Good boy, Rake. Bring it to me."

Greg took a step toward the shadowcat, but Rake scampered away, dangerously close to the chained wyvern, and stared back at Greg defiantly. The wyvern shot forward, snapped its chains tight, and bounced harmlessly backward.

"Rake, watch out. What are you doing? We need to get that to Nathan. He's the only one who knows how to use it."

Rake dropped the amulet and screeched for Greg to come take it, but when Greg tried, he snatched it up again and moved even closer to the wyvern.

"Rake, this is no time for games."

The wyvern lunged again, its jaws snapping shut just short of Rake's tail. Greg backed off a step, not trusting the strength of those chains. Maybe it was just a wyvern, but it still looked a lot like a dragon to him.

As if aware of Greg's thoughts, Rake screeched again, and Greg suddenly understood. If the amulet could be used to control a dragon, maybe it would work on a wyvern, too.

Perhaps it was coincidence, but Rake seemed to calm. He grabbed the amulet in his mouth, ran forward and dropped it at Greg's feet. The wyvern watched the movement intently and fought against its chains, but Rake kept just out of reach.

Greg debated the possibility that the beast was just toying with him, waiting for him to move closer. He pushed back his fear, swept up the amulet and held it out.

"Stop," he commanded, and the wyvern instantly froze in place. "Sit."

The wyvern sat.

From behind, Greg heard panicked shouts. Ruuan swept toward the castle entrance, unleashing a jet of fire that bore a trough in the lawn right up to the gate.

When Tehrer struck the castle earlier, a few stacks of spireling warriors had been toppled by flying debris. Apparently Mordred's spell only protected them within their living towers. Now men and spirelings alike were running about in chaos, trying to dodge the searing flames.

"Don't move," Greg shouted at the wyvern. He rushed to the post where the beast was tethered and unhooked the chains that bound it.

"Bow," he commanded, and the wyvern lowered its head so Greg could climb aboard.

"Up," Greg shouted before he really had time to think about what he was saying. The wyvern took to the air. It beat its wings with a flurry and soared easily between the remaining spireling stacks, weaving between them like a child at play.

But the wyvern possessed no magic to hold Greg in place. With the same strength he'd used to grip Tehrer earlier, Greg latched onto the wyvern's scales to avoid being flung to the ground.

"Go," he shouted. "To Ruuan."

Without hesitation, the wyvern turned and sped toward the castle. Distracted by those fleeing below, neither Hazel nor Ruuan saw the tiny threat coming. A glimmer of hope dared to enter Greg's mind. Then, at the last second, he screamed for the wyvern to change course.

Running just ahead of Ruuan's flames, barely remaining true to his name, was Lucky. Greg had no choice but to force the wyvern to dart ahead and scoop the boy out of harm's way.

The element of surprise was gone. Hazel held out her palm and conjured another of her emerald green fireballs.

"Watch out!" Greg screamed.

The wyvern had no desire to disobey. Still clutching Lucky's robe in its jaws, it dodged nimbly aside.

Compared to a dragon, the wyvern was little more than a gnat, hardly worth concern, but its small size gave it an agility Ruuan could never match. If Greg could just get past Hazel's defenses, separate her from her amulet as she'd done with Nathan . . .

"Help!" Lucky screamed, still dangling from the wyvern's jaws, and Greg briefly wondered if his friend was feeling particularly lucky at that moment.

Again Greg ordered the wyvern to attack, and again Hazel ordered Ruuan to protect her.

The dragon had no room to protect itself. Ruuan barely soared between the towers of angry spirelings as the wyvern flew easily behind, able to use its wings far more effectively within the narrow gaps. Hazel had to expend all her magic just to keep the wyvern's jaws at bay. If Greg only knew a spell he could use against her, he could launch an attack of his own.

Again Ruuan arced toward the castle, dodging blows from spireling axes the entire way. Below, Greg could see Priscilla trying to look up at him, but her mother had clasped a hand over her eyes to protect her from seeing. At her side were Melvin and Marvin Greatheart, cheering Greg on, and next to them Kristin, staring up at him wide-eyed, her mouth dropped open in horror.

At least she's not staring at Marvin, Greg thought to himself in one unexplainable moment. Then he realized Kristin's mouth was open not in horror but because she was calling out to him. For an instant he could swear she said, "Use the force." Then he realized it was something else entirely. Something about holding his course. She must really believe what everyone had been saying about him being a hero.

If only it were true.

"Down," Greg screamed, and the wyvern dropped toward the ground. Greg ordered it to fly in low under Ruuan's belly.

Even if Ruuan had been able to wound Tehrer in these softer tissues, Greg didn't hold any hopes of the wyvern doing the same to Ruuan. Fate of the kingdom or not, he didn't know if he'd have felt right about hurting Ruuan even if he could. No, he'd ordered the wyvern there because it was the one spot Hazel couldn't see.

Now, as Ruuan continued to soar about the yard, antagonized by the constant pounding of spireling axes upon his scales, Greg and the wyvern soared easily along below him, waiting for the witch to make a move.

Greg knew Ruuan's magic would protect Hazel from falling, as long as she remained between the spikes running along the dragon's neck and shoulders, but what if she wandered off to either side? If he guessed right, Hazel wouldn't be able to tolerate not knowing where he was. She'd creep around the dragon's back for a better look.

Only how would he know when she was away from safety?

Lucky paused in his incoherent screaming long enough to yell something helpful. "Now, Greg, now. To your left."

But where Greg thought Lucky meant Greg should move to his left, Lucky really meant Hazel had moved to Greg's left. Greg ordered the wyvern to dart around Ruuan's rib cage, only to find himself face-to-face with the witch.

He couldn't say he liked the expression he saw there.

Neither did the wyvern. It spotted Hazel's amulet and looped around so quickly, Greg could barely hold on.

This is it, Greg knew. This was the moment he would plummet to his death and fulfill the prophecy.

But fate had something else in mind. The wyvern's tail lashed through the air as it turned, and—if this wasn't proof that having Lucky swaying from the wyvern's jaws was influencing this battle, Greg couldn't imagine what could be—swatted the amulet from Hazel's outstretched hand.

The change in Ruuan was instantaneous. The dragon reared and pitched. Any magic he might have been using to hold Hazel in place, he was not wasting now.

Hazel let out a screech. As if in slow motion, she veered away from the dragon's back, toppled end-over-end toward the ground, screamed words lost beneath the wind.

And then her screams cut off abruptly.

Ruuan didn't pause to witness the witch's fate. He took off toward his spire as if just now succumbing to a long elastic band that had been stretched tight between them.

With a roar, the proud wyvern arced around for a victory lap, making a show of rolling over as Ruuan had done. Greg held on for dear life, knowing his ordeal was not over until he touched safely down. The wyvern flew him directly over top of King Peter and Queen Pauline, and there were the two girls cheering and waving up at him.

"You did it!" screamed Priscilla.

"You're a hero!" added Kristin. And then she said something he never would have expected. "I love you!"

Greg was so dumbfounded, he forgot to tighten his grip during the wyvern's next roll. Launched off his perch, he barely managed to hang by one hand as the wyvern spun through the air, throwing him first one way, then the other. His fingers strained to their limits. And then, as if in slow motion, he watched them give way.

For a few brief seconds the world spun in front of Greg's eyes. He witnessed the ground rush up to meet him, soaring faster and faster, and then, suddenly it struck with unbelievable force.

Greg's vision cut off in an instant, as did the noise of the spirelings cheering, and the pungent smells of billowing smoke and charred grass.

And indeed, the very essence of life itself.

Just as Simon's prophecy had predicted, the Mighty Greghart was dead.

Dark Magic

"No!" screamed Kristin. She rushed forward to where Greg's body lay lifeless in the charred grass.

Priscilla pulled free of her mother's grasp. She ran to Kristin and fell to her knees, and the two girls clutched each other, not daring to believe.

"It's true," Melvin cried, running up with his brother Marvin. Tears ran down his face as he announced to the crowd what all others feared. "The prophecy came true. The Mighty Greghart is dead!"

"Let me through, boy," came a voice from behind. Mordred had broken free of the circle of magicians and had just now reached the spot where Greg lay. He pulled back his hood and stooped to place an ear over Greg's heart, his greasy black hair hanging heavily across Greg's chest.

"Well?" sobbed Priscilla.

"It's true," he said, and even his voice revealed a hint of remorse. "The boy didn't make it."

"No!" Priscilla screamed.

Kristin released an indistinguishable noise and threw her arms around Greg. She begged him to quit playing around, to get up and tell them this was all a joke, but Greg didn't move. King Peter stepped up behind Kristin. He pulled her away and hugged her to him, and Queen Pauline did the same for their daughter.

As if the sight of Greg lying dead weren't horrible enough, a sickening thump sounded to their right, and all turned to witness Lucky's crumpled body bounce off the lawn. Above, the wyvern screeched and tore off toward the Enchanted Forest.

King Peter rushed over, followed closely by Marvin Greatheart, who looked down at the boy and said, "That doesn't seem lucky at all."

The king bent and checked on Lucky, and after a moment sat back to regard the others. Tears ran down his face as he shook his head and closed Lucky's staring eyes.

"No!" screamed Priscilla. She dropped to Lucky's side, but no matter how much she hugged the boy and told him she loved him, it was not enough to bring him back, and she could do nothing but weep.

The dozens of towers of spirelings melted like ice sculptures on a hot griddle. Within seconds Nathan came running up to join the others, fear in his eyes. "Quickly. We have but a moment. We need the two amulets. They should be in the grass."

Not one of those who heard him knew what Nathan intended, yet throughout the yard, men and spirelings alike dropped to their knees and began combing the grass. There were enough spirelings present to require each to cover only a few square yards of lawn, but many others lay dead or wounded, hindering the search.

Suddenly a thunderous gasp sounded. Hundreds of thousands of spirelings all turned at once to stare at the very same spot. At the center of the focus, a lone spireling stooped and picked up a small object on a chain.

"Found one," he said.

With the speed of a spireling, he rushed to Nathan, who was bent over Lucky's lifeless body. Nathan took the pentagram-shaped amulet that had been forged so many centuries earlier and laid it across Lucky's chest while the others continued their search.

Even though they sensed how important it was to find the second amulet, Priscilla and Kristin watched to see what Nathan was about to do.

"Hold on," said Mordred. He stepped over no less than a dozen spirelings as they searched on hands and knees through the grass. "What form of foolishness is this?"

"It is not foolishness," Nathan said calmly. "It's a spell I learned in the Void. I think it may save him."

"The Void?" Mordred gasped. "Why on Myrth would you go there?"

Nathan scowled. "Perhaps to learn the type of spell I'm about to use now." He brushed back Lucky's hood, only mildly startled by the sight of Lucky's bald head. Placing a hand on Lucky's forehead, he closed his eyes and forced himself to the same state of relaxation he used to help him focus in chikan.

"But the boy is dead," insisted Mordred. "Only evil magic can return him now."

"Quiet. Evil is a word used only by those with limited understanding. Now, we're wasting precious time."

Mordred was about to object again when King Peter stepped up behind him, his robe wafting out behind, and placed a hand on the magician's shoulder. "Leave him be, Mordred. He knows what he's doing."

Nathan took Lucky's right hand and placed it over his own heart. "Princess Priscilla," he called.

Priscilla quickly turned away and pretended to search the grass. "No, come here, child, quickly."

Priscilla hopped up and rushed to Nathan's side. He beckoned her to kneel next to Lucky and instructed her to follow his example and hold Lucky's left hand over her heart. She grabbed it, tears flowing down her cheeks, and pressed it against herself so fiercely, Nathan worried she might push it right through her own chest. He warned her to be careful and then closed his eyes again and began to chant.

The bright morning sky immediately began to darken. Ominous black clouds rolled in, as if poured from a giant cauldron, and thunder sounded as lightning danced between them, high in the sky.

"Dark Magic," said Mordred. "This is—"

King Peter silenced him with a single wave of his hand, as if he held a magician's power. Nathan continued chanting, and the thunder grew stronger. So much lightning streaked across the sky that the day grew bright again in spite of the heavy clouds blocking out the sun.

Kristin was patting the same spot of grass over and over, her eyes fixed on Nathan. "What's happening?" she asked when Priscilla's flowing hair began to lift away from her ears.

Priscilla's hair rose until it stood fully on end—even the longer strands that had not been hacked off in the Netherworld. Her eyebrows raised, and her eyes somehow gave the impression they were wide with fear, even though they were closed. The turmoil of lightning above rivaled any fireworks Kristin had ever seen. She suppressed a scream as her own hair began to rise as well.

Throughout the yard everyone paused in the search to see what was happening. Suddenly the sky burst open with a thunderous boom. A single bolt of lightning shot into and through the amulet resting on Lucky's chest, lighting the boy up like a light filament. Electricity surged up his arms and into Nathan and Priscilla, lighting them up as well. Panicked screams and gasps of horror rang out through the yard, but the lightning remained, a steady stream flowing into Lucky's chest like a roaring waterfall.

Kristin turned away and hid her eyes under her arm, as the image was just too bright, but even then the intensity of the light managed to pierce her flesh and bones. The incredible roar of thunder shook her to her very core, until she just knew she would collapse.

And then it stopped.

The intense roar cut off in an instant. Overhead, the thunderclouds began to dissipate. Within seconds they'd completely disappeared, letting back in the light.

With hope in her heart, Kristin whipped her head around, but all that had changed was that now there were two more dead bodies lying next to Lucky's. The scream she released spoke for all of those present.

King Peter fell to his knees, his wife at his side, and dropped his head to his daughter's chest. Mordred checked on Nathan, and Melvin and his father struggled to hold up Princess Penelope's limp form.

"Fool!" Mordred nearly spat. "He got what he deserved for messing with Dark Magic." But Kristin could see there was a tear in his eye all the same.

The hundreds of thousands of spirelings looked on uncertainly. It seemed quite pointless to find the other amulet now. But then Melvin released his hold on Penelope to point at Lucky. Norman struggled alone against the princess's limp form for a few seconds before toppling backwards with her on top of him.

"He moved," said Melvin. "I saw him."

All eyes turned toward Lucky. Smoke drifted up from the boy's chest, where the Amulet of Tehrer, now gone, had rested. The material of his robe and the tunic he wore beneath had been dissolved away, and a black stain the size and shape of the amulet was burned into his chest.

He opened his eyes slowly and blinked against the bright sunlight. "Where am I?"

A cheer rose up throughout the yard, but neither King Peter nor Queen Pauline joined in. The queen hugged her daughter against her chest with the same ferocity Priscilla had hugged Lucky's hand.

And then Priscilla began to stir as well. Queen Pauline gasped, and a second cheer rose up through the yard, even louder than the first.

Nathan opened his eyes and pushed himself up on trembling arms. "Did it work?"

Mordred, who had been holding his hand and doing his best not to weep, made a show of throwing it down. "Fool!" he spat. "You could have been killed."

Nathan didn't notice. Having spotted Lucky sitting upright, he rolled over and hugged the boy, stroking what should have been Lucky's hair.

They'd have probably gone on this way for some time if Kristin hadn't brought them back to reality. "What about Greg?" she cried.

"The other amulet," said Nathan. "Has no one found the Amulet of Ruuan?"

The multitude of spirelings jumped back to the hunt, sifting through every blade of grass with a speed only one born to the Canaraza race could manage. But no one seemed capable of finding the second amulet.

Rake scurried through the crowd and crawled up onto Lucky's legs. Lucky seemed somewhat shocked, as the shadowcat had never shown him much affection.

"It's okay, Rake. I'm fine."

Rake bared his fangs and shrieked with such intensity, Lucky scrambled backward, sending the shadowcat flying.

"There it is," Priscilla moaned, as she was too exhausted to shout.

All turned to see the Amulet of Ruuan lying in the crumpled grass where Lucky had been lying. Queen Pauline grabbed it and extended it out by the chain toward Nathan, but stopped in mid reach, the smile on her face dissolving.

"Oh."

Nathan stared weakly at the circular amulet in her hand. Comprised of five pieces, four identical pie-shaped wedges surrounded by a single ring, the amulet held more power than any artifact ever created in this world. But a triangle of light beamed through the amulet as it swung easily from its chain.

One of the inner sections was missing.

"No," gasped Nathan. "This won't do at all."

A Love Shared

"We must . . . find . . . the other . . . piece," Nathan gasped. He dropped back to the grass, too weary to speak.

Everyone, even King Peter and Queen Pauline, garbed in their elegant robes, dropped to their hands and knees, overturning every blade of grass, but try as they might, no one could find the missing wedge of metal.

King Peter paused when he noticed Mordred sitting upright and motionless, his eyes closed. "Mordred," he scolded. "I know you and the boy have had your differences, but you must help in this."

Mordred did not answer at first. Then his eyelids drifted open. "I think I see it."

"What are you talking about?" King Peter asked.

"A spell, Sire. I began working on it when I was gathering the pieces of Ruuan's amulet for Hazel a few months ago. It is not an easy task, as artifacts of this nature have a way of eluding magic, but I . . . well, let's just say I called upon a bit of knowledge I learned before I came under your service."

"You've used Dark Magic is what you're saying," King Peter said, hope lighting his eyes. "Well, it's about time. Where is it?"

Mordred frowned. "I'm not sure. I need all these spirelings out of here."

King Peter turned to the nearest spireling and commanded him to leave. The spireling paused, a distant look in his eyes as he consulted with Queen Gnarla through their silent bond, and suddenly every spireling capable of walking shot to the edge of the yard as if a huge spireling-filled bomb had exploded.

For the first time since the battle, it was possible to see all who had fallen. King Peter gasped as he took in the sight of the thousands of dead scattered throughout the yard.

A few of the injured tried crawling away, but with limited success. Mordred's eyes had fallen closed again, and playing about his hood was an odd black light one witnesses would later describe as a hundred bats swarming to tear at Mordred's face.

Mordred's eyes popped open. He looked a few yards to the east, where a spireling warrior was dragging himself slowly toward the Enchanted Forest.

"There," he said, pointing at the injured spireling.

The spireling's eyes grew wide as several men swarmed on him to see why Mordred had singled him out. Marvin Greatheart helped him to his feet, oblivious of the fact that both his legs were broken, but the spireling didn't cry out until Mordred ran toward him, his magician's robe fluttering out behind, and reached toward his face.

Mordred's hand extended past the rows of razor-sharp teeth to the spireling's shoulder, where lodged in his chain mail, nearly hidden from view, was the tiny wedge of metal they sought.

The spireling's eyes grew wider still. As he witnessed Mordred pry loose the tiny section of amulet, so did all of his kind. From the edge of the yard in all directions erupted a roar of approval, and the implosion of spirelings back to the center of the yard was a sight no human or spireling was likely to ever see again.

Mordred rushed to Nathan's side and pressed the tiny wedge into the hole in the amulet Rake had helped them find. In an instant the metal flashed and fused together. Mordred helped Nathan to his feet and over to where Greg lay unmoving in the grass. The two of them knelt beside Greg's body, and Nathan struggled to take Greg's hand in his own.

Mordred reached out to stop him. "Nathan, are you sure you want to go through with this?"

Nathan nodded, clearly too drained to speak. No one voiced the fear, but all wondered how the magician could possibly survive a second experience like the first.

"You'll be killed," Mordred warned. "And what of the Amulet? The last was destroyed. Do we really want to lose an object of such power?"

Nathan's eyes softened as he took Mordred's hand in his own. "We . . . must. You and I." He tightened his grip on Mordred's hand and stared into his eyes, as if seeing into the man's soul.

Mordred looked confused, but then their two hands began to glow, and Mordred's lips separated in a silent gasp. The two magicians remained that way a long time while the others looked on, wondering if they should be doing something . . . anything.

Finally Nathan's eyes rolled up into his head. Mordred pulled his hand back and shook it, staring wide-eyed at Nathan's unconscious form. Obviously he didn't know what to say at first, but then he placed one palm on Nathan's heart and took up Greg's hand in the other, pressing it against his own chest.

"I'll do what I can, old friend," he whispered to Nathan. His eyes darted around the yard. "I need someone who loves the boy."

King Peter, Queen Pauline, Priscilla and Lucky all fought to be the first to Greg's side, but Kristin won in the end. She knelt beside him and took his other hand in hers without being asked, pressing it firmly to her chest.

Mordred's eyes dropped closed. He began to chant as Nathan had done. Nothing happened for a long while, but then the telltale clouds began to coalesce, and the day darkened. Thunder rolled in. Lightning flashed and darted across the sky.

Unconsciously those in the crowd edged away from the spot where Greg lay, figuring Mordred's skills in the Dark Arts were likely not as polished as Nathan's.

The intensity of thunder grew, just as before. Those in the crowd took another step backward. When the expected bolt shot from the sky to strike Greg in the chest, everyone screamed and dove to the ground. This time the electricity traveled up Greg's arms into Kristin and Mordred, and on into Nathan, as Mordred still held one hand over his old friend's heart.

The others cowered away from the sight and sounds for what seemed an eternity, and then just as before, the lightning cut off suddenly, and the thunderous echoes rang out through the kingdom for several long moments.

All looked to where Greg lay, his tunic and even the spireling chain mail burned away, his chest smoking from a circular hole etched into his skin. At his side, Kristin lay, unmoving. Priscilla scooped her up in her arms and tried to revive her, to no effect.

Nathan and Mordred lay at Greg's other side, looking no less dead than Greg.

"What's wrong?" shouted Lucky. "Why didn't it work?"

"Wait," King Peter told him. "It took a moment before."

They waited, hundreds of thousands of them, without a sound, barely breathing. Moments passed. Then, a slight movement in Greg's eyelids.

A roar erupted throughout the yard like none that had ever been heard before, for Greg was a hero of unequaled measure to the spirelings, and his loss would have been impossible to accept.

"He's alive!" Lucky shouted. He leaned forward to wrap his arms around Greg.

Princess Penelope looked torn between hugging Greg and holding Kristin, who still hung limply in her arms. Then Kristin began to stir, and Priscilla squealed with glee. She hugged the girl so tightly, her mother had to pry her arms away so Kristin could breathe.

Mordred was the next to stir. Then all waited to see some evidence of life from Nathan. The magician did not move.

"I was afraid of this," Mordred gasped, and even in his current state, his impatience was clear. In his mind he probably jumped to his feet. To everyone else it looked as if he slowly erected himself out of spare parts.

"Come," he squeaked.

While the few who managed to hear him stared back, not knowing what he wanted, every one of King Peter's magicians pushed past the crowd and took up hands in a circle around Nathan's unmoving form. They bowed their heads in silence, and Greg could swear he saw a faint blue light passing between their fingers, though after what he'd just been through, he was seeing odd lights no matter which way he looked.

When Mordred's legs began to shake, Marvin Greatheart stepped forward to help him stand. A hush had fallen over the crowd once more. They waited in silence, until finally Mordred opened his weary eyes.

"What's wrong?" asked King Peter. "Is he going to be okay?"

Marvin tried releasing Mordred, but immediately the magician began to sink. After a brief frown, Marvin raised a fist. In it he clutched the cloth of Mordred's robe. Like a puppet, Mordred raised his head and spoke, and more than a few in the crowd checked to see if Marvin's lips were moving.

"I—I don't know," admitted Mordred. "While all of us are skilled in the art of healing . . . there's something . . . not right . . ."

"Yeah, he looks dead," said Melvin.

"Quiet, son," said both his father and King Peter.

"I've never witnessed . . . someone in this state before," Mordred said, panting. "I have a partial understanding after what I just experienced, but . . . I'm afraid this is an area unknown to me. It has something to do with the . . . Dark Magic that was cast here today. I'm afraid, it's quite possible we can do nothing to revive him."

"No," Greg cried. "I'm the one who was supposed to die, not Nathan."

"You did die," said Melvin. "Your part in the prophecy is over."

"But Simon never said anything about Nathan dying," argued Lucky. "This isn't right."

"Well, he never said anything about Nathan not dying either," Melvin pointed out, and even though Greg knew he was just stating the truth, he wanted to punch the boy now more than ever.

"Quick," said Mordred. "Get him to the Room of Shadows . . . Our power is strongest there."

The circle of magicians dropped their hands at once. So did Marvin, which meant he had to scoop Mordred off the ground before he could carry him toward the castle. Four magicians lifted Nathan and followed the others inside. Instead of wasting time using the gate, they filed in through the gaping hole in the castle wall, where Tehrer had met his more permanent demise.

King Peter and Queen Pauline followed at their heels, completely ignoring the damage to their home. Lucky, who was recovering quite well, helped Greg stand. Priscilla supported Kristin, and the four of them followed the others inside. Even Melvin managed to slip past before the king's guards stepped up to block the crowd.

"Too much help can be as bad as not enough," one guard announced.

Inside, the magicians proceeded to the anteroom where Greg had seen them on many occasions. Perpetually burning torches rested in sconces lining the walls, and shadows flickered and danced about the empty room. Aside from Tehrer's foot taking up half the space, it was exactly as Greg remembered it.

The magicians laid Nathan out in the center of the remaining floor and formed their circle again. Seeing the worried look on Greg's face, King Peter took up Greg's hand in his own. Kristin moved in behind the two of them and slipped her arms around Greg's waist, and Priscilla hugged them all as they waited in silence.

"What's taking so long?" Melvin asked, and was nearly knocked flat by all the shushing.

Greg felt Rake brush against his shin. He tried to stoop to pick the shadowcat up, but couldn't bend with such a gathering of people attached to him.

Rake didn't stay long anyway. He scooted between the magicians' feet and climbed onto Nathan, stretched out each of his four legs in turn, and made a big show of settling down on Nathan's chest, turning several circles before he got it right. In a second he was purring, the only sound in the room, aside from the occasional falling stone.

The penetrating tone tempted an already tired Greg to pass out, but he fought to keep his eyes open. Finally, miraculously, Nathan stirred.

Rake feigned a look of annoyance, hopped down from Nathan's chest and, true to his kind, quickly disappeared into the shadows.

"He moved," said Lucky. "I saw him."

Greg stared at Nathan, disbelieving. Nathan's head teetered first one way, then the other, and finally rolled toward Greg. His eyes dropped open, and a faint smile came to his lips.

"Looks like Simon ended his prophecy too soon."

Lucky to be Back

Greg held Rake cradled in his arms. The shadowcat lay with its head lolling to one side, staring at the ground, where it clearly would have preferred to wait. Greg tried to appease the creature by scratching under its chin. Finally Rake relaxed and allowed himself to enjoy the attention. The shadowcat might have even started purring, but was probably smart enough to know Greg would fall asleep and drop him.

Nathan was resting in one of the castle chambers. Although he'd saved Greg's life, he'd paid dearly for the effort. Greg tried talking to him earlier, but barely got a word out of him. Actually, he barely got three.

"Talk to Mordred," Nathan had said, and as little as Greg liked that idea, he'd gone out in search of the magician and found him in King Peter's study, reviewing the written words of the prophecy.

Kristin, who hadn't left Greg's side since he woke up on the lawn outside the castle, tagged along with him. Greg wouldn't have wanted it any other way, though it did prove a bit embarrassing earlier, since Greg's tunic had burned away during the lightning strike, and Queen Pauline had insisted on applying a soothing ointment to his bare chest. The mark of the Amulet of Ruuan was burned deep into his skin, a permanent brand that he was going to have a lot of trouble explaining to his parents.

Lucky was there in King Peter's study too, and much as with Greg and Kristin, Priscilla stood by his side, afraid to leave him for even a moment. Lucky had foregone his familiar orange tunic and tights and was dressed in a robe of soft white fabric. The outline of the pentagram burned into his chest was barely visible through the light cloth. Priscilla was wearing, of all things, a dress, and Greg had to admit she looked very beautiful, though at the moment he had an idea she preferred Lucky be the one to notice.

Earlier, Norman Greatheart had tried to gather his two sons and head home, but Melvin had demanded they stay until Greg and Kristin were sent back. He stood beside them now in the king's study, staring at

Mordred along with the others.

Mordred looked up from the scroll laid out before him. "What do *you* want?" he said, his voice filled with slightly less disdain than usual.

"We were curious about what happened out there today," Greg told him. "Nathan said I should talk to you."

Mordred frowned. "Just when he and I were starting to get along."

"How did you know how to save Greg?" Priscilla asked. "You always claimed you didn't know Dark Magic."

"I don't," said Mordred. "Oh, I remember a few things. There was a time when I was foolish, like Nathan. But that was long ago, and those memories do not come easily."

"Then how did you cast that spell today?" said Lucky.

Mordred looked very uncomfortable with the question. He hesitated a long time before answering.

"When Nathan . . . touched me, the way he did, something odd happened between us. I have never felt anything like it, or even heard of such a thing occurring."

"What was it?" asked Priscilla, and Lucky's face reddened as she squeezed his hand, waiting for a reply.

"It was as if our souls bonded. Almost as if I had lived all of his life experiences. I knew the things he knew, felt the things he felt. I was him, and I can only imagine he was me."

Greg shuddered. The thought of becoming Mordred for even a moment . . . He had no desire to know the type of thoughts that circulated through the magician's mind.

"He loves you very much, you know," Mordred said to Greg. Then to the others he added, "All of you."

"You felt that?" Greg asked.

Mordred's expression was completely unreadable. "Yes."

"Did you feel it too?" Priscilla asked. "The love, I mean."

Mordred looked away a moment and then regarded the princess with the same unreadable expression he'd used on Greg.

"I understood Nathan's motivation in living the life he has chosen. I know now why he pursued the Dark Arts against all my warnings. He sacrificed our friendship, lived his entire life alone for one purpose and one purpose only: to save this kingdom. I always believed that was why I'd chosen the path I took, but now . . . I'm not sure I could have protected us today." Greg was surprised to see him smile. "I at least know I couldn't have protected you."

"Will he be okay?" Greg asked. "Nathan."

"He will recover," said Mordred, "but I'd be lying if I said he won't be changed by the events of this day—as will we all. I can't say if that change will be for the better or worse, but . . ." He paused and drifted into a moment of deep reflection. "Life will be different. Let's leave it at that."

"What are you doing now?" Kristin asked, nodding to indicate the scroll rolled out on the table.

"Just reviewing some old information from a new perspective. It can actually be quite helpful at times. Our best sources of new information are often those we thought we'd already exhausted."

"And what have you learned?" Priscilla asked him.

Mordred leaned back in his chair. The smile that eased across his face reminded Greg of Nathan the day they met in the Molten Moor so long ago.

"Only that Simon Sez is one incredible man."

Greg slipped his journal into his pack and shifted Rake to the other arm so Melvin could shake his hand. The boy then tried to steal a kiss from Kristin, but she saw him coming and turned her head in the nick of time.

Marvin patted Greg on the back, a good-bye suitable for one hero to another, and then Norman tried to do the same, crackling several bones in his wrist and elbow. He turned to Melvin. "Let's go, son."

"But the magicians haven't sent them home yet."

Once again everyone had gathered in the Room of Shadows, with all of the king's magicians lining the walls, their faces invisible beneath their hoods under the flickering light of the gloomy chamber. Nathan sat in the only chair in the room, still recovering from his ordeal but, according to Mordred, doing quite well under the circumstances. King Peter and Queen Pauline were there too, but Penelope was conspicuously absent, having offered a quick good-bye and scuttled off to paint her nails or something equally important.

The king couldn't thank Greg enough for everything he'd done to save the kingdom. Over and over he apologized for trying to talk Greg out of coming.

"Don't worry about it," Greg said. If the truth were known, he found it hard to believe he hadn't listened to the king's advice to start with.

Queen Pauline kissed Greg's forehead. "Return soon. Let us know how you're faring."

"Ah, sure," said Greg. He was just glad he no longer had Ruuan's ring. That was one temptation he planned never to succumb to again.

Priscilla hugged him as if she were never going to let him go, to which Kristin made the same noise Rake sometimes did just before coughing up a hairball. Finally Priscilla released Greg and hugged Kristin.

Lucky stepped up and smiled at Greg. His ragged stubble had been shaved clean. "Well, we did it again," he said, holding out his hand for Greg to shake.

Greg smiled back at him. "I guess we did."

The two boys hugged while the magicians began their chanting. Before long Greg felt a change in the air. The space in front of him split open to reveal a sea of planets, soaring past like bottles on an assembly line, waiting for Lucky to randomly point out the one in countless billions that would take Greg safely home.

Lucky glanced over at Greg and winked. "You know, you're lucky I was there with you," he said, just before pointing at an unassuming blue sphere that was attempting to sneak by unnoticed.

"Now!" Lucky shouted before Greg could respond.

As if someone had yanked a carpet out from under his feet, Greg felt the world shift. The hard stone floor of the castle gave way to soft dirt, and Greg realized he was now standing on the trail through the woods near his own home on Earth.

Kristin's arms were latched around his waist. Greg nearly yanked free, but stopped when he felt the softness of her touch.

"That was incredible," she shouted, as if Greg weren't standing inches from her.

"You get used to it."

She released him and glanced around the woods. The light was failing, as they had returned to the same moment they'd left this spot, and evening was setting in.

"It did happen, didn't it? I mean, I didn't just imagine all of that, did I?"

Rake peeked out from behind Greg's neck and chattered at her.

"No, it really happened," said Greg.

"Did I mention it was incredible?"

Greg smiled and took her hand in his own. They started walking toward Kristin's house. Her parents were sure to be wondering where she was.

"You know what's incredible?" Greg said. "Lucky. Did you hear what he said just before we popped out of there? I was *lucky* he was with me."

"Well, you were."

"How do you figure?"

"Well, if he hadn't distracted the witch, you might never have defeated her."

"But he didn't—? It was the wyvern that—"

"And who knows what might have happened to you if he hadn't been on that wyvern with you? The way the thing was twisting and rolling about. It's a miracle you weren't thrown off."

"Yeah, but—?"

"And then it was pretty lucky he fell on top of the amulet Nathan used to save you. Anything might have happened to it if it had just been lying about."

Only then did Greg realize she was joking.

"You laugh," he said, "but I'll bet he's going on right now about how lucky he was in that battle."

It was growing cold, and Kristin wrapped Greg's arm around her. "Well, now *that* I'm going to have to agree with."

"What? The boy was *killed*. He fell out of the sky and died. Kaput! Dead as a doornail."

"Yeah, well, so were you."

"Exactly. I don't consider myself lucky."

She nudged her head into his cheek and pulled his arm tighter around her. "Well, maybe you should."

Greg felt the softness of her hair and the warmth of her body against his own. When she put it that way, he found he had a hard time disagreeing.

About the Author

BILL ALLEN may be described as an unusual man who has accomplished an unusual many deeds. In fact, it has been said that if you total up all the things he claims to have done, he cannot possibly be less than seven hundred years old. No one knows if this is true. All we know for certain is that for many of those years he's been living in Florida with his wife, Nancy, writing software by day and, well, mostly sleeping by night. Every now and again he writes stories, too.

Made in the USA
San Bernardino, CA
18 October 2015